£1.50

THE QUESTION

Jane Asher's first novel, *The Longing*, was published to great acclaim in 1996. Celebrated British actress of stage and small screen, she is also well known for her many other activities, especially her books and journalism and her successful cake-making business. She lives in London, with her husband and three children.

Acclaim for *The Question*

'As accomplished a writer as she is professional cake-maker, or indeed, actress . . . Asher convincingly portrays the complexities of her characters' inner lives, while retaining our sympathy for her tormented heroine, even when her actions are at their most dubious.' *The Times*

'What a smasher, Jane Asher' *Daily Mail*

'Having thrown a fistful of feminist balls into the air, Asher handles them beautifully . . . she keeps the entire plot moving as effortlessly as a well-tuned car.' *Birmingham Post*

'A well-plotted story of betrayal and revenge' *Independent*

'A sometimes sinister yet always intriguing tale' *Jersey Evening Post*

'A genuinely page-turning and suspenseful read with a twist in the tale of which Roald Dahl would be proud' *Publishing News*

'*The Question* dissects with surgical accuracy the corrosive jealousy which spreads through every fibre of the central character . . . Read it and shiver' *Yorkshire Evening Post*

'At turns terrifying and ridiculous, immensely sad and funny' *Telegraph*

Also by Jane Asher

The Longing

JANE ASHER

THE QUESTION

HarperCollins*Publishers*

The characters and events in this book
are entirely fictional. No reference to any person,
living or dead, is intended or should be inferred.

HarperCollins*Publishers*
77–85 Fulham Palace Road,
Hammersmith, London W6 8JB

Published by HarperCollins*Publishers* 1999
1

The Author asserts the moral right to
be identified as the author of this work

ISBN 9780007809493

Typeset in Spectrum by
Palimpsest Book Production Limited,
Polmont, Stirlingshire

Printed in Great Britain by
Clays Ltd, St Ives plc

Many thanks once again to Rachel Hore,
Lucy Ferguson, Jenny Parr and Carole Blake and my
appreciation to Kathleen Venner for her inspiration.

For Clare

Chapter One

'So how was your holiday?'

'Wonderful, thank you, Mrs Hamilton. Absolutely wonderful. You can never be quite sure about the weather out there, but we were really lucky — it was gorgeous. Jackie got really burnt and I was covered in freckles, as usual, but we really enjoyed ourselves.'

Eleanor grimaced a little to herself as she continued listening to Ruth's chatter, the girl's tone and the liberal sprinkling of 'reallys' as grating to her ear as ever. She smoothed a hand across her upper lip to wipe away the tension she could feel settling into the muscles around her mouth, then hunched up her shoulder and gripped the receiver against it with her chin. She reached out to pull the kettle closer towards her along the hardtop, tilting her head to examine more clearly the distorted reflection in its rounded chrome surface, feeling the usual jolt of unpleasant surprise at seeing the clarity and depth of the lines running from nose to mouth.

'Lucky you!' she volunteered, the flat calmness of her voice giving no indication of the intense scrutiny she was giving herself as she peered even closer at the image in front of her.

'Oh yes, we were. Really lucky. Getting that late booking was a real stroke of luck, and Mr Hamilton letting me go a week early like that too. We only got back on Friday evening and it still seems a bit like a dream.'

Eleanor stretched her mouth downwards and raised her eyebrows, pulling the soft skin of her face into an elongated, surprised O and the eyes into inquisitive rounds that challenged her in the reflection. The lines lengthened and thinned but remained stubbornly in place. She forced her lips into a grin – wide, huge and humourless – and gripped the receiver again with her hand as she turned her head from side to side to check the profiles. Now that the lines were buried in the flesh of her cheeks they were more acceptable, the forced smile giving them an excuse to be there. She relaxed a little, even allowing a little genuine warmth to creep into the still maintained rictus of her lips. Her hair was looking good, she decided. The new girl had cut just enough to add some bounce and style without giving her that shorn look she hated. And the colour was perfect – exactly the right amount of Russet Brown to warm it up and soften the grey without looking overcoloured and hard around the tidemark, as John always called it. Suddenly she pictured Ruth's thick, dark red hair spilling and curling, as she knew it must be, over the receiver as she talked on, and felt an uncomfortable little stab of envy pinch deep inside. The grin dropped a little and she sighed.

'Anyway, Ruth,' she interrupted, 'I wanted to show

Martin Havers some new swatches I picked up the other day. Lovely colours. And not unreasonable.'

'For the—'

'For the show house. Manchester one.'

'Oh right, yes. Do you want to come in, or shall I—'

'No, I'll come in. It's curtains I'm talking about. You know.'

'Yes, Mrs Hamilton, I'm with you now. Do you want to—'

'I'll come up to town tomorrow. Do you know if he's particularly busy or will any time suit him?'

'I'll put you through to Mr Havers' office in just a moment. Did you find a good yellow after all that? It was a yellow you were after wasn't it?'

'Yes, I did. How clever of you to remember. Gorgeous. A lovely yellow.'

As she spoke, Eleanor could see herself spreading the large sample of lemony cotton piqué across Martin Havers' desk, acknowledging his appreciative reaction with a satisfied little nod of her head. She pictured folds of it gathered and ruched and blowing from open sunlit windows into the magnolia-washed rooms of the new house. She was happy planning the schemes for the company's more upmarket developments; the chance to spend a little more on fabrics and paint finishes made her feel less uneasy about the cheaper end of her work on the lower cost estates, where budgets were so tight as to give her no option but to plump for inferior, crudely patterned man-made furnishings that she knew she would never be able to live with herself.

'Mr Havers' line is engaged at the moment, Mrs Hamilton, but I'll keep trying. Did you want a word with Mr Hamilton? He's around somewhere but he seems to have slipped away from his desk. He has a ten o'clock meeting booked so he's bound to be back in a second.'

'No, don't worry, I don't need to speak to him; it was only to fix a time to come in and see Martin. I'll ring back later on – or he can ring me. There's no mad rush. Yellow curtains can wait till I've walked George.'

'Talking of yellow – I love Mr H.'s new tie. All those swirly things on it – very unlike his usual.'

'Well, I'm obviously in my yellow phase at the moment. I think it perks him up; very jolly. Certainly better than the usual old dark red. Anyway, Ruth, I'll see you next time I come up. I'm so glad you had such a good holiday – and just ask Martin to give me a ring later.'

'Yes, of course, Mrs Hamilton. Nice to talk to you. 'Bye.'

• ∾ •

As Eleanor walked out of the large, tastefully decorated drawing room into her large, tastefully decorated hall she brushed a hand gently through the front of her hair, then patted the soft curls at her neck. Going up the stairs she automatically straightened her back and pulled in her stomach, vainly trying to flatten the persistent bulge that swelled from below the waistband of her camel skirt to the creases at the tops of her thighs. She paused at the window on the half-landing one flight up and squinted at the faintly reflected outline that she could just make out against the dark background of the shadowed lawns beyond. She sighed a little, pulled the muscles even tighter and moved briskly up the next flight and towards the bedroom, vaguely wondering, as she so often did, why she bothered to worry about her face and figure. John, she knew, loved her just the way she was. Indeed, he never stopped reminding her of it. He was aware and appreciative of the way she dressed; of the trouble she always took over her hair and makeup; of her neat nails and polished shoes (well groomed, as her father had described it), but the relentless signs of ageing that Eleanor acknowledged were creeping into every aspect of her body had never affected his feelings for her and seemed to have no bearing on the inevitable ebbs and flows of the physical side of the marriage. Their sexual relationship came and went in slowly moving cycles of which she was only indistinctly and intermittently aware. On odd occasions she would find herself lying in bed mulling over the evolving shapes and patterns of her marriage, like some infinite, dreamlike version of the earth's surface – giant plates imperceptibly shifting over millennia to meet in slow motion crashes for a few centuries, before gliding away from each other again into frigid separation. There were periods when she would realise, without surprise or even regret, that they hadn't made love for several weeks – even months. Certainly there had not, at least since the early days of their relationship over thirty years ago, been times when it had been more frequent than weekly, and, for her part, their supposedly joint decision to have no children had given their sex life an aspect of pointlessness that added to her lack of enthusiasm. Sometimes, during her night-time musings, she would admit to herself that John had talked her into the policy of childlessness; that she herself would have welcomed the 'disruption' and 'diversion' from their 'comfortable life' that he was so adamant had to be avoided, and at times she hated herself for having acquiesced so easily. In the main, however, she convinced herself that she had fully accepted the idea, and felt no lack at either the absence of offspring or the irregularity and unadventurousness of their love-making. The comforting friendliness and companionship of the partnership was enough, and she had long ago understood that John's libido had gently dwindled, as hers had, to the stage where the occasional routine coupling was all that was needed to keep both parties satisfied.

She walked into the salmon quietness of the large bedroom and made to cross to her dressing table, but stopped suddenly in the middle of the room, her gaze fixed on the window in front of her, but seeing nothing.

At first she couldn't think why she knew so certainly that her life had changed for ever. She stood suspended in mid-step, frozen into immobility by the shock of the knowledge that as yet had no substance or reason. Her mind wildly flashed back over the past few seconds, seeing in disjointed, back-to-front snatches the moments leading up to the present one. She saw herself entering the room; then her steps into the doorway; then the walk across the carpet of the landing; then her feet taking the last few treads up the stairs — no, her mind had been calm then; she could sense from this distance her normality on the stairs. It had been somewhere between the top of the stairs and——

Eleanor walked quickly out of the bedroom and back onto the landing, hoping she had been wrong; silently screaming at whatever force was controlling this pivotal moment in her destiny to transform what she knew she was about to see lying on the couch in the dressing-room next door.

She had no realistic hope of changing the fact that the yellow snake would still be there, coiled, waiting, on the velvet surface, just as it had been when she saw it those few moments before, but she forced herself to believe that she just might be able to make it change into something less portentous; differently patterned; differently coloured: less deadly. From where she now stood she could see only one blue arm of the couch: the seat and the other end being hidden by the frame of the open dressing-room door. She leant her body the last few inches sideways needed to clear her view, tilting her head to peer reluctantly at what she didn't want to see. As she moved, the unfocused white gloss moulding in the foreground of her vision slipped away to the side like a curtain pulled back from a sickening tableau.

It still lay there, just as she knew it must; the dark blue pattern along its length pulsing against the bright yellow background. As she stared at it, mesmerised by its unassuming yet deadly presence, she could feel the poison already seeping into her soul. She marvelled at the intricacies of her subconscious; only now in retrospect beginning to work out consciously what she had known instinctively in that first millisecond of awareness when she had passed the open door of the room that lifetime of a few short moments ago.

She stayed unmoving, fascinated, trawling through the evidence logically and calmly, still, in spite of the reptilian silk in front of her, harbouring a tiny seed of hope that something had been missed, that the inevitable conclusion could be changed or avoided. But the facts that forced themselves on her attention chafed at her relentlessly, like some horrific piece of logic leading inexorably to one answer:

I bought the new tie only last week.

The tie is lying here in front of me.

Ruth has been away on holiday for two weeks.

Ruth only arrived back on Friday evening.

Therefore, class,

John is not wearing the tie today.

Ruth hasn't seen John for two weeks until this morning.

Therefore, again,

Ruth hasn't seen John's new tie.

But she has just told me she likes his new yellow tie.

Conclusion:

Someone is lying.

Discuss.

Eleanor's immediate instinct was to rush back to the phone and get through to Ruth again; to demand an explanation and to scream her panic down the line. Then she thought better of it: that was too easy. Over the phone Ruth could bluff her way out of it; she wasn't stupid. A physical confrontation was needed – a trip up to town and a storm into the office as in a scene from a film – the avenging wife crashing through into the heartland of her husband's empire, denouncing, shaming. But picturing the faces of receptionists, secretaries, junior managers, turned towards her incredulously, young eyes agape, lips parted in expectation and enjoyment of the wonderfully embarrassing scene unfolding in front of them, made her quiver in disgust and humiliation. She forced herself to be still and breathe quietly for a few moments before slowly moving across the landing and towards the stairs.

Back in the kitchen she walked over to the kettle and plugged it in, only half aware now of the reflection of the whitened face that stared back at her. There could, of course, be a perfectly rational explanation for this, she told herself. She was getting it all entirely out of proportion. But then why did her whole body tell her something was so dreadfully wrong? Going over it again she tried to work out just what it was that was making her feel so threatened. If Ruth had been away till Friday night then there was no possibility of her having seen the new tie, that was incontrovertible. But perhaps there was another tie? She must have meant a different one. Was there another tie she could possibly have seen that might just have fitted the description of swirly things on yellow? That she could describe as 'new'?

As the water in the kettle began to mutter and growl around the heat of the element, Eleanor struggled to remember what tie she had seen John wearing as he had left in the morning. She could see him coming out of the bathroom, his thick grey hair still wet, brushed neatly back as always. In her mind's eye she watched him walk out of the bedroom, his tall figure slightly stooped in the white towelling dressing gown. They had been chatting about the week ahead of them, as they always did on a Monday morning, shouting to each other from bedroom to dressing room, Eleanor sitting at the dressing table carefully sponging beige foundation onto her moisturised face.

'So I'll stay up till Thursday, darling,' John had called out to her, 'probably. It depends how it goes. I might leave it till Friday, but I'll see. Abbotts are nearing finishing the plans on Devon and I want to work through them before they're finalised. And year-end reports are getting horribly close. Have we anything on?'

'Not really, although I told Amanda we might drop in on them for a drink at some point, but the weekend'll be fine. Is Devon going to have more ghastly whirly ceilings?'

There was a silence. Eleanor knew John found it particularly irritating when she criticised the inferior plaster finishes on the housing estates, but there was something about the depressing combed half-circles of thick white plaster applied quickly and cheaply to their ceilings that she found objectionable and dishonest and she could never resist saying so. To her eye, combined with the sprayed-on roughcast exteriors, the ceilings gave the houses the impression of shoddy goods covered quickly with an unattractive veneer of mock sophistication.

'John?'

'Yes. Probably. Well, of course, yes.'

She could hear the annoyance in his voice but went on, enjoying the predictability of the marital friction that she knew she was inflaming, puffing powder over her face as she talked. 'I'd just love to see you live in a house like that, that's all.'

John didn't bother to reply, but continued dressing next door in silence. Eleanor could hear the slight squeak of hinges as he opened the old mahogany wardrobe, and the faint clink of metal as the hooks of the clothes hangers were pushed together as he sifted through his jackets.

The hinges squeaked again as the wardrobe was closed. Eleanor brushed brown shadow across her eyelid as she half listened to the rustle of cellophane as John took a shirt from its laundry wrappings, and then to the whip of cloth as he briskly shook it free of its folds. She was waiting for the moment when he would come back into the bedroom to proffer first one, then the other arm for her to do up his cuff links. Until she saw his face she felt unable to judge his mood, and unsure as to whether it was worth pursuing the ceiling conversation or whether the annoyance factor was too great to be overcome. Not that she felt particularly strongly about the poorly finished ceilings, but it had become an interesting and long-running challenge to get John to admit that he thought them as ugly and vulgar as she did. The unspoken words that were passed via the briefest of looks on both sides during such discussions were as revealing as those that were actually uttered. A quick glance from beneath John's raised eyebrow silently asked Eleanor why she couldn't appreciate that everything that she now enjoyed in the way of lifestyle was paid for by the very ceilings that she so abhorred. Eleanor's returning smirk conveyed that she was, indeed, only too aware of just what it was that paid the bills but didn't he realise that there existed men who could provide for their women to a standard as high – or higher – than he did without having to compromise on moral or aesthetic standards? The toing and froing of question, answer, recrimination and impatience would often continue for some time, the silent conversation bouncing between them like some invisible ball.

The click of the kettle's switch as it came to the boil snapped Eleanor back into the present as she still struggled to picture John as he had walked back into the bedroom. However hard she tried to remember, the tie he had been wearing refused to materialise, but it was quite clear to her that he must have worn one of the relatively limited choice of safe, striped ones that he tended to revert to unless pushed by her into something else. His natural instinct was to quiet conformity, and she would certainly have noticed if he had worn anything even remotely similar to the brightly patterned yellow of the one still pulsing its terrifying implications from the couch upstairs.

She made the tea automatically, hardly glancing at the plastic jar of tea bags, the carton of milk or the bowl of sugar as her hands found what they needed by feel, pro-grammed by years of having made these same movements in the same way day after day to be able to judge precisely and unconsciously the distance from kettle to cup, spoon to bowl and carton back to fridge. While her body moved calmly and routinely, her mind was flying, darting back and forth over days, looks, months, expressions, smiles, phrases, excuses, years, laughs, absences – anything that might now be possibly construed as a clue. Some memories and images came back relentlessly over and over again: the times she had rung the flat and had no answer; the smile he gave her every time he drove off to London; messages from the office to say he couldn't get back to the country as expected; his voice blowing a kiss down the phone at the end of his regular evening call. The pictures in her head were crescendoing to a visual scream of unbearable misery that battered on her mind's eye from within. She picked up the mug and took a gulp of scalding tea that burnt her mouth and shocked her into a moment's respite from the mental cacophony.

But, like a red ant crawling over a stretched white sheet, a single, relentless image crept into the stillness and clarity of her emptied mind. Hair. Red hair. Long red hair curling over a receiver.

Ruth's hair.

Chapter Two

That Monday morning George didn't get his walk after all. Eleanor shut the puzzled black Labrador in the kitchen, grabbed her bag from the hall table, locked the front door and drove the Range Rover down the A3 towards London. She had no idea what she would do when she got there, realising after just a few miles that the potentially perfect excuse of the yellow curtain material was lying neatly folded on her desk in the study.

'Idiot!' she shouted out loud at herself, then, 'Idiot!' again at the very thought that she should need an excuse at all; she, the wronged woman, as she was now convinced she was: the innocent.

'He's the one who needs the excuse. Bastard!'

She turned on the radio and listened for a few seconds to the Classic FM jingle played on a harp, wondering, in spite of herself, how many versions of the miniature theme existed, and whether the composer could possibly receive royalties every time it was played.

'No, of course not. They must have done a sort of all-in deal.'

She smiled to herself at her own absurdity, then suddenly frowned and, feeling an uncomfortable tightness in her throat and a fullness behind her eyes, knew she was in danger of starting to cry. She slowed the car down and looked for somewhere to stop.

In the lay-by she switched off the engine and looked out of the window at the cows in the field next to her, their tails flicking away the flies as they grazed, moving slowly across the ground as they tugged at the grass, lifting their heads occasionally to stare around them as their mouths worked at it, jaws sliding sideways in continuous motion. Eleanor felt a deep sadness as she watched them. Had she failed John? What was it he had needed from her that she hadn't been able to give; that the red-haired Ruth had supplied instead?

'Sex, I suppose,' she muttered out loud. 'Middle-age crisis; male menopause, or whatever they call it. But what do I have to go on? Why do I feel so sure something's wrong? What do I really know? And I must stop talking to myself — I've got to think.'

She stopped and felt herself calm a little. She didn't like the way her usual ordered, logical intelligence had deserted her, and began to think through the evidence that had prompted the horrible certainty of John's unfaithfulness. She tried to remember a previous occasion when she had felt like this, but couldn't. The feeling was utterly alien. In all the years of marriage, through periods of intense irritation with each other, through the times of boredom, of friendship, of comfortable familiarity, she had never once had the slightest suspicion that he might be having an affair. It seemed to her all at once pathetic that she hadn't. With newspapers packed every day with stories of desertion, divorce and infidelity she couldn't think now how she had ever felt secure. Even the bastions of her upbringing had deserted her over the past decade: the sleazy goings-on of Tory MPs had become regular reading in the once safely staid pages of her *Daily Telegraph*.

A string of attractive, available secretaries and PAs from John's years at the office paraded in front of her mind's eye. She saw them all in bed with him – first individually, then in a romping, orgiastic group.

The vision filled her with a terrible, furious, nervous energy, and she hurled herself onto the steering wheel and turned the key violently in the lock, holding it pushed as far forward as it would go while the starter motor churned loudly and impatiently. A smell of hot oil reminded her to relax her grip, and the key sprang back in the ignition and the engine purred into life. She released the handbrake and pulled out of the lay-by, hardly glancing in the wing mirror as she did so.

By the time she pulled into a meter bay opposite the office in Portland Place she was calmer. As she reached for the door handle she paused and glanced at her watch, then sat back into the seat again. Why see Ruth before she had to? The idea of a meeting with her was agony: both the possibilities of confronting her with what she knew – or thought she knew – or of avoiding the issue and behaving as normal seemed utterly impossible. In another five minutes or so Ruth would leave the office for lunch as she always did, and Eleanor could talk to John on his own. Quite what she would say, she hadn't begun to consider. She just knew she had to look at him; to search the face of the man she had thought she'd known for so many years and who now felt like a stranger. This man who was 'carrying on' with his beautiful red-haired secretary was a figure from a novel or television programme; not the familiar, boring, comforting, predictable husband of thirty years.

She watched as, a few minutes later, Ruth's tall, slim figure stepped through the black-painted double doors of the large house and moved down the pillared stone steps. A lightweight beige raincoat was pulled in tightly round her waist, and as she glanced up at the sky, wrinkling her nose in disapproval at the small specks of rain, Eleanor was dismayed to take in the unlined, pale, but prettily freckled skin and clear, shadowless eyes, seeing the attractive face quite differently now that it belonged to a rival rather than a friend. Ruth turned in Eleanor's direction to reach over one shoulder for her leather knapsack, and Eleanor made to sink down in her seat. Realising even as she did so that the Range Rover was as identifiable as she was herself, she sat up again and stared straight at the young girl, daring her to raise her eyes; ready to tackle whatever greeting might be given, prepared to rage inwardly at the attitude of friendly innocence she felt sure would be assumed. But Ruth pulled a tiny telescoped umbrella out of the bag and, without glancing towards the car, began to unfurl and extend it as she turned away again and walked northwards along the wet pavement. Once she was out of sight, Eleanor stepped from the car and crossed the road, ignoring the sprinkling of fine rain that marked her coat and spotted her shoes.

·∞·

'Darling – I'll be with you in a minute. Ruth's at lunch, but I'll get Judith to fetch you a cup of tea – or do you want coffee?'

Eleanor couldn't rescue herself from the lurch of shock she felt in the pit of her stomach at hearing Ruth's name in John's mouth in time to answer before his head had disappeared again from around the door of the office. She had looked up just in time to catch the briefest glimpse of a dark red, striped tie at his neck, and it was all she could do to stop herself leaping up from her chair and following him. She tried to pull herself together enough to call for coffee in as normal a voice as she could muster, but he was shouting to her from the corridor before she could manage more than an intake of breath.

'Do you want to see Martin? Ruth said you were bringing something to show him.'

It was hopeless. The second mention of her name had hit her in the stomach again, and she felt once more the dangerous threat of tears and decided to keep her mouth shut. She knew John wouldn't wait for a reply – much of the time his questions were thrown out rhetorically in any case, and she was well used to being ignored when replying to them, particularly in the context of the office. If she didn't answer, he would just stride on in whichever direction he had been going before he had diverted from his route long enough to cast a quick greeting at her where she sat in the luxurious outer office. She had tried to search his face in the couple of seconds it had been in front of her; anxious to catch traces of the new person she was now dealing with. It was disconcerting to find him looking the same as ever, and again she felt a flash of panic and guilt at the assumption she had made and at the guilty verdict that she had so quickly imposed on him on a single piece of evidence.

She took a well-worn gilt compact out of her handbag and began to powder her nose and cheeks, trying hard to ignore the contrast that the picture of her face in the tiny mirror made with the image of the upturned face of the young girl squinting into the rain that she had seen a few minutes before.

'Thank you, Judith.'

The tea was put down on the coffee table in front of her. She looked up, suddenly anxious that something in the tone of her voice had given her away; half expecting to see curiosity or sympathy on Judith's face, but meeting only her usual expression of bland indifference.

'Mr Hamilton says he won't be long. Anything else I can get you, Mrs Hamilton? Did you want to see Mr Havers?'

'No, for goodness' sake, why does everyone think I want to see Martin? And I did ask for coffee, Judith.'

'Sorry, Mrs Hamilton, I thought Mr Hamilton said

tea. And I thought Ruth said you were coming in to see Mr Havers.'

Eleanor knew that Judith was right and that the slight tone of resentment in her voice was completely justified, but that didn't prevent it from annoying her. How dare she come back at her like that? What gave her the right to—

'Did you want me to change it for coffee?'

'No, no, leave it now. Leave it. Tea's fine.'

She looked at Judith's large, tightly skirted bottom and hips as she walked away from her and felt a wash of sweaty dread break over her. Could she be another one? Now she no longer knew John, he could be capable of anything. But he hated fat women; he had always said so. But even as she thought it she knew that 'always' had no meaning now: the man who had 'always' didn't exist.

She looked around the office at the large modern watercolours, cream sofas and glass coffee table and tried to identify something else that was badgering for her attention at the back of her mind. It took a few seconds to identify it: she was hungry. Her usual routine of toast and marmalade first thing, followed by morning coffee and biscuits an hour or so later to the accompaniment of *Woman's Hour*, had been abandoned in the morning's upheaval, and it was only now that she realised she had eaten nothing since a small supper over fifteen hours before.

Eleanor was solidly built; shaped in a way that had changed little since spreading into a traditionally English pear-shaped middle age in her mid-forties. Her intake of food had varied little over the years: although she sensed that the energy she expended was a little less every month that passed, she did nothing to adjust the amount of fuel that sustained it, secretly a little mocking of those of her friends who had joined in the general drift towards diet and exercise. Gyms and aerobic classes were for those younger than she, and were even to be looked down on for encouraging an unhealthy awareness of one's own physical condition. Missing a meal was not something to be taken lightly, and even in her present emotional state, the demands of routine were pressing and unavoidable.

She considered calling Judith again and asking her to send out for a sandwich, or to bring her a plate of biscuits from the office kitchen, but suddenly seeing again in her mind's eye the meeting with John that was inevitable if she stayed, she decided to use her hunger as an excuse to herself to go, and quickly picked up her coat and bag and left.

She turned the car round and drove down one of the side roads towards Marylebone High Street, thoughts of the quiches and rolls she knew would be in the window of her favourite coffee shop juggling for position with an image of Ruth's slim frame balanced on one hip on a corner of her desk as she nibbled at a crispbread or sipped at some mineral water.

'Coffee and a Danish pastry, please.'

'Cappuccino, espresso or filter?'

It had taken an enormous effort on Eleanor's part to bring her voice into a semblance of normality long enough for her to give the order, and the strain made her dizzy. To have it countered with a question fired back at her so quickly took her by surprise.

As the young waitress gazed down at her, Eleanor opened her mouth to try to answer but suddenly stopped; hit by a terrible uncertainty. The choice of coffee seemed suddenly impossible. How could she make a decision if she didn't know who she was? She found herself stuttering and panic-stricken: unable to reply or even look the girl in the eye. The waitress's obvious embarrassment just made it worse, and it was a relief when she muttered something about coming back in a moment and, putting a menu down onto the polished wood surface of the table, moved away towards another customer.

Eleanor took stock. It was so extraordinary for her to be out of control like this. It was new, and it frightened her. Yes she suspected her husband of having an affair, but surely she could deal with this as logically and calmly as she always had with problems? Why did she feel so completely incapable? Even her physical surroundings seemed to be all at once abandoning the rules: the marble floor tilted away from her into the shadows; the walls looked warped and soft; the table sloped and buckled. She rested her forehead on the palm of her hand for a moment and closed her eyes. In the relative calm of the pink world of her inner eyelids she could see more clearly, and suddenly understood. Not only was John not the man she thought she had known: she herself wasn't the same woman, either. Her position in an ordered, comfortable, middle-class world was turned upside down, and by living with a man who had been lying to her for — how long? — she had unwittingly colluded in a nonsensical pretence. For so long she had read in magazines of women resenting their position as 'somebody's wife' and had always thought their worries childish and irrelevant: now she could see — could feel — what they meant. If she wasn't the happily married woman she had thought she was for so long she seemed to be nothing.

By the time the waitress returned she was able to order, and after downing the cappuccino and chicken sandwich that arrived within minutes, she felt fortified and more resolved. Sensing suddenly what she must do, she paid the bill and went back to the car, smiling slightly in her newfound sense of purpose and direction.

She swivelled the driver's mirror down towards her until she could see herself clearly and reached into her bag for a comb, pulling through the dampened but still glossy-looking brown curls until they were arranged to her satisfaction, pleasantly surprised to see that her makeup had survived the ravages of emotional upheaval and that, once a quick swipe of lipstick had been applied to her mouth, she was in reasonable shape to tackle the next stage of this extraordinary day. As she moved the car smoothly out of the meter bay and made her way towards the flat in Nottingham Place she felt almost excited. The sense of terrible anticipation that she had had since the morning's discovery had taken on an aspect of nervous energy that was almost sexual in its physical attack on her. A sensation that was somewhere between a desperate need to urinate and a thrill of excitement fluttered between her legs, and she squeezed her thighs together as she drove to try and contain it.

The only meter she could find was in Paddington Street, but as the rain had stopped the five-minute walk to the flat didn't seem too daunting, and the thought of the fresh air was good. She would install herself comfortably in the sitting room and await John's return in the evening; by the time he arrived she would have planned her assault on him carefully enough to prevent his wriggling out of it; she would be ready to counter any excuse he might have with a crystal-clear, logical comeback. Her step was purposeful and almost confident. A clarity and overwhelming need to know everything had taken over from the blind panic.

Eleanor walked with her upper body thrust forward from the hips as if her head were more eager to reach its destination than her feet, but the look of assurance it gave her on this occasion belied her inner struggles: to the onlooker the tall, middle-aged woman in sturdy shoes and Burberry raincoat striding quickly along the shiny London pavements appeared to have not a care in the world.

But that stride was to be stopped in its tracks by something so startling and yet so obvious that, even as she stood transfixed in horror, she wondered at herself for not having foreseen it. From where she watched, twenty yards or so away on the other side of the road, she was able to see quite clearly the attractive, neatly belted girl with red hair, carrying a bulging supermarket bag in one hand, approach the large dark red brick block of flats and turn into the entrance. How stupid she was! Where else did she think they would have met, for goodness' sake? What had she imagined — a quick fling on the sofa in the office? A willing body pressed back onto the desktop, skirt pushed up; knickers pulled down? Secret kisses stolen by the photocopier?

Eleanor could feel the calm clarity of the last few minutes evaporating even as her mind scrolled relentlessly through the horrifying images; images that, intolerable as they were, she knew now were less terrible than the reality must have been. As she saw Ruth's figure receding into the gloom of the flat's main entranceway they were superseded by images more tranquil, more domestic and far, far more hurtful. Ruth cooking an amusing little Italian meal in the tiny kitchen of John's *pied-à-terre*; John creeping up behind her, sliding his arms round her waist and kissing the nape of her neck in a clichéd movie version of cosy domesticity. Eleanor stirred herself and made to cross the road before she had to let them move into the bedroom and onto the white-framed Heal's bed she had chosen with such care. Some things were not to be looked at — at least not for now. Anger drove her in through the front door of the flat and towards the confrontation she now felt was inevitable — and even to be welcomed.

· ∞ ·

The darkness of the inner hallway was comforting; she was less exposed in here, and more able to let her face reveal the anguish and fury which fought for expression in the set of her mouth and the tension in the muscles round her eyes. She stood still a moment to listen, tilting her head upwards towards the stairwell, expecting to hear the hum of the lift's motor making its way up to the third floor with its hated cargo. But there was nothing; just the distant sound of a television set. She frowned, puzzling over the speed at which Ruth had apparently managed to get into the lift and up to the flat in the short space of time that it had taken Eleanor to follow her in, then tutted to herself at her stupidity.

Of course, she thought, she's gone up the stairs. Just because I always take the lift it doesn't mean she does. She's young and fit – even if she was carrying that shopping. No doubt she does aerobics, or step or whatever it is now. Gym. She goes to the gym. In a leotard and tight shiny Lycra leggings. She puts her hair up in one of those scrunchy things and her face goes shiny and red with the effort of toning herself. Honing herself. Honing and toning. John likes her honed. He likes to see the gleam of sweat on her neck, the tiny droplet of moisture running down from the damp hair. He puts his mouth to the—

'Oh shut up, you silly woman!' Eleanor snapped at herself out loud and made her way towards the lift.

She stepped out at the third floor and turned to shut the old-fashioned metal lift gates quietly, not wanting to alert her prey to the avenging eagle in camel skirt about to descend on her. As she pulled the outer gate across, she suddenly panicked, all at once completely unsure of what she would say, what she would do, when directly facing the horror of looking Ruth in the eye. She could see how the girl would greet her: an immediate smile of recognition and pleasure at the sight of her boss's wife, a flicker of guilty knowledge at the realisation that she shouldn't have been found here in his flat, at the possibility that this woman in front of her knew that the husband was not only a boss but a lover, then a quick and smoothly accomplished murmur of excuse and explanation.

Eleanor took the door key from her pocket and crossed the worn maroon-carpeted landing towards the front door of the flat. She held the key out in front of her, waving it about slightly as if pushing aside the irresolute thoughts threatening to stop her momentum, like a blind man feeling with his white stick for objects in his path. As she made to push it into the lock, she stopped again and listened. Still nothing but the distant sound of audience laughter from the television. She almost believed she could hear her heart beating, but knew it was the sensation of it throbbing against her chest that she was aware of, and that the two senses of feeling and hearing had become confused. As she turned the key in the lock, surprised to find her hand far steadier than her thoughts, she shut her eyes tightly against what was about to be revealed by the opening of the door.

Chapter Three

Eleanor took a deep breath and pushed open the door. The bottom edge of it brushed over the cream carpet with a faint swishing sound as it swung away from her, and she opened her eyes and looked into the darkness of the flat's unlit hallway. She frowned a little, surprised into a mixture of relief and disappointment to find no lights on and to hear no signs of life coming from the kitchen at the other end of the passage.

'Hello?' she called out bravely into the silence.

Nothing.

She stepped into the hallway and closed the flat door behind her, feeling rather as she thought a lion tamer must when shutting himself into a cage with one of his animals, uncomfortably aware of the possible presence of her rival in one of the rooms in front of her. She coughed loudly as she walked along the length of the hall, unsure now whether she wanted to see the dreaded glimpse of red hair or not as she looked quickly into first the lavatory, then the bathroom, kitchen and sitting room.

She moved towards the bedroom and was annoyed to

feel her heart begin its dramatic thumping against her ribs again. As she breathed in deeply but quietly in an attempt to calm it, or at least to give it more space in the uncomfortable tightness of her chest, she sensed for what seemed like the hundredth time that day the terrible urge to cry. She couldn't remember ever feeling as alone as she did at this moment. To be creeping towards her own bedroom – or at least the bedroom she occasionally shared with John on her rare visits to London – in dread at the thought of finding the beautiful young girl she had convinced herself must be inside, was so miserably humiliating that she longed to turn to someone and appeal for the sympathy she knew she deserved for being placed in such an impossible situation. She even found herself crying out from some dim place in her soul for her mother to comfort her, a person and presence she hadn't thought of with any particular warmth for many years.

By the time she entered the bedroom, registered it as empty and collapsed in frustration and fury onto the bed, the storm had broken, and she burst into the kind of relentless and exhausting tears that she hadn't experienced since childhood.

But she didn't let them last for long. If Ruth wasn't here in the flat, where the hell was she? Had Eleanor fantasised that it was indeed the same girl that worked for her husband whom she had seen entering the building ten minutes ago? Could her overstimulated jealous imagination have created this *doppelgänger* of Ruth to taunt her and mislead her? Eleanor suddenly found herself feverishly examining yet again the early morning's evidence that had begun the nightmare she had been living in ever since. Once more she trawled her memory for the tiniest hint of uncertainty or ambivalence. But even as she did so, she knew she was right. Some deeply rooted female instinct told her not to waste her time. There was an affair going on. And she had seen Ruth walk into this very block of flats. Ignoring the puzzling question as to where the girl could possibly have got to, pushing aside visions of her escaping from a bathroom window or hiding under the kitchen sink, she rose instead from the bed in a movement of intense but controlled energy and began to search the bedroom and bathroom for any evidence, however tiny, of an alien female's occupation, certain that nothing could escape the concentrated scrutiny she gave to every corner, examining everything as intently and revealingly with every effort of her mind as with the needle-sharp beam of a finely focused torch.

After twenty minutes or so she gave up. She was certain that no other woman had occupied the room, or, if she had, she was so extraordinarily clever at covering her tracks that Eleanor knew she was no match for her. She carefully tidied everything back in place, splashed her face with cold water in the bathroom sink and made her way out of the flat and back towards the lift.

After waiting by the gates for a couple of minutes and hearing no sign of life she abandoned it and decided to walk, much less daunted by the thought of going down three floors than she would have been at having to climb the stairs coming up. The time it would take her to get back down to the ground floor stretched ahead of her rather comfortingly; the three or four minutes spent in the no man's land of the stairwell would give her a further chance to recover and take stock. She was aware again of the sounds of the television she had heard earlier, and as she made her way down the stairs it became louder, reaching a climax on the first floor, where it clearly came from the open door of one of the flats. The sheer ordinariness of the varying notes and cadences of the human voice, interspersed with bursts of clapping or laughter, was deeply reassuring, and Eleanor glanced up at the door as she passed, catching a brief glimpse of a grey-haired woman in the doorway. She heard the door close quietly behind her as she went on down, muffling the noise of the television, and she reached the ground floor in a better state of equilibrium and calm.

The journey back to Surrey was uneventful. She still had no idea what she would do next, but managed to put away the car, open up the house, read the note left by the cleaning woman and attend to a frantically welcoming dog without feeling the need to know. She surprised herself by reaching for the telephone and dialling her brother in Gloucestershire, unsure what she would say to him but satisfying some deepseated urge to make contact with someone.

·∞·

Andrew picked up the phone in dread. For the last few years he'd always hated answering it, knowing he would find it difficult to hear what the person on the other end was saying and, even worse, knowing he might well be completely unable to identify them even if he could hear them. What appeared to be the entire collapse of his memory system, at least as far as names and faces went, caused him much embarrassment and annoyance, and at times like this, when Catherine was out of the house and he had no option but to pick up the receiver, he felt very hard done by.

'Hello? Winstead 354?'

'Andrew? Andrew, it's me.'

Now that was familiar. He felt a huge sense of relief wash over him as he recognised the voice of his sister, and the fact it took him a split second to remember her name seemed amusing rather than serious.

'Nellie. How are you?'

'I'm fine. Well I – no, I'm fine.'

There was a small pause, and Andrew panicked slightly at the thought that something was expected of him. He went quickly over the conversation he'd had with Catherine that morning before she left. Was there any message he was supposed to do, have done, give to somebody? It wasn't Nellie's birthday or anything was it? It wasn't his own birthday, surely? He smiled to himself. No, his internal address book and mug shot files might be completely out of sync but he did at least know that his birthday was a good few months away. But it was odd, Nellie ringing up like this out of the blue. The occasional call she made to them was more likely to be at a weekend than in the middle of a Monday afternoon.

'Everything all right?' he asked.

'Yes, of course. How's Catherine?'

'She's fine. She's off shopping in the village. Stocking up after yesterday. We had one of our parish dos. She put on the most marvellous spread.'

'Oh, right.'

There was another silence and Andrew shifted his weight off the more arthritic of his hips and cleared his throat. The small hall clock made the odd grating noise that it did before chiming, echoing in the polished quietness of the cottage hallway, and he turned to look at it.

'She should be back soon,' he went on. 'She's been gone about three-quarters of an hour. How's John?'

Well, yes, thought Eleanor, of course he's going to ask that. It's only normal. The huge significance this simple question has for me is irrelevant to him.

She opened her mouth to give him some sort of non-committal reply, then stopped, struck by the thought that if she were to answer with any sort of truth at all she would have to say she had absolutely no idea. How was John? Was he happy? Guilty? Miserably wretched and bored with his life of compromise; at having to come back to his worn old wife every weekend after the joys of Ruth's firm young flesh? Or did he revel smugly in his cleverness at having deceived her, enjoying the rest and comfort of a well-ordered Surrey home after the rigours of his London life? She couldn't stop a short grunt of disgust spilling out of her mouth at her own stupidity.

'What?'

'Nothing, Andrew. He's fine, thanks. I thought I might pop down and see you both for a few days — are you a full house at the moment?'

Why did I say that? she thought. She had had no idea she was going to ask before it had slipped quickly out, but even as she waited for him to answer she found the thought of an escape route rather comforting.

'No, no, just us. Yes, of course, Nellie, come any time you like. Just you, or could John manage a few days?'

'No, just me. Not immediately, I don't think, but maybe in a week or so. I'll give you a ring. There are a few things I need to ask you.'

This last sentence filled Andrew with foreboding. Even as a practising vicar he had hated to be confronted by other people's problems, much preferring the ceremonial and administrative side of his job to the shepherding and nurturing of the flock that was an inescapable part of it, and since retirement he had been even more uneasy at having to discuss anything of any personal depth. For a man who had spent all his working life representing or at least acting as an officer for the Church, his reluctance to discuss matters of the spirit or of emotional depth was a tiresome handicap, but one which he had managed to overcome by hiding behind the comforting rituals of the job. He had coped quite happily with his parishioners' divorces, bereavements, illnesses and deaths by not only using the designated paragraphs from Prayer Book or Bible, but by trotting out the well-used formulaic words of comfort that he had copied from older and wiser colleagues during his training. But if anyone ever looked him in the eye and attempted a direct conversation with him about what he really believed in himself, or tried to tell him, really tell him, about their passion, agony or a dark night of the soul, he would dip his head in embarrassment and change the subject.

Now there was something in the way Eleanor had spoken that made him think that something very emotional indeed was about to come his way, and he curled his toes at the thought of having to face it.

·∞·

After lunch the office always tended to quieten down a little, and John found a moment to pop over to see Ruth across the corridor.

'Oh hello, Mr Hamilton,' she smiled at him, 'how was the lunch?'

'Good, thank you, Ruth, very good. That's all well on course and the client seems very happy. The last house should be finished next week. Thanks for all your help on that as usual – and the food was excellent, too. We should use that place again.'

'Yes, right, I'll make a note of it. Did you want me for some letters now?'

'No, don't worry, we'll leave it for now. Come and do them about four, would you?'

'Of course, Mr Hamilton.'

Just as John turned to leave he remembered what he had come to ask her.

'Did you manage to get that spot of shopping done for me, Ruth?'

'Yes, of course I did. It's fine. Everything's fine. Much better, in fact. Much better.'

She gave him a little encouraging smile and he nodded back at her.

'Jolly good. Thanks again. See you at four.'

He walked back to his own office and shut the door behind him, feeling more settled than he had during the morning, now that things seemed to be getting sorted out. Ruth had become indispensable during the five years she had worked for him. She was pleasant-looking, too. What was it she was wearing today? He knew he wasn't too good at women's clothes, but he tried to picture her attractive body as he had seen it seated at the desk not a minute before. Pale blue. That was it, wasn't it? A pale blue jumper of some sort; pleasingly tight. Her pretty red hair fastened up in one of those slide things. Very nice. He smiled a little to himself and shook his head. He gave a little sigh as he smoothed his straight greying hair back with both hands and then sat heavily into the leather swivel armchair behind the desk, hitching up both knees of his trousers automatically as he lowered himself into it, regretting the Stilton and biscuits he had unwisely indulged in after the chicken, but congratulating himself on having stuck to mineral water. He shook his head a little and smiled to himself as he thought, not for the first time, how lunches had changed since before he had become chairman. In those days they had taken place in the office dining room and lasted two or three hours; good, rich food – three courses minimum – always accompanied by plenty of claret, a Sauternes perhaps with the pudding, and port with the cigars. A certain sleepy fullness hung over everybody who had taken part for the rest of the afternoon – certainly there was not much work accomplished, or if it was it had always been a wise precaution to look over it carefully the next morning. On taking over on his father's retirement, John had moved quickly to curtail such enjoyable excess, and, just as he saw his friends in the City doing, he cut his own and all the staff's lunch breaks to a maximum of one hour when taken as part of the normal office routine, or an hour and a half when entertaining clients. The in-house catering had had to go: pleasant though it was to be cooked for by a regular small team who knew one's every taste in food and drink, it was an extravagant indulgence that the company could do without.

The plans for the development of fifteen four- to six-bedroomed detached houses on the estate just outside Manchester were still spread out across the desk, and he pulled them over towards him, swivelling the large photostatted sheet round to face him. He was particularly proud of this project: the houses were going to look elegant and well-proportioned, with just enough garden round each one to give a feeling of privacy, in spite of his having insisted on squeezing in one more than the originally scheduled fourteen. He had listened to his architects' arguments about angles of building height, diagonals of wall relative to ground span, proportion of garden size to number of rooms, but he was convinced the illusion of space given by the carefully planned hedges, arches and strategically placed walls would make up for the small amount of land he took from each plot. His speech to the planning officer had been masterful, even if he did say so himself.

It wouldn't be long now before they finished the final plastering, and the interest from local estate agents had been extremely encouraging. He particularly wanted a quick turnround for these, and reached for the phone to check on the progress of the show house, and to remind himself of the date of its opening.

'Ruth, get me Martin, would you? Did Mrs Hamilton show him the colour schemes this morning? I didn't see her go – did she manage to get together with him, do you know?'

'I don't think she did, Mr Hamilton. I didn't see her go either, I'm afraid. Do you want me to try and get hold of her?'

'No, don't worry. Just put me through to Martin, would you?'

He wondered idly why Eleanor had gone without saying goodbye – hadn't she asked for a cup of tea or something? Usually she would bring her drink into his office and fill him in on her latest ideas for design, but maybe she'd had somewhere to go on to today. The large variety of charity work, church organising and general local do-gooding that she was involved in meant he was never quite sure what she was talking about when she discussed anything relevant to their life in Surrey. Perhaps she'd had something to go back to this afternoon – but then it was odd that she'd bothered to come up to town at all. She certainly wouldn't have driven in just to meet Martin and show him her samples; there must have been something up in town for her to do. He knew it was no good his thinking back over their conversation this morning; she had said something about her plans, but as usual he hadn't really been listening. During such conversations he generally managed to reply often and noncommittally enough to convince her that he was interested and aware, but all he could remember from this morning was a vaguely uncomfortable feeling that she had brought up the old whirly ceiling business again, and that he had half known she had unwittingly hit the nail on the head in that particular instance. The Devon houses weren't going to be one of his better schemes: they would sell because there was a desperate shortage of houses in that area of this particular type and price bracket, but they were overpriced and ugly, and the sooner they were finished, sold and forgotten, the happier he would be.

He gave up waiting for Martin to come to the phone, and instead pressed the speed dial button on the telephone that was programmed for the Surrey number, ready to leave a warm and thoughtfully interested conjugal message on the machine to greet Eleanor when she returned, but was surprised to hear her voice answer in reality, rather than via the rather strained message that she had recorded on the answering tape.

'Hello?'

John thought she sounded quieter than normal, almost hesitant. Eleanor's middle-class tones usually had a quality of stridency about them that cut across the most crowded of rooms; this softly spoken one-worded question was almost inaudible.

'Eleanor? It's me. Are you OK? You haven't got a migraine or anything, have you?'

'No, why should I have a migraine? I thought you were Andrew ringing back.'

'Because you came into the office and then just disappeared. I thought you must have an appointment in town, so I was surprised to find you answering the — Andrew? Andrew, brother Andrew? Why should he be ringing?'

'Because I rang him.'

'Oh I see.'

There was no doubt about it; there was something very peculiar in her tone. John couldn't quite put his finger on it. After thirty years he prided himself on judging her moods and state of health very finely; knowing exactly when to leave her alone and when to indulge in the comforting husband scenario he knew he was so good at. But this one was a bit of a puzzle.

'Why were you ringing Andrew?'

'I just felt like it.'

'You felt like it? You haven't felt like ringing your brother for as long as I can remember. Had to, yes; felt you ought to, plenty of times, but not wanted to off your own bat. Not that I can think of. Is he all right?'

'Yes, he's fine.'

There was another pause, and John found himself getting irritated by this mysterious laconic exchange.

'OK, I'll leave you to it, then. Are you coming up tomorrow?'

Yes, thought Eleanor, no doubt I am. No doubt I am.

'No, I'll be here all day.'

'Right. I'll ring you this evening, anyway. 'Bye, darling.'

''Bye.' The tiniest of pauses. 'Darling.'

Chapter Four

Eleanor went up to London for the next three days running. She managed to cancel or postpone most of her local meetings and social arrangements without causing too many problems, getting back to the country each day in time to fulfil at least some of the prearranged appointments. She surprised herself by being calmly efficient in her lying; smoothly explaining that John had had a change of schedule in one of his developments, and that her interior design work had been brought forward. She had no worries that her subterfuge would be found out — her life in Surrey was so separate from John's in London that the two rarely intertwined at all. She was quite well aware that John understood almost nothing of the time she spent apart from him during the week; she knew even as she chatted to him on a Sunday evening or Monday morning of her plans for the week ahead that he neither understood nor cared about the people and places she was describing. It had never worried her; she had found it rather sweet the way he bothered to grunt or reply occasionally in roughly the right places so as to keep her happy, and the monologues – which in effect was what they were – were delivered as much to herself as to her bored husband. Now, however, she found herself thinking quite differently about his lack of interest in her life, although it was proving very useful when it came to her surreptitious excursions up to town.

She divided her time between watching the outside of the office and that of the flat, happy to sit calmly in the car for hours at a time; parking it carefully so that the likelihood of it being identified was kept to a minimum. She still occasionally thought she might be imagining that there was any problem at all, but as she churned over it, time and time again, she knew more definitely all the time that she was right. The possibility that Ruth had happened to be at the same block of flats as John's purely by chance, coupled with the knowledge of the tie and the way she had clearly lied about not having seen him over her holiday added up to only one conclusion. Eleanor didn't know quite what she was waiting for. She just knew that if she gave it long enough, something or somebody would reveal a further clue, give her a little more evidence, a little more knowledge. Two questions dominated her thoughts as she tried to penetrate the superficial smattering of facts and find the truth. She couldn't leave it alone. It was like an itchy patch of skin she kept fiddling with and picking at; worrying at the inflamed place until it would break open to reveal the ugly sore underneath. How long had the affair been going on? And did John think he loved

Ruth, or was it a short-lived sexual encounter that had already begun to fizzle out? Either way, Eleanor wasn't at all sure how she would react when she finally made her move; if indeed she ever did make a move at all. She had considered more than once doing nothing, returning to Surrey and pretending nothing had changed, that she had never heard Ruth mention the yellow tie, and never seen her in Nottingham Place.

But she knew that wasn't possible. Never again would she be able to look John in the eye, never again hear him tell her of his evenings in town or his nights in the flat without being aware of the possibility that he was lying.

On the Thursday she made sure she got back in good time to the country, unsure as to whether John might be returning that evening, and wanting to see that everything was looking as normal as possible for his homecoming, and that she herself was calmly ready to tackle the awkwardness of having to face him for what was in effect the first time since the weekend. Their Spanish cleaning woman, Carla, given the extra time allowed by three days completely alone in the house without the coming and going of Eleanor, had tidied and polished more than usual, and Eleanor spent some time rearranging things, opening up windows and scattering signs of life about to make the house feel more as if it had been inhabited as normal during the past three days.

She didn't know whether to feel angry, relieved or disappointed when John's call came at six o'clock. It wasn't as if it were anything new, of course, and many times over the years she had been rather pleased to have another night on her own in front of the television when she had been expecting to cook for John and spend the evening with him. But this time she found herself listening wryly to his call and realising that she had no way of knowing now whether what he said to her contained a word of truth.

'So I'll stay up till tomorrow darling, and leave a little early in the afternoon. Are we still on for the drink with Amanda, or didn't you fix it?'

'No, I haven't called her. Any problem today? Any particular reason why you're not coming back tonight?' Is Ruth feeling a bit randy? Hasn't she had enough this week? Eleanor mentally interpreted the conversation on both sides as it continued.

'No, not really. Just a bit more on than I thought, that's all.' It's not her. It's him. He wants to spend another night next to her: to play with her firm, high breasts, to kiss her unlined, smooth face.

'Well, I'll see you tomorrow then, about fourish as usual. Have a good evening.' I hope she gives you a heart attack as she f— as you make love.

'Yes, OK. Thanks, darling. Have a good evening yourself. I'll see you tomorrow.' He's thanking God he's got one more night away from me, you tired old bag.

As soon as she had put down the receiver, she knew she would go up to the flat again the next day. It felt like her last chance; once he had come back and spent all weekend at home she knew she would weaken into either saying something too soon and give him the chance to cover up the truth, or she would do nothing and let the suspicions fade away into a permanent, grumbling misery. The flat seemed like the best bet for a final throw: at the office they were used to his wife appearing with no notice; they would be too practised at their deceit. The flat she virtually never visited except when with John after an evening out together. If Ruth was seeing him there with any kind of regularity there was a good chance of her being caught.

No – of course! she suddenly thought. How could she have been so stupid? It wasn't during the day that she would catch them – it was now, this evening, at night. He had rung with his excuse – bastard – and now knew his wife was safely at home as usual. Now was the time they'd be together, and now was the time she'd catch them.

She threw a jacket over her brown long-sleeved dress, picked up her bag and quickly locked up the house, catching the dog's reproachful glance as she walked out through the kitchen.

'Oh Christ, I haven't fed you, have I, George? Never mind, I'll do it when I get back. Be a good boy.'

She installed herself in her usual discreet parking place from where she could clearly see the front entrance to the flats, and waited. After ten minutes she began to feel impatient, and looked at her watch. Seven forty-five, she muttered quietly to herself. On a hardworking day he'll stay at the office until seven thirty or eight, and reach the flat about eight fifteen. Give it another ten minutes or so.

But then a sudden quiver of something like frightened

excitement ran down the inside of her belly as a thought struck her. Or does he? Has he been getting back to the flat far earlier than I've ever known? Has he been ringing me after he's eaten, or made love, or lain in the bath with her, or whatever they like to do together when they first get there after work? Telling me he's just got back, when they've been relaxing there for an hour or so with their drinks and their self-satisfied, smirking, knowing looks into each other's eyes?

Anger ripped through her body and jolted her muscles into sudden, intense action. She almost leapt out of the car, slammed the door shut and ran over the road towards the building, not bothering, for the first time in her life, to lock the car, and intent on only one thing. To find them. Together. Now.

Too impatient to wait for the lift, she half ran, half walked up the stairs to the third floor, getting out of breath by the time she reached the second-floor landing, but refusing to let herself stop and rest until she had reached the flat and discovered what she felt sure was the lovers in their lair. She went straight for the door and inserted the key without hesitation, still fired by the furious indignation that had possessed her since she had left the car.

But once more the flat was empty.

This time she didn't bother to look around or to search. She felt completely out of her depth, outwitted by a pair of conspirators, who, even now, she felt were watching her somehow, and laughing at her. Almost tearful in her frustration, and reluctant to return to the loneliness of the car, she began once more to walk slowly down the stairs, anxious to put off the decision of what to do next or where to go, and trying in some small way to recapture the relative serenity she had found the last time she had walked slowly back down from the flat in the warm, dark silence of the stairwell.

The door of the first-floor flat was ajar once more as she passed it, but this time there was no sound of a television, and the quietness surrounding her was deep and total and made her feel uneasy. She found herself missing the cheerful sound of the audience laughter that had reassured her those three days before. Once again, her footsteps creaked on the old floorboards of the landing, and she could hear her breath still escaping in little pants after the effort of the climb up.

As she started to go down the final flight of stairs she heard the sound of the door behind her being pulled further open. Almost as if she could feel it through the back of her neck, Eleanor sensed something extraordinary was about to take place. It seemed as if she knew exactly what she was going to hear just a split second before it happened, and it was almost calmly that she paused on the stair to listen, as the quiet, hesitant voice spoke gently into the twilight of the landing.

'Ruth, dear, is that you? Is that you, Ruth?'

·∽·

Eleanor turned round quickly just in time to catch a glimpse of the same grey-haired woman she had seen before. She thought she saw a flash of something like anxiety in the hooded eyes behind their gold-framed glasses as they looked into hers for a fraction of a second, but as Eleanor moved back up onto the landing and towards the door, it was closed quickly and firmly against her.

She stood outside it and considered. She wasn't sure why she felt so certain that this woman was the key to answering the questions that had been plaguing her for three days. She could see, even in the state of suspicion and unease that clouded her normal logical practicality, that there were alternative explanations. Yes, it was possible that here was another coincidence: that this woman knew another Ruth; or that it was the same Ruth but here on an entirely innocent mission: that this friend of hers, or relative, just happened to have a flat in the same building as John – or not even just happened to, but had taken it on John's recommendation. Ruth was an efficient, helpful PA after all; she knew about this place; she must ring John here in the evenings to deal with problems or prepare him for the next day's meetings. She could well have suggested this location for her friend or relative and fixed it up for her.

But nothing that suggested itself to Eleanor's weary mind could convince her. Even as she dismissed every alternative, she was walking slowly towards the closed door, certain that every step was bringing her closer to an explanation; willing now to face anything in the desperate and relentless need to know the truth.

She pressed the small white push button on the side of

the door and heard the bell ring out quietly inside the flat. She thought she heard some movement inside, but after a few seconds it stopped, and the landing was as silent as before. She pushed the bell again, and then again, angry at the way this woman, whom she knew to be somewhere inside and listening, was ignoring her. Couldn't she feel her pain, this person a few feet away from her? Wasn't the lonely humiliation on this side reaching out to her on the other through the thickness of the wooden door? Surely she must be able to sense it? Eleanor rested her forehead on the surface of the door and closed her eyes. She pressed her finger back onto the bell push and held it there while she focused all her mental effort on the questions that still burnt into her brain, feeling almost as if she could transmit them by the force of her will into the flat beyond. Never having been a particular believer in the sisterhood of women, or in the idea of some sort of communion of the female spirit, she nevertheless now found herself appealing to some primitive common bond between herself and the woman on the other side, whom she knew now could, if she wanted, give her the answers she needed so desperately.

Please, she found herself silently begging, please, please tell me. Open the door and talk to me. I'm in agony here – can't you feel it? You don't look like a bad person; you can't want me to suffer like this, surely?

Her head suddenly jerked forward as the door moved. For a confused second she wasn't sure if she had somehow pushed it with the weight of her body, but as she lifted her head and recovered her balance she found herself looking straight into the glittering lenses of the woman who stood in front of her, holding the edge of the open door.

'You'd better come in.'

Her voice was still quiet, but the eyes behind the glasses had lost their anxiety and gazed back into Eleanor's almost challengingly.

'Yes. Thank you.'

The layout of the flat followed the same pattern as that of John's, but in reverse, and, as she followed the rather dumpy figure of the woman in front of her through the hallway and into the sitting room, Eleanor had the uncanny feeling that she was walking into the one upstairs, but in a surreal version that had somehow been changed into a mirror image of itself. She was half aware of the differences in colour and décor, but couldn't shake off the dreamlike feeling that she was somewhere she had been before, and that it was the woman in front of her that was the visitor, and that it should be Eleanor ushering her into the sitting room and onto the floral sofa, not the other way round.

The woman sat down opposite her in a small armchair, keeping well to the front of it and leaning slightly forward as if ready to jump up again at a second's notice; wary of relaxing her guard in front of her visitor. They looked at each other for a few moments, and Eleanor was able to examine more clearly the straight, cropped grey hair, the long, unmade-up face behind the glasses, and the thick-waisted body. She was wearing a brightly coloured green blouse with short cape sleeves that revealed plump, mottled arms above reddened hands that were clasped firmly together on her lap, and her patterned skirt was stretched tightly across between her legs just below her knees.

'I know who you are,' the woman said at last, the hint of North London accent more obvious now in the stillness of the room. 'I suppose I always knew this would happen one day.'

'Yes,' answered Eleanor. 'And you're her mother, aren't you?'

'Yes. I'm Barbara.'

Eleanor felt surprisingly calm. In control. She looked around the room, automatically and professionally assessing what she saw, unable to help herself mentally rearranging the furniture, changing the fabric of the curtains and removing the gathered frills on the pelmets and the bottoms of the armchairs.

'Do they see each other here?' she went on, the tone of her own voice sounding to her ears as normal as if she were passing the time of day with a social acquaintance, rather than confronting the mother of her husband's mistress. No, not mistress – the word gave her too much dignity; it trembled with echoes of the beautiful courtesans of the past; of spoilt, Armani-clad, pouting lovers of the present. Whore. That was nearer to it. Whore. Eleanor surprised herself with the succession of degrading labels that sprang now one after another into her mind, screaming to be heard: her husband's whore; bitch; tart; harlot; trollop.

The woman hesitated for a split second, and Eleanor thought she saw again a flash of anxious uncertainty as she looked down at the floor.

'Well, yes. Of course. Of course they do.'

Eleanor couldn't help herself. The recently acquired composure that had held her body and voice in check since entering the room deserted her in a wave of furious revulsion. *Of course? Of course they do?* How dare this woman sit before her so calmly? How dare she look her in the eye and answer her the way she did? What kind of disgusting morals could allow her to parade her whore-bitch-daughter to John's caressing, fondling fingers and then discuss it with his wife as if nothing was wrong? Her anger erupted in a sudden, violent rise from the sofa and a tirade of abuse spewed out at the startled face looking up at her.

'What do you mean, of course? How can you? How can you sit there and talk to me – how can you face me? What kind of woman are you? Don't you have any— haven't you any— for Christ's sake, how dare you? For God's sake – how dare you? I don't understand you, I can't understand you – you're disgusting, you disgust me, you all disgust me!'

The woman looked white and frightened, and rose slowly from the chair as if semi-paralysed by the ferocious anger of Eleanor's attack, her eyes like a rabbit's hypnotised in a car's headlights, her body backing slowly from the heat of the assault as Eleanor went on.

'How long? How long? Just tell me that. Do you watch them? Do you watch your daughter while my husband screws her? Do you?'

The woman gasped and held a hand to her face as if Eleanor had hit her. She finally managed to speak, in a voice filled with what appeared to be a genuine sense of shock, confusion and sheer horror.

'What do you mean?' she said, 'What are you saying? Don't – don't say such things. You don't know what you're saying. They couldn't—'

'Don't cover it up – it's too late now. I've found you. I know. I know what they do. How can you, as her mother – how can you let it happen? How can you?'

Eleanor made a sudden move towards the woman, filled with a terrible urge to hurt her, to make her hurt as much as she did, to tear the agony out of herself and force it onto this terrified creature in front of her. Even as she raised her hand to – what? hit her? pinch her? slap her? – some deeply ingrained moral sense rebelled against the physical violence she had so abhorred all her life, and she felt her own arm blocking the fury of her instinctive revenge and become heavy and slow as it resisted the force of her anger. The momentum that her arm already carried sent it flailing towards the other's chest, where it landed in a clumsy, painful shove into the flesh of her upper breast, pushing her victim backwards as she gave a yelp of distress.

'Oh my God!' the startled woman cried, clutching at her breast with her hand, trembling as she backed away from her attacker. 'Oh my God! You must go now, please, go, just get out – please.'

Eleanor herself was backing off now, shocked by her own violence, filled with a confusing mix of horror at her own savagery and hatred for the pathetic woman in front of her.

'Yes,' she panted, out of breath from the eruption of violence and from the battle with herself to contain it, 'yes I'm going. I can't talk to you now. But I will. Don't think I'm one of those wives who are going to take this. Don't think I'm going to make it easy for you, or for your whore of a daughter.'

She was moving towards the door now, but stopped again to turn and look at the woman with terrifying hatred and anger in her face.

'And don't tell him I've been here. Don't tell him anything. I'll make things very unpleasant for you if you do. Just remember that.'

She backed away, still trembling in little waves of after-shock from the horror and humiliation of the encounter, keeping her head still turned to face the frightened, watery eyes behind the glasses watching her as she left the room. As she opened the front door she heard a movement behind her, and looked back to see the woman standing at the open door of the sitting room, still holding her breast with one hand.

'I need to think,' said Eleanor, sounding horribly feeble and conciliatory to her own ears. 'You may have to leave here. I don't know what arrangements you've — you may have to leave, that's all. And Ruth. I won't make it easy for either of you. You or your daughter.'

She closed the door behind her and began to make her way down towards the ground floor. Just as she reached the last step, she heard the door open again on the landing up the single flight of stairs behind her. A voice, still sounding frightened but given more confidence now by the relative safety of the distance between the two of them, called down to her with an urgency fuelled by genuine bewilderment and confusion.

'What do you mean? I don't understand. What has Ruth to do with it? My daughter's name isn't Ruth. What do you mean?'

Chapter Five

Eleanor kept going down the stairs. The emotional and physical turmoil of the encounter had left her shocked and bruised, and she couldn't at first make any sense of what the woman had said to her. Not only the meaning or implications of it, but even the words themselves wouldn't form any kind of pattern in her head; they seemed to float about in their own mysterious limbo, creating strange sounds and echoes but not transmitting any clear signal. It wasn't until she was crossing the street outside, jumping automatically out of the way of a car coming down Nottingham Place, headlights full on and flashing irritatingly into her eyes for a moment as it passed, that she began to appreciate what had been said. She needed to be still to concentrate, so took a moment to open the car door and get in before going over the words that were beginning to arrange themselves into a comprehensible order in her mind.

'My daughter's name isn't Ruth.'

Yes, that was the crucial phrase. That was the bit that didn't fit, that made nonsense of the understanding she had felt sure she had of the whole situation. How could it be? The woman had admitted she was the girl's mother, there had been no doubt, no hesitation about that. Did Ruth have another name? Was that just for the office: an assumed name to cover some horrible original one? Did her mother know her as Charlene, or Kylie, or Tracy? Or call her Freckles, or Ginger, or Bimbo, or Bitch or Slag or— Hold on, hold on. Calm down. Keep thinking clearly for a moment.

But even as she tried these names against the picture she conjured up of the chic red-haired girl, she knew she was on the wrong track. They didn't fit her any more than did the accent, clothes and general aura of the woman who was her mother. Or wasn't her mother. And, in any case, Eleanor had heard the woman call out to her. She had heard her call 'Ruth' down the stairs at her. It just didn't make sense.

She sighed and buried her head in her hands to think. She knew she would have to go back, would have to talk to that wretched woman again, but at the moment she just couldn't bear it. She sat in the shadowy quietness of the car, the only noise that of the occasional passing car and the hum of traffic from the busier streets nearby, and despaired.

•∞•

John Hamilton rose from his desk, stretched his shoulders backwards and grunted with the effort and relief of it. He shook his head a little, feeling his jowls shake and a loose lock of greying hair flop forward over his cheek, then reached for the finely striped grey jacket that hung over the back of his chair. It was unlike him to have taken it off in the first place, but this late in the evening and at a time such as this, when the office was almost empty, he indulged himself in the small luxury of sitting in his shirtsleeves while, tonight, he'd checked through the initial draft of next year's budget. He was about to pick up his briefcase, when he remembered that he hadn't yet made his usual call to Eleanor, and he glanced at his watch as he went to pick up the phone.

Eight fifteen. Later than usual, but not too late to ring her. Anything after ten, and he would hesitate, never sure if she might be taking the chance to have an early night while he was away in London and when she didn't have an evening meal to prepare. He perched on the edge of the desk and listened to the sound of the phone ringing. One, two, three – up to six double rings, then he heard the familiar click of the machine switching on, and Eleanor's brisk tones announcing the fact that she wasn't in and to please leave a message.

'Good, good, good,' he muttered to himself as he waited for the long beep. He wasn't in the mood for a chat, and the fact that she was obviously out at one of her local dos meant he could get away with a message instead. He hadn't a clue where she was, but knew he could leave a message ambiguous enough to cover the possibility that he ought to know.

'Hi, darling. Only me. Sorry I didn't get a chance to ring earlier, but it's budget time and I've only just finished. I had no idea how late it was till I stopped. See you tomorrow night, darling. Hope all's going well with you. Thought I'd ring now in case I didn't speak to you later. Poor me! Back to my bachelor pad, now, and the delights of baked beans. I might give you a ring when I'm there, but if not I'll speak to you tomorrow. Lots of love.'

He was proficient at leaving messages; never sure why so many people stuttered and hesitated when confronted with the silence of the waiting tape. He was very happy to talk into the anonymous quietness; relaxed in the knowledge that he would not be interrupted, that he could put across what he wanted to say in his own time and without the distractions of any interjections or observations before he had finished. His messages to the office staff that he would dictate into a pocket recorder while driving to and from Surrey, or at home in the evenings, were legendary. Firm, detailed and leaving out nothing, they were delivered with greater clarity and confidence than when he spoke to the staff in the flesh, when there was always a tiny element of something approaching shiftiness in his behaviour: a certain reluctance to look the other person in the eye for more than a few seconds, after which he would glance away, or down to a paper on his desk, or at an imaginary speck on his sleeve.

He smoothed the flopping strand of hair back over his head with his palm, picked up his case and left the room, satisfied that he had dealt with everything that needed to be done, and that he could look forward to an evening of relaxation and comfort, and maybe a little enjoyable — no, he would think about that later, when he had eaten.

·∞·

As he rounded the corner into Nottingham Place, a green Range Rover pulled out from a space about opposite the flat and accelerated away. He manoeuvred the BMW into the space smoothly, took out his case from the front seat and walked over the road, setting the car alarm and locking the doors with a satisfying click as he pressed the small pad set into the key. He kept hold of his silver keyring but let the car key swing round on it as he searched quickly through the other keys with one hand to find the one he wanted.

Eleanor sped up Nottingham Place, anxious now for only one thing: to get back home and lie in a hot bath. She had sat for another twenty minutes in the car, half waiting for John to arrive, half terrified that he would, but she suddenly felt she couldn't bear to wait any longer, and that the only hope of restoring any feeling of sanity was to get back to familiar surroundings and wash away the horror of the day in a scaldingly hot scrub in the safety of her home. Now that she was on her way she felt better, and she switched on the radio to try to stop her mind starting again its relentless trawl over the evening's events.

John took the lift to the third floor and let himself into the flat. He flung his case onto the cream sofa and sat down next to it, reaching across to the telephone on the small glass-topped table next to him, picking up the receiver with one hand and dialling with the other.

'Hi. Me. I'm home . . . What's the matter? . . . OK, yes . . . Are you sure? You sound— . . . Good. . . . Well then, late fish and chips d'you think? . . . OK, no hurry . . . they're open till eleven . . . I'm going to have a bath . . . Pour me a drink in about half an hour or so . . . 'Bye.'

He lay his head back on the sofa for a moment and closed his eyes, then suddenly rose and took off his jacket as he walked out of the sitting room and down the hallway. He flung the jacket on the bed, then moved into the bathroom and leant down to turn on the taps, standing up as the steam hit his face and turning to confront himself in the mirror over the basin. He wiped away the condensation that was already beginning to gather on the glass, then turned his head from side to side as he examined himself, considering a shave but knowing even as he half-heartedly felt his chin with one hand that he probably wouldn't bother. He picked up a comb from the shelf below the mirror, and swept it back through his hair, tutting a little in irritation at the way a long, loose strand would break free of the smooth shape and drop over one ear, or flop onto his forehead. He liked to keep his hair this long, he liked the way it swept right back across his head in silvery grey stripes and reached halfway down his neck, where it broke in the tiniest of neatly trimmed curls, but even with the small swipe of gel that he added to it to smooth it sleekly into place, the occasional lock would insist on escaping.

After the bath he felt good. He went to pick up his shirt and boxer shorts from the tiled floor, but a twinge in the small of his back stopped him and he grunted and straightened again.

'Oh, never mind, Mrs Whatsit can do it,' he muttered to himself, and gently pushed them with one foot towards the white laundry basket in the corner. He hummed quietly as he walked into the bedroom, put on a clean short-sleeved sports shirt that he took from the neatly filled shelves of the fitted wardrobe and some beige slacks that were hanging from metal clips on one of the mahogany hangers. He pulled on a pair of maroon leather mules and took his wallet out of the pocket of his jacket, which he then flung back onto the bedcover.

He went into the sitting room, picked up his keys and then walked out of the flat and made his way quickly down the stairs to the first floor. He glanced down at the silver keyring, picked out one of the several Banham keys that were hanging on it and pushed it into the lock of the first-floor flat door.

He closed the door behind him and turned round. A young girl was standing at the other end of the hall, watching him.

'Hi!' John said. 'How're you doing?'

'OK.'

As John put his keys into the pocket of his trousers and walked towards her, she turned away and moved into one of the rooms that led off the hallway.

Eleanor reached the house at nine thirty and headed straight for the bathroom, where she turned on the taps and pulled off her clothes in a burst of furious, unhappy energy. She felt polluted, dirty and degraded, and as she pulled down her pants and unhooked her bra, she was tempted to throw them into the rubbish bin under the basin, but instead opened the linen basket and chucked them into the gingham-lined inside.

The water was too hot even for her skin that had been toughened by years of scaldingly hot baths, so she added a little cold as she swished it about with her hand. She reached out towards the little shelf inset in the tiles above the bath, and hovered for a moment between the choice of the two aromatherapy oils – one labelled for relaxation and the other for revival. So what if you need both? she thought to herself. She almost smiled as she considered mixing the two in a desperate attempt to bring her poor body into some sort of balance. The woman she had been a few days ago who had added a little oil to her bath in the morning to revive herself and a few drops of the other one to relax should she have taken an evening bath instead, was a creature from another planet. It would take more than oil to either restore or relax her now; the old body that had taken such a battering in the last few days could probably never be restored again – at least not to its previous state. Perhaps it could only function usefully and efficiently again if it could be transformed into something that was altogether less ambitious, like cutting up an old dress to make dusters, or chopping up a piece of furniture to make firewood.

She chose the bottle for 'revival', feeling that relaxation was so utterly out of the question that it would be perverse even to attempt it, and after adding a few drops and mixing them in, climbed into the now bearably hot water and lay back. She was astonished to find herself closing her eyes and slipping into a semi-doze, smiling to herself at the apparent ineffectiveness of the oil, but was jarred awake by the sudden ringing of the telephone. She began to clench her stomach muscles in the effort to pull her body out of the comforting suction of the water, but frowned and let go again, allowing her head to rest back again onto the cool enamel of the bath. What the hell was the point in answering it? Nothing could bring her good news, she was sure of that. She knew there was a lot more misery and discovery to come but she just couldn't face it at this moment. She wanted to stay disembodied and removed for a few more minutes before having to tackle anything else; and if – oh if – she could even get a few hours' sleep before she was expected to take in any more she thought she just might be able to survive.

After several rings she could hear the answering machine click on in the sitting room, and then the distant sound of her own recorded voice – the voice of another age. She tried not to listen any more, willing herself to think about nothing but the warmth of the water and the pleasant feeling of it lapping over her stomach, but the sound of John's voice forced her to pay attention. She couldn't hear clearly enough to pick up every word, but even at this distance could make out the familiar tone of reassuring cheerfulness that he used to talk to her on the machine. The dutiful husband trying in vain to say goodnight to his faithful wife, and leaving instead a fond, loving, caring message. She almost screamed out loud at the outrageous dishonesty of it, at the sleek practised way he would be giving her a little bit of news from the day, or sharing a quick anecdote.

'Shut up!' she shouted out loud, then quickly clamped a hand over her mouth, frightened that he could somehow hear through the machine. So what? she thought, and wondered why it mattered to her. She had done nothing wrong – why did she feel frightened at the idea of John finding out that she was onto him?

'Because I don't trust him,' she said out loud. Well, of course you don't, you idiot, what else do you think all this is about? she thought, scornful of her own naïvety. No, she mused, I don't just mean that. It's more complicated than that. And she thought of all the years of little lies and deceptions that she had watched John indulge in without any compunction. It hadn't seemed to matter too much when she had been party to them all: a little twisting of the truth to make a higher percentage profit here; a small distortion of the facts to secure a deal there. How easily and smoothly they had all been accomplished! And somehow, even when he had patently been in the wrong – or at least been in the shadowy no man's land where the perception of what would be the right thing to do is carefully avoided so that no choice appears to exist – John always managed to emerge looking as if he had behaved with integrity and honesty. She sometimes wondered whether he fooled everyone but her, or whether they could all see, just as she could, that something a little less straightforward than appeared was hiding behind the front of confidence and honesty. In their arguments, however forcefully Eleanor put her case, and however much she knew her point of view was the valid one, he always made her appear to lose – even to herself. Although she could see the hints of insecurity hovering behind his eyes, she could never seem to force them out into the open, and would later think back over their conversations and marvel at the way he had yet again managed to manipulate them to his own purposes.

If he could twist things so easily in a simple argument, Eleanor knew she was going to have to be very, very careful when confronting him with – with what? What would she say to him?

'You're having an affair.'

'Oh, really? With whom, may I ask?'

'Well – I thought it was Ruth, but now I think . . .'

'Yes?'

'I mean – I think it's Ruth, but she's – she's not Ruth. Or not called Ruth. If you see what I mean. I think she may have a different name, but I'm not sure if—'

'What the hell are you talking about?'

'I've met her mother.'

'Whose mother?'

'I've met the mother of the woman you're having an affair with.'

'So, I'm having an affair. You don't know who she is, or her name – or anything about her – but you've met her mother. Is that right?'

'Yes. Well, you were wearing the wrong tie, you see . . .'

It was hopeless. She could picture him listening, watching her, arms folded over his chest, impatience and anger growing in his face at every blustered accusation. She would need to know and understand far, far more before she would be ready to tackle him. For now she had to have time to think. If he could be kept unaware of her suspicions for a little longer it would give her a breathing space in which to move.

'So lots of love, darling, hope you're having an early night. I'll speak to you tomorrow. 'Bye!'

He lifted the end of the last word in a cute, baby voice that made her feel like throwing up. She sat up quickly, reached for a towel and stood up, pulling out the plug and drying herself briefly but adequately before stepping out of the bath and wrapping the towel round herself as she walked out of the bathroom and into the sitting room, where she arrived just in time to hear the beep at the end of John's call, and a series of clicks as the machine reset itself. She waited impatiently while it finished its whirring and winding, then, once the small red light let her know it was settled, she pressed the Play button and listened to the two messages that were stored on the tape. There was the one that he had left at eight fifteen, a casual, everyday, uninteresting message about budgets or something. She hardly listened. Then the recent sickening one – loving, understanding and oh so calmly self-satisfied.

A small part of her wondered yet again if she could possibly have been mistaken in everything she thought she had found out. He sounded so utterly confident and plausible: it took her breath away to consider the efficiency of his lying. To have known he had been living a double life, a life of pretence and deception, of planning and brilliant juggling of times, dates and telephone calls had been hard enough to believe. Now that she could hear him doing it, it seemed even more unreal, and more preposterous.

She didn't want to see him. Suddenly she couldn't bear the thought of facing him — either to have to try to maintain the pretence that everything was normal or to risk blurting out the muddled accumulation of semi-facts that made up her evidence. By the time he came home the next evening she knew she must be gone; and gone without his knowing that anything was wrong. In the morning she would pack a few things and leave before he returned. Perhaps this was the time to go to Andrew's. When she had rung him and suggested going to stay with him she had done so without thinking, not at all sure whether she had any intention of really doing so, or whether it was simply a comforting idea, to be imagined but never undertaken in reality. Now it suddenly seemed a good idea.

But as she walked back into the bedroom and moved towards the bed she stopped, suddenly overcome with revulsion. He had lain there. He had lain there next to her and chatted about his week; slipped an arm round her shoulders; drunk the tea she had brought him. And all the time his body and mind had been betraying her.

She couldn't do it. She couldn't bring herself to get back into the sheets he had fouled with his lies. She wanted out. She would go now. Tonight.

She picked a selection of easy, comfortable clothes, threw a minimum of cosmetics and washing things into a sponge bag and put it all in a small suitcase. What else do people take when they're leaving home? she thought to herself, feeling like a character in a film escaping the law, or eloping. Passport! That was it — you took your passport. 'Oh don't be so melodramatic,' she said out loud, but walked into the sitting room and over to the desk, where the spare keys to the small wall safe were kept in a secret compartment at the back of a drawer, the originals being on John's own keyring.

As well as the safe keys, the bunch held spares to the office, house, cars, and to the London flat. John's efficiency was sometimes irritating, but now Eleanor found herself grateful that he had bothered to duplicate everything so carefully. She searched through the large bunch, pausing for a moment to wonder why he had bothered to make two spares for the flat, when all the others were copied on the ring only once. Probably for *her*, she thought, or for another tart if he decides to pick up a different one. No — wait a minute — what a fool I am!

She searched back through the keys to find again the two Banham ones and then held them up together, letting all the others fall back onto the ring. As she held them positioned exactly one over the other, she took a close look at the pattern of the teeth. They were different. There was no mistaking it. Only one of these keys was to the flat, the other was to — Well, of course, to the other flat. *Her* flat.

She fetched her handbag from the hall and took out her keyring and looked quickly for her own key to the flat, then held it turned so that it caught the light from the hall lamp in a flash against the metal. Now she could just make out the worn number engraved into the hilt: 47669. A quick look at the spares and she knew she had been right. The Banham keys were for two different locks. The unworn, shiny new spares revealed their numbers more easily: 47669 and 64533.

She took her passport from the safe, locked it, and then removed the key number 64533 from the ring before replacing the set in the back of the desk. She picked up her bag, case and coat from the hall, called George to her, and made her way quickly downstairs and towards the car.

Chapter Six

The key fitted. Of course. Eleanor gently pushed
open the door of the first-floor flat and peered
round behind it, half expecting to see the grey-
haired woman cowering in the corner like a frightened
animal, but finding only a metal stand filled with a
collection of sticks and umbrellas. In the deep shadow
thrown by the door she thought one of them looked
suspiciously like an old umbrella of John's, but, fearing
she would explode in a hysterical tirade of fury if she
looked more closely and found she was right, she turned
her head away and quietly closed the door behind her.

As she walked slowly along the hallway she became
aware of music coming from somewhere in the flat.
It was some sort of rock or pop – Eleanor was never
quite sure what to call it – and she tried to make
out which room it was coming from. In this mirror
image layout of her own flat upstairs, it didn't take
her long to realise that the music came not from the
main bedroom as she had expected, but from a small
room on the other side of the hall, which in her own

flat was used as a storeroom and occasional spare bed-room.

As she approached it she was astonished to find how calm she felt. Her earlier misgivings about John's discovery of her suspicions had, for the moment, disappeared, and she felt almost elated at the possibility of finding him with his tart. They might even be — and she rolled the operatic-sounding phrase around her head in ghastly anticipation — *in flagrante delicto*. No, she wouldn't allow them that: it sounded far too dramatic and romantic: *delictos* could only be *flagrante* on silk or damask sheets in main bedrooms to the strains of Mozart or Puccini, not in little boxrooms to the accompaniment of Oasis or whoever it was. They might even be . . . *at it*. That was better.

It took a split second to register what confronted her when she opened the door. It was so utterly different to what she had expected that she almost found herself mumbling a quick excuse and backing out again, but she stopped herself just in time and stood for a moment taking it in.

A girl was staring back at her from the bed. A girl on her own. Not Ruth. *Not Ruth*. No red hair — just rather lank-looking mousy brown; no attractively long, shapely legs — the pair sprawled across the covers were thinnish and a little mottled. And the face: so young, so — (but how could it be?) — innocent. And so terri-fied.

Good. That was good. The girl's obvious fear gave Eleanor courage and she was able to take a quiet breath and assume what she hoped was a look of controlled cynicism as she thought quickly of what to say.

But the girl beat her to it. She shifted a little and wiped a hand quickly over her top lip, then pulled her skirt defensively over her knees as she kept looking at Eleanor. 'Who are you?' she whispered. 'Who are you? How did you get in here and what do you want?'

'I'm – no, wait. Why should I tell you who I am? Tell me first who you are, and why this key fits your flat.'

The girl opened her mouth a little as if about to answer, but instead shook her head fractionally and stared back as if mesmerised by Eleanor's intimidating gaze.

'Come on – tell me,' Eleanor repeated more forcefully. 'Who the hell are you?'

'I'm Susan. Susan Hamilton.'

Eleanor gasped as if someone had hit her. The effect of the girl's words was immediate and devastating. It had never occurred to her that her husband's mistress might take his name, and it enraged her to feel that it might give them any kind of link, that the sameness of surname made them somehow equal in their positions in the Hamilton household; that she had quite suddenly been reduced to being a member of the Hamilton harem; no better and no worse than the other woman still staring at her from the bed; simply another of the females kept for John Hamilton's pleasure and comfort.

Eleanor's obvious discomfort seemed to give the girl back a little control, and she looked slightly less frightened as she spoke again. 'Now, please tell me who you are and what you want.'

But the thought of giving this person the satisfaction of knowing they had something in common was unbearable. A name, a man, a prick: none of these things could she yet own up to sharing with her. If the woman was stupid enough not to realise that Eleanor was John's wife, then she certainly wasn't going to tell her just yet.

'What are you doing here? Is this your flat or your mother's? Where is she anyway? Come on, answer me, you pathetic little whore.'

Eleanor was startled to see the girl's face begin to crumple, and hated herself for almost feeling sorry for her. She was new enough to the horror of the extraordinary past few days to feel shocked by the ferocity of her own violent feelings and by the language which she found herself using, and she couldn't help feeling a jolt of guilt at seeing how the harshness of her words had affected the other woman. She looked no more than twenty or so – and the messy brown hair, still pressed onto one side of her head in a sweaty mat from lying on the bed, made her look doll-like and very vulnerable. She was blinking fast, and Eleanor found herself hoping desperately that she wouldn't cry; she didn't think she could cope with that without giving in and breaking down herself.

'Well, it's my mum's flat,' the girl answered very quietly and with a funny little tremble in her voice, her flattened vowels contrasting markedly with Eleanor's definitively middle-class, strident tones, 'or – no – I suppose it's my dad's really. I don't – no, I don't really know. I mean it's both of them's. It's –' She looked up at Eleanor with such terror in her eyes that it was all the older woman could do to stop herself instinctively from reaching out to reassure her. 'Oh look, I'm sorry – I don't know what you want, but please don't hurt me. Please don't. Tell me what you want and I—'

'Hurt you?' said Eleanor incredulously. 'Hurt you? What on earth makes you think I want to hurt you, you stupid creature? In your world maybe that's what people do, but I – what possible reason do you have to think I would want to hurt you? I just want to know what right you think you have to – to –' Eleanor searched frustratedly for the right word, and hated herself for being unable to produce anything remotely strong enough, '– to – to screw John Hamilton.'

The girl looked as if Eleanor had hit her. She leapt back against the headboard and gasped, her eyes filling quickly with the tears that she couldn't now keep at bay, and her knees pulled in tightly to her chest as if she were trying to squeeze herself into as small and insignificant a shape as possible. She looked so genuinely horrified that Eleanor began to experience an unpleasant feeling creeping up her body from somewhere deep in her bowels that she was making some sort of horrific mistake, that the cringing girl in front of her was, after all, a complete innocent, and that she was enmeshed in something that she had as yet no understanding of whatsoever – that her wild, blind stabbing at the truth had done nothing but terrible harm.

'I'm sorry,' she found herself saying. 'I – I think I may have . . . Look, for God's sake, let me understand this, once and for all.' She heard her tone sounding a little softer, and saw the girl's face relax infinitesimally. She went on, trying to keep the firmness in her question, but anxious not to frighten her quarry again into closing up completely: 'Are you John Hamilton's mistress?'

The girl again looked utterly astonished, but the fear seemed to have receded a little as she hesitatingly began to answer.

'No! No, of course not.' She let her body loosen a little from its coiled, tense position against the bed head, and looked straight at Eleanor, her eyes watery from her crying, but with more confidence in her voice than before.

'I wish you'd tell me who you are. I don't understand. Are you my auntie? I told you, I'm Susan. I'm his daughter. John Hamilton is my dad.'

·∽·

Eleanor was so completely thrown by what she had heard that she couldn't think where to begin. To her amazement, her body seemed to take over command from her mind, and she found herself moving into the room and towards the bed, then bending her knees and sitting on its edge, her back to the girl and her head dropped forward. She sat for a moment in silence, too shocked to speak; numbed from the implications of what she had heard. After a few seconds she lifted her head again and turned towards the girl, who was watching her with a calmer, but still wary, look on her face.

'But, I don't see −' Eleanor stopped again, all at once aware of just how much she didn't see, of just how drastically her world was changed. She had thought up to this moment that she had failed in any way to accept the fact that John had been having an affair behind her back; now she could see that she had in fact come to terms with it more than she had realised. This new bombshell made her aware that, before it was dropped, she had already in some way moved on from being shocked by what she thought was the discovery of his infidelity. Suddenly that seemed so simple: so uncomplicated. A mere affair. That happened all the time — almost *de rigueur* in these times of acceptable divorce and second marriages. Why had she been so ridiculously upset? She felt that if she could cancel the last few seconds, the last few words, and go back once again simply to be dealing with a matter of straightforward adultery then she would have no trouble at all. How innocent that seemed now, and above all, how wonderfully uncomplicated.

'If you're his daughter,' she went on, but even as she said it she felt as if she were play-acting. The words didn't have any real meaning, they sounded like a joke, or like some-thing said by somebody else, 'if you're his daughter, then that woman — your mother, you say — that woman—' But she couldn't get any further. The picture that presented itself in her mind as she realised the implications of what she was about to say was so ludicrous and so impossible that she couldn't bring herself to let it be said.

The girl was still watching her, quietly, curiously, and Eleanor studied her face for a moment. She was pretty; in spite of the messy, lank hair and white, shocked face she could see that. Was it imagination that made Eleanor now notice an echo of the shape of John's jaw in the girl's mouth or the outline of his profile in her cheekbone? There was something in the look, something that made her know that it was true; that John's genes were in this girl.

'But you still haven't told me who you are,' the girl said, 'and why you're here. What do you want? What is it? What's the matter?'

It was extraordinary to find herself being looked to for answers when she herself felt so utterly confused. Eleanor opened her mouth to reply, but couldn't think where to begin. She just stared back at the girl for a moment, then suddenly pulled herself upright and covered her bewilderment with an assumed and completely false confidence. It was time to take charge.

'Well, Susan – if I may call you that. I think – Look, sorry, just a moment. Are you really – I mean, is it true? Is John Hamilton your father? Really?'

'Yes. Yes, of course he is. Why, what's wrong?'

So there could no longer be any doubt. The girl's face was so transparently honest in its look of terrified incomprehension that it left no possibility of any other explanation. It was real.

'Well, Susan, I think we may have found ourselves in a rather extraordinary situation. I have—' Eleanor suddenly stopped. Some instinct told her to be careful. To be very careful what she said, before she destroyed in an instant something delicately constructed without her knowledge in the years that had led up to this moment. She sensed quite clearly that if she were to dig out the truth of what had been taking place behind her back, then the way she handled this girl in the next few moments was of extreme importance. One move too far and she could cause this confused creature before her to snap shut like a little frightened shellfish, keeping the secrets of this other life to herself. Eleanor needed to know far, far more before revealing her hand, and before committing herself to telling this girl the fantastic truth of their situation.

'My name is Eleanor. It doesn't matter who I am, at the moment. I'm afraid I've been very confused, and I'm sorry I've upset you.' She managed a small hint of a smile at the irony of it all, and was strangely pleased to see the tiniest glimmer of a smile back from the exhausted-looking girl in front of her. 'Do you know where your mother is, Susan? And —' as she began to speak the words she heard them echoing like some extraordinary fantasy in her head — 'and your father?'

'They've gone out to fetch some fish and chips. For a treat.'

Eleanor laughed out loud, startling the girl in front of her and making her shift backwards on the bed.

'How often does John — your father — come here? How old are you?'

'I'm nineteen. He comes — well, most evenings, really. After work. You know.'

'But just during the week, you mean?' Eleanor realised there was a ridiculously optimistic place in her head that still searched for a way out; that a part of her secretly thought there was still a chance that there were two John Hamiltons, and that the one who lived here with his wife and daughter was not the same as the man to whom she had been married for thirty years or more.

'Yes, just during the week. He – Why, why do you ask that? You are his sister-in-law, aren't you? He goes to stay with you at weekends. He's always done that. I think it's a bit weird, but Mum always explained that you weren't very well and that he had to look after you. Since your husband died.'

'Did she? Did she really?' Eleanor raged at the thought of the discussions that must have taken place over the years. Of the deceit, the humiliation that had been heaped on her unknowingly.

'My dear girl, I don't know what they've told you, the pair of them, but I am – No, never mind.' The strong instinct to preserve her own secret as long as possible had taken firm root, and Eleanor pushed aside the conflicting but pressing desire to shock this girl into recognition of the reality of the situation by confronting her with the truth.

'Susan, tell me – do you know someone called Ruth? With red hair?'

'Ruth Tranter? Who comes and—'

'Yes, Ruth Tranter, that's right.'

'She works for my dad. And she helps Mum when she needs things. Sorts the accounts out and things. She did some shopping for her on Monday when she wasn't well. Stuff like that.'

Eleanor felt a minuscule jab of relief to know that the beautiful redhead was a go-between and not a mistress: the implications of treachery and deceit would have to be faced later.

'Can you tell me, Susan — if you can remember — when did you last see her? Ruth, I mean.'

'On Monday. I said. When she—'

'No, before that. I mean the last time before that.'

'Well, I think she's been on holiday for a bit. So we haven't seen her much since — no, wait. She popped in on Friday night when she got back. Mum's had flu, you see, and Ruth came round to see how she was.'

Eleanor could feel her heart racing as she went on. 'And was your dad there, Susan? Did your dad—'

'Yes. He doesn't usually see us on a Friday, of course, but he came for a bit because Mum was ill.'

Eleanor felt a twinge of bitter triumph as she understood. That was why John had been unusually late home for the weekend. And that, of course, was when he had been wearing the tie.

She pictured the cosy little scene. Ruth, John and Susan gathered sympathetically round Barbara's bed, the yellow tie falling forward as John had leant down to plant a kiss on the woman's sweating, lined forehead. An amusing comment from Ruth about the brightness of the yellow, a little laugh from them all at the trendiness of the design. The image made Eleanor want to retch, but she shook it aside and went on.

'I must apologise for some of the things I said to you. I'm afraid I got a little confused. You mustn't take any notice. Do you think you could forget some of the — I mean, I really said some stupid things and I'm very sorry.' Eleanor hesitated a second, then, seeing a temporary way out of the immediate situation, tried to keep the bitterness out of her voice as she said, 'Your mother's quite right. I haven't been very well and John — your father — has to look after me. He's been very good about it all these years.' She almost smiled at the irony of finding herself defending the man who had betrayed her, but at the same time felt herself warming to the task of maintaining the delicate edifice of deception that she was uncovering little by little from the muddy ground she had unknowingly trodden for so long. She must continue to portray herself to the confused girl as a crazy old woman who didn't know what she was saying. She needed time to think before she dared let the truth come out, and sensed that the girl might clam up completely if the existing fantasies were crushed too quickly. She had to find out all she could before the inevitable happened and everything came out into the open.

'But John has had this flat for over twenty years or more — no, I'm sorry, I don't mean this flat. His flat. Or his other flat, perhaps I should say. Upstairs. Did you know about that?'

'Yes, of course. Flat six. On the third floor. He often goes up there to sleep. When he has lots of work on. And sometimes he just goes straight there from work, and doesn't come down here at all. But not usually.'

There was a pause, and Eleanor fancied she could almost feel the grinding of Susan's brain as it struggled to assess the meaning of this sudden materialisation of a hitherto unseen aunt in her room. The girl looked straight at Eleanor, the tone of her voice entirely matter-of-fact now, and without the smallest hint of self-pity.

'Why did you come here? And why did you say those terrible – I mean, what did you mean? And what did you want?'

'You'll just have to understand, Susan. Just have to believe me when I say I didn't mean them. I was upset about something and I – I get very confused. As I said, I had a bit of a shock today and I think I took it out on you.' Even as she said it, she found herself silently appealing to some inner judge to take notice of the exquisite satire echoing behind the understatement in this brief description.

'And why haven't you ever come to see us before? Why haven't we been to see you? At your house? Where Dad goes all the time?'

'Well –' Eleanor hesitated, hating the snarl of lies she was enmeshing herself in ever tighter under the innocent gaze of the girl – 'well, what does your father say about that?'

'He doesn't like to talk about it. And I suppose it's – it's just always been like that, you know. Ever since I can remember. It seems funny now, but I suppose I've just got used to it. It's all right, isn't it? I mean, you promise there's nothing bad that's happened? Something you're not telling me?'

There was something so touching about the girl's appeal for reassurance that Eleanor found herself wanting to comfort her, to make things better for her.

'Of course not,' she said, reaching a hand out across the floral bedspread and delicately touching the tips of Susan's fingers with her own. 'Everything's just as it always was.' She looked down at the pattern of entwined green leaves and pale pink roses on the chintz between them and took her hand gently away from Susan's and lifted it to her face, rubbing the space between her eyes with one finger as she felt the threat of tears advancing from her throat. 'Tell me, Susan, do they seem happy, your mum and dad? Don't answer this if you don't want to, but I'd just like to know that they're OK.'

Eleanor amazed herself at her capacity to lie so smoothly while at the same time feeling genuinely emotional; the slight hint of tears in her voice fitted so well the apparently sincere need to reassure herself about the wellbeing of her 'brother-in-law' and his 'wife' that it was confusing to know that it was the very thought of their being happy that was making her want to cry.

'Oh yes, you mustn't worry about that. They row some-times, of course, but they're still very happy together. My dad worships her really. More than he does me, anyway.' She gave a little laugh. 'All my friends say I'm really lucky. But then they don't know.' She stopped and looked down for a second. 'Lots of them have divorced parents, you see,' she went on, looking straight at Eleanor again. 'Or single mums. You know – some of them never knew their dads at all. Or they've got stepfathers. They think I'm lucky.'

She frowned slightly and bent her head to try to see into Eleanor's face.

'Are you crying?' she asked quietly. 'What's the matter? You don't look like someone who'd cry, somehow. You look too – oh I don't know. You just don't look as if you would.'

'Sorry, Susan. I'm not really crying – I'm just a bit

tired, that's all. I didn't think I was someone who'd cry either. I thought I was — well, I cried when my mother died, I remember that, but that was just at the funeral and it was a different sort of crying somehow. I'm not really crying, don't worry.'

What was making her so anxious to protect the girl? It wasn't just the necessity of keeping her only witness in a state of innocence long enough to prise as much information out of her as possible; it was more than that. Eleanor felt an extraordinary mixture of anger and pity. When Susan looked upset it hurt her. She was quite taken aback to find that she cared about what the girl was feeling; that her own awareness of the lies in which Susan had been brought up made Eleanor somehow responsible for seeing that from now on she was hurt as little as possible. In her innocence Susan obviously still felt secure; for the immediate future Eleanor knew she must preserve this tenuous security. Not yet need she know that her parents were adulterers and liars. Not yet need she know that she was the offspring of an illicit affair.

'Susan, may I ask that you don't tell anyone about my coming here? I know that's a lot to ask, but I'm sure you can see now that I'm sorry — very sorry — that I burst in on you and frightened you the way I did, and that I just got a bit muddled about things. It would be much easier for me if we could just forget all about it. Do you think you could do that?'

Susan hesitated and Eleanor knew she would have to put more pressure on her if she was to convince her to keep quiet about this extraordinary incident.

'I swear to you, Susan, that it can only do good if you say nothing. I've been very silly and I wish I hadn't done it now. Haven't you had times when you just longed to be able to pretend something had never happened, and that you could go back to the way things were before it did?'

'Well, yes, of course I have.'

'Then please, please just give me this chance. Don't let them see what a fool I've made of myself. Please.'

Eleanor could see she was winning through. The girl's concern was focusing on this mysterious aunt before her, apparently still in danger of breaking down. She had no thought for herself any more.

'Yes.' She paused and looked earnestly at Eleanor. 'Yes, of course. If that's what you'd like. But are you sure you're all right?'

'Yes, Susan, I'm sure. I'm fine,' answered Eleanor matter-of-factly, then, after a moment's hesitation, in a move that took Susan by surprise as much as it did herself, she suddenly reached out both arms and drew the startled girl towards her across the bed, clutching her tightly in an awkward, trembling embrace. 'I'm absolutely fine.'

Eleanor smiled to herself as she tried to picture Andrew's reaction to her arrival. It would be nearly three o'clock in the morning by the time she reached Winstead, and he and Catherine were always in bed by ten. He had sounded puzzled enough by her phone call, and by her suggestion that she 'pop down to see them for a few days' or what-ever she had said, but this middle-of-the-night arrival was really going to throw the system. She could just imagine Catherine's rather silly, startled face beneath the hairnet as the doorbell woke her, and Andrew's strained, confused look under the tousled white hair as he peeped round the chained front door.

'Poor old things!' she said to herself. She felt odd. Very odd. Almost excited, she thought, if such a word could possibly be used to describe a woman in her unhappy position. Rather as one does immediately after the first terrible reaction to news of a death or some horrific disaster, when the immediate shock is beginning to be absorbed and before the endless grinding depression sets in. The kind of moment, she thought, when someone suggests making a cup of tea or getting a drink, and a strange euphoria descends on the company; an excitement at the very change in the everyday routine, at the *specialness* of the moment; at the transportation, even by such misery, of the leading players to a status of being different. Special. To be looked after, noticed, cosseted.

'Except who is to cosset me?' she said out loud, and clucked her tongue at the hint of self-pity she could feel the words produce. 'Good old Andrew and Catherine, of course! No doubt they'll cosset me in their own peculiar way.' She could imagine the well-meaning lecture her sister-in-law would give about her handling of the situation. She could picture the embarrassed squirming from Andrew – but at least the tea or the drink would be forthcoming. 'Better than nothing,' she muttered. 'Better than nothing.'

She thought back to the extraordinary scene in the flat.

It had all been too much to take in, and she still didn't feel she had really begun to understand. In spite of her original plan that she should get as much as possible out of the girl while she was willing to talk, she had soon realised that the chances of the missing parents returning was far too high to risk staying any longer. The thought of having to face either John or the girl's mother was unbearable, and after she had indulged in the snatched comfort of that extraordinary hug, it hadn't been long before Eleanor had made her move. She had felt almost guilty at leaving Susan behind, but was reassured by the thought that the girl merely thought she'd had a visit from a batty old aunt, and that so far nothing had changed in her relatively comfortable, secure world of two apparently loving parents. Eleanor's knowledge of the truth of the girl's situation coloured her view, and she had to force herself to remember that so far no one but she and the girl's mother knew that anything had changed.

As she drove through the blackness of the Gloucestershire countryside, the sharply focused beams from the Range Rover's headlights whitening the surface of the narrow lane and throwing the long grasses on the verge into bright relief against the darkness behind them, she tried to make sense of the swirling emotions that were beginning to battle with her precarious sense of wellbeing. A mistress — and a child. A child. What did that make her feel? Had John wanted this daughter? Had the woman got pregnant and forced him to look after them both? John had always been so smug in the childlessness of their marriage, so sure that they were happier, calmer, certainly better off than those of their friends whom they saw go through the mess and trauma of having kids. Eleanor, of course, had never been quite so certain. If she was honest with herself, there had been many times when she had felt a stab of regret, an emptiness, a horrible creeping feeling that perhaps something wonderful was missing from her life. Particularly when the menopause had overtaken her from behind, unexpected and unavoidable. She hadn't realised until her periods slowed, stuttered and spattered to a halting stop nearly ten years ago at the age of forty-eight, how much she had depended on the theoretical possibilities that their existence had given her. She had felt not only depressed at their ending, which her doctor assured her was 'to be expected', but positively angry. All the years of pads, pains, tampons and mood swings. All for nothing. All wasted. But at least it had always been a shared decision, a shared view – she had always comforted herself in the occasional moments of disquiet by congratulating herself on what a good marriage they had, and how their closeness owed not a little to the fact that they were unburdened by the responsibilities of children.

'Huh!' she said out loud, and smiled grimly at the irony. Now she knew that the marriage had been preserved, not because of the bond between them and the lack of children at all, but in spite of – or even because of – the existence of a mistress and her – what? Love child? No, she couldn't countenance the idea of 'love' in any way connected with John and that dreary, grey old woman. Bastard? It sounded too old-fashioned even to be insulting, and even as she spoke the word in her head she pictured the face of the confused young girl in the bedroom, and knew that wasn't at all how she felt. The child was an innocent; there was no doubt about that. The child could not, must not, be blamed.

Then, as Eleanor took the car smoothly round the winding bends of the lane, enjoying the way the empty road and the silent darkness echoed her mood, a thought suddenly occurred to her, and made her brake quickly and slow the car to a crawl so she could examine it.

'I'm a stepmother,' she whispered to the night ahead of her behind the fly-spotted glass of the windscreen. 'How extraordinary: I'm a stepmother. I have a stepdaughter.'

Chapter Seven

The horrors didn't begin until much later in the night – or morning, as it was by then. Eleanor woke suddenly, at the sound of an unnerving gasping, and it took a few moments to realise that she had made it herself. The room was light, in spite of the heavy old-fashioned brocade curtains, and as she opened her eyes she could clearly see the worn pattern of chrysanthemums embossed on them and the large, tasselled pelmet drooping at their head. The way they hung in deep, straight folds filled her with foreboding, and she looked away from them and down to the surface of the bed. The eiderdown had slipped sideways and was hanging halfway to the floor, revealing an unevenly hand-crocheted patchwork blanket underneath. She pulled the eiderdown back into place and took a quick look round the large, high-ceilinged room, examining her own fear and trying to find out what it was that had woken her into such uneasiness.

The furniture was heavy and dark: a dressing table, topped by a swivel mirror; a large double-doored wardrobe; a chest of drawers with a cream, lace-trimmed mat on its top and a couple of upright chairs tucked against the wall. There was a mustiness in the air, which Eleanor knew was emanating partly from the eiderdown now tucked beneath her chin.

It wasn't that she had woken without being immediately aware of the new situation in which she found herself. The few hours of sleep she had had since arriving at two fifteen in the morning had been spent in dreams of intense clarity; she had known the moment that her own disquieting sounds had disturbed her exactly where she was and what had taken place the previous day. But there was something more that stirred in her unconscious; something that she knew she hadn't until then allowed herself to be aware of or think about, and, whatever this unpleasant knowledge was, it was creeping up into her head and scratching at her consciousness, demanding to be acknowledged.

She lay her head back into the lumpy feather pillow and stared at the ceiling, reluctantly allowing the thought to push its way into her mind and form itself slowly into a picture that she would be forced to look at. And there it was. She could see it, clearly and in detail. She could avoid it no longer, and she cringed into the bedclothes and screwed up her face at the terrible truth of what she saw. John and – that woman. John and that old woman: that dumpy, unattractive, frumpy old woman. He was touching her, he was kissing her, fondling a sagging breast, pushing down wrinkled, cheap, nylon underwear and moving on top of her. Eleanor could see a withered thigh and a mottled, puffy belly.

'No!' she cried out loud and turned her head to the

side and away from the terrible picture, the smell of mothballs and damp nylon sickening in her face as it fitted so well the images that still forced their way into her consciousness. 'No!' she said again, more quietly, 'I can't bear it. He doesn't do it now. They don't do it now. It must have happened—' She stopped, counting back nineteen years and trying to remember how life had been then; where she was; what she was doing. She felt that if, by some impossible process of elimination, she could pinpoint the exact moment of Susan's conception, then she might be able to understand it, and possibly even to accept it, as something less horrifying than it appeared at this moment. Nineteen – no, twenty years ago. There must be a reason; an excuse: something that could provide an explanation. Where had he met the woman? Had Eleanor been ill, perhaps, or away for an unusually long time?

But even as she tried to think back over the years, she realised she was beginning to make excuses for him. Supposing she *had* been ill, or away, or they had been going through a bad patch in the marriage – so what? She had remained faithful all through the thirty years; why should she try to find an excuse for John's having failed to live up to her own standards? She knew why, of course. For her own sake. Because she wanted to find a reason: needed to, desperately. Because if she couldn't, the only possible explanation was far, far worse to contemplate. This was no one-night stand: he had stuck by this woman and her child; provided them with a flat; visited them regularly. But that was good, wasn't it? He had made a terrible mistake and he had done the right thing.

But the image of him and *her*. Making love. Making love. Eleanor knew now what it was that had woken her. Not the humiliation, not the fury at having been deceived. It was jealousy. A raging, unbearable jealousy that tore at her guts and tunnelled into her groin. She could see now that, without being aware of it at the time, she had at first felt an enormous sense of relief to discover that her rival wasn't the beautiful, clever Ruth, or even the young, innocent girl on the bed, but the unremarkable, dowdy, middle-aged creature peering out from the door of Flat 2. But now she could see how stupid she had been: it was much worse that her husband's lover was so ordinary. There must have been something far more than physical passion to bring John together with someone so plain, so unstylish and so . . . so . . . she searched for the right word, and hated herself for knowing what it was even as she tried to avoid it – so *common*. A seductive figure, or a heavy-lipped mouth and thick blonde hair, might have gone some way towards explaining the initial affair, but even allowing for the passage of twenty years Eleanor couldn't imagine that there had ever been an irresistible physical attraction.

She pushed the covers back and sat up, flinging her head forwards onto her chest as a wave of dizziness hit her. She took some deep breaths before slowly shifting herself to the edge of the bed and swivelling her legs sideways so that they hung down from the old-fashioned, high bedstead towards the floor. She leant onto her right arm and lifted her left wrist to her face to squint at her watch: the watch John had bought her for an anniversary present six – seven? – years ago. Did he give *her* presents?

Did they celebrate anniversaries? There was so much she needed – not just wanted: needed – to know.

She made to reach for her handbag to find her reading glasses, but stopped as her brain made sense of the fuzzy figures she had seen on the dial. Six twenty. Where would he be? And what was he doing? With her, or without her? Would he have tried to ring Eleanor at home last night, and been surprised to get no answer? Although she felt utterly unsure about so many things, there was one thing of which she was certain: she still wasn't ready for a confrontation. It was important that John was kept unaware of the discovery for just a little longer, while she found out everything she could, and thought out what she wanted to do.

'How stupid,' she said out loud, realising she had left the woman's flat without getting the telephone number from the girl, not knowing, even if she had had it, whether she would have risked ringing it, and perhaps being confronted by John's voice at the other end. But, although as a rule Eleanor had waited for John to ring her in the evenings from London during the week so that she hadn't risked disturbing him in the middle of some work, there had also been many, many times over the years when she had had to contact him late at night or in the early hours to discuss a domestic crisis or pass on an urgent message. And she'd always found him in the flat when she had rung unexpectedly. So maybe he didn't ever stay with the woman and her child? What had the girl said? Maybe, after all, he had simply done the right thing by them, had set them up in a flat and continued to visit the girl over the years to fulfil his fatherly obligations, too ashamed of what he had done to tell Eleanor, but never again touching the woman or feeling anything for her other than guilt, obligation and pity.

Drunk. That was it. He must have been drunk, and the woman, desperate for affection, had seduced him. It was hard to imagine such a thing: the word 'seduce' didn't match her in any way at all, but yet again Eleanor tried to picture the enormous change that twenty years might have wrought. She could see the woman as a little secretary – a temp, probably – when the fat had been a pretty plumpness, and the grey, wispy hair had been thick and brown. He had felt sorry for her: a rather pathetic little thing who hadn't known anyone in the office. He'd had too much of that ghastly cheap wine they always had at the Christmas parties and she had got him on his own on some pretext in his office and pushed herself against him by his desk, forcing him to look down at her cleavage and—

'Stop it!' Eleanor spoke out loud again and stood up, knowing she had to move, do something physical or she would go mad. She looked for a telephone on the bedside table, but then remembered the only extensions on this floor were in Andrew and Catherine's bedroom and out on the landing. Andrew and Catherine's bedroom – how cosy that sounded. Familiar, domestic, loving. She knew she was in danger of veering off into another bout of self-pity, so she grabbed her cardigan quickly off one of the upright chairs and quietly opened the door and crept out onto the landing.

She dialled the London flat, certain she would get

no answer, but ready to leave a simple message on the machine to tell him she was at her brother's, but was astonished to hear John's voice after only a couple of rings.

'Yes?'

There was a pause, while she held her breath, unprepared for this direct confrontation.

'Yes? Eleanor, is that you? Are you all right, darling? What on earth are you doing up at this hour?'

'Yes, it's me.' She was astonished to hear his voice so calm and so – unguilty. But of course, he'd been talking like this for twenty years. For twenty years he had been speaking to her with the knowledge of his other life clearly in his head; this telephone conversation was for him no different than any of the other many thousands they had had with each other since the – what could she call it? How could she label it? – the affair? Too simple a word. Too innocuous-sounding for the event that had overshadowed her life for so long without her knowing it.

There was another pause, longer this time. Then she went on, in a whisper that she hoped didn't sound hesitant but which was essential if she were to avoid waking the others in the bedroom just along the landing, 'I'm at Andrew's. I'm going to stay here for a bit.'

'But when did you— Why are you there? Are you all right?' John sounded serious, as he always did on the phone, but there was a hint of something different in his voice, which, if she hadn't known him better, she might almost have fancied could be fear. Could he know that she knew? Had that woman, after all, told him of their encounter?

As another silence threatened, Eleanor felt her usual compunction to fill it, to make things easy, to lessen the awkwardness of the moment, but she sucked her lips in over her teeth and pressed them tightly together, determined not to speak. She didn't trust herself not to give something away. In all likelihood he knew nothing, and all her efforts must be directed to keeping it that way as long as possible.

'Shall I ring Gordon?' he asked at last. She knew that tone of voice; it was the one he used whenever she was unwell, or appeared to be upset or depressed for no apparent reason. It was intended to signal worried concern, but had always seemed to Eleanor to contain a hint of patronising superiority, an implication that only a woman, or, more particularly, only Eleanor, would react in such a way, and that all could be explained in terms of hormones or female oversensitivity.

'No, no, I'm fine. There's no need to ring Gordon. I just felt like a bit of a change, that's all. And I didn't feel tired last night so I decided to drive down here late and avoid the traffic.' She was amazed at how calm her voice sounded; how plausibly the lies oozed from her mouth. It was simple. No wonder she had been deceived so easily all these years: the process was almost enjoyable. The sense of power in knowing that she now knew more than he did gave her strength. She felt suddenly in control: only she could see that the smug security he must feel in the clever juggling of the double life he had maintained all this time was now a paper-thin film stretched tautly over his nasty little lies, just needing her decision to prick it for it to tear wide open. He thought he was warm, safe, covered: only she could see that in reality he was naked, exposed and shivering.

'I don't know, Eleanor. It's very strange of you to drive off like that. You could at least have told me you were thinking about it. And why did you ring so ridiculously early? What do you want?'

'I—' It took just a split second for her to find an answer. 'Do you know, I didn't realise how horribly early it was until I was talking to you. I am sorry, darling — were you asleep?'

'No, it's OK, I was awake anyway. It's just unlike you to wake so early, that's all. What did you want?'

'Just to tell you I was here. In case you wanted me for anything.'

'Oh, right. How long are you staying?'

Why do you want to know? she thought. *Why do you want to know?* Oh God, help me.

'A few days.'

'I see. Well, I'll stay up in town then, if you're not going to be home. Get a bit of work done.'

She closed her eyes at the stab of pain his remark had buried in her chest, then bit her lip until she was able to control her voice again.

'Martin is still waiting to see you, don't forget,' he went on.

There was a short pause, while Eleanor considered the other universe that had existed four days ago; the one in which she had been on her way to see Martin Havers.

'Are you sure you're all right?' John asked again.

'Yes, I've told you — I'm feeling fine. Sorry to worry you. I'll give you a ring tonight, darling. Have a good day.'

'Yes, you too. Give my best to Andrew and Catherine. Speak to you later. 'Bye, darling.'

''Bye. Darling.'

She put the phone down and gazed at it for a moment, grappling with a terrible realisation that had crept up on her during the call without her being aware of it. Suddenly she knew exactly how she had been able to call him all these years at times of the day — or night — when he couldn't possibly have been expecting it and yet always found him at home. Or apparently at home.

'Oh, for God's sake, I'm such a *fool*!' As she suddenly became aware of her naïvety, Eleanor found herself collapsing into the tears she'd been holding back unconsciously all night, and she gulped out the words as she shouted them at the senseless instrument in front of her. 'You've got an extension down there, you bastard! You've got another extension! I've been talking to you all these years and you've been— You bastard! You — you—' She couldn't find the words she needed to berate him with; frustrated in her lack of expletives, she was aware that there were terms that existed that, if she only knew them, she could spit at him to release her misery and anger. What she now saw was that the pathetic prissiness of her limited, middle-class, middle-aged language had no vocabulary for the way she felt, and her inability to express herself only added to her despair.

A noise on the landing made Eleanor look up from the phone to see Catherine's frightened face peeping round the edge of the bedroom door opposite. She looked frail and papery without her makeup, and her expression of fascinated nervousness beneath the pink hairnet made Eleanor long to poke out her tongue at her, but instead she covered her contempt with a thin smile and whispered across to her: 'Sorry. Sorry to wake you. I'm all right. Sorry – a little bit of marital friction, that's all. Nothing serious. I'll talk to you in the morning. Go back to bed.'

She wiped her face with her hand and stood up as Catherine's head disappeared again and the door closed.

Chapter Eight

'I don't know, Andrew. I just can't see the point of any of it, somehow. It's all become completely meaningless. What the hell is the point of it all?'

'Ah, well, yes indeed.' Andrew tried to cover his discomfort with a suitably concerned and thoughtful expression, but had a feeling his sister was far too canny to be fooled by the flimsy façade of his noncommittal waffle into assuming there was any real insight behind his words. 'We all tend to get that feeling from time to time, you know. It's part of the – um – human condition and so on.'

'Yes, Andrew. Well of course I realise that. I don't for a moment assume I'm the only person who's ever felt like this. But you see it's more than that. I don't just mean that there seems to be no point; I suppose I'm trying to say that there also seems never to have been any point. And that kind of wipes out the whole of my life. I just can't remember what I'm for. Oh dear, I am talking nonsense, aren't I? Never mind, Andrew. It's just a middle-aged crise. Or old-age crise, I should say.'

'Nonsense.'

They were walking in the garden, George exploring ahead of them, Eleanor feeling chilled in the early autumn morning, but enjoying the feeling of the air on her bare arms beneath the short sleeves of her cotton frock. She had fully intended to unburden herself to him when she had first asked Andrew to come outside with her, hoping to find comfort in the knowledge that she would no longer be alone with her terrifying secret, but after her first few words she had changed her mind. A glance at his carefully assumed expression of benign understanding had made her wince, and she had suddenly felt like just one more dilapidated member of his flock; a number on a list for him to deal with and then tick off as part of the job; a supplicant scheduled to receive the allotted quota of sympathy before he moved on to someone else, or walked back into the house to relay everything to Catherine. Her initial words had been vague enough for her to change tack without any appreciable swerve, and she had diverted her speech into describing a generalised, sourceless fear and depression. She hoped the ensuing discussion might yet bring her some relief without having to let him in on the truth.

Andrew was holding his hands behind his back and dipping his head in what he hoped appeared to be a suitably serious and sympathetic posture of friendly accessibility: the wise, all-knowing priest, who is shocked by nothing, and endlessly understanding. He had assumed such poses before when confronted, as he inevitably had been many times over the years, by human misery; each time hoping that the external appearance would somehow find itself mirrored in a true depth of understanding, but always aware that part of him was standing back and watching as he played the role expected of him. Once again, as on so many previous occasions, he felt the inadequacy of his experience; his life had been so sheltered and so limited that the times he came up against the emotional crises of human nature left him flailing. He knew that somewhere inside himself was the capacity to give true support and understanding, but the instinctive closing up that the approach of emotion produced in him always got in the way. He could sense quite clearly that Eleanor had been about to confide in him, and he was ashamed at the relief he felt at her obvious decision to keep it to herself after all. He knew this was the moment he should persuade her to tell him everything, to let go and trust in him and God to offer peace and understanding, but somehow the thought of his own sister opening herself up to him was too difficult to take. He stopped and stood still for a moment, and as he did so Eleanor turned and looked at him.

He's getting old, she thought. My big brother: my shy big brother is getting old. She thought of the thick dark hair that had always grown straight out from the top of his forehead in a horizontal fringe, cute and strokable as a child, but intensely irritating to him as a teenager, and felt a pang of pity at the sight of the thinning grey strands that had taken its place. The kindly, florid face, half hidden behind horn-rimmed glasses, still held the look of permanent slight anxiety that she had known all her life. Now she knew she was causing it, and she reached a hand onto his shoulder and squeezed it.

'Don't worry, Andrew, I'm not really asking you for any answers. Nor any advice, either. It's just that I haven't got anyone else I can talk to now.'

'What about John? You can talk to him, can't you? It's very easy in a marriage to skim over the surface for most of the time, but believe me, if you try one can —'

'No. No, unfortunately that's not possible.'

'Ah.'

So it's the marriage, thought Andrew. He felt rather relieved. He had assumed something far more sinister than a bad patch in her marriage; something darker, more complex, more — metaphysical. If John had been playing around, or drinking or even whacking her about a bit — well, these things could be got through, passed over, survived.

'Eleanor, you have to understand that marriage never stands still. The times of—'

'Andrew, it's all right. I told you — I don't expect any answers. It's not John. Or at least, not in the way you think. I've just lost heart in it all. Not marriage, I mean — in life. A bit. At the moment. But I'll be fine. Don't worry — it's just good to get away for a while and clear my thoughts.'

She turned and began to walk again, looking down at the ground just as her brother had before.

'Is there anything I can do to help?' he said.

She was surprised to hear the tone of gentle enquiry in his voice, and glanced up into eyes that, for a moment, had lost all their usual shuttered nervousness, and looked into hers openly and with genuine interest.

'No, just let me mope about here for a while, that's all,' she smiled.

Andrew was still looking at her, and a small frown grew between his eyebrows in a little fold of reddened skin, falling easily into its familiar, well-worn creases. He bit his lower lip and made a small grunting sound, and Eleanor almost smiled as she felt the effort to communicate going on behind the hesitant exterior.

'We all live a lie, Eleanor, you know that, don't you? I mean to a certain extent.'

'How do you mean?'

He paused again, and smacked his lips apart. She fancied she could almost see the waves of energy produced by the battle within him between the urge to make some sort of direct, heartfelt admission and the stronger instinct to turn and flee – or at least to cover the inner turmoil with a comforting platitude.

'Well. Catherine and I – of course, we haven't been what you'd call husband and wife for many— I mean— Oh dear, oh dear, this is— No, no, I'm sorry I can't burden you with this.'

'Andrew – oh Andrew, I'm so sorry. I'm so selfish. It's not burdening me. Not at all. You never talk to me about your life; about your marriage. Of course it's not burdening me. I just always assumed that everything was fine.'

'Yes, well, of course. One would. But no, we haven't been fully – we haven't made love for many, many years now. She doesn't enjoy it, you see. Well, she never did, really, I don't think. And of course that's her privilege.

But it does make for — what shall I say — a rather bleak old time of it, on the whole. I always envied you and John so much. You seemed to be so — so loving.'

There was a silence for a moment as they walked on. Eleanor was surprised to find that his reference to John didn't at this moment bother her; it was as if he were talking about someone she hardly knew, someone not connected with her or her life at all. She found herself concentrating on her feelings of pity for the bewildered man by her side. There was something immensely touching about the way he had confided in her, the sadness of his feelings still conveyed in the peculiarly British matter-of-fact shorthand that betrayed in a few clipped phrases the agony of years of loneliness.

'But you still care for each other? I mean, you're good friends, if I can call it that, aren't you?'

'Oh yes indeed. In fact, I'm making a terrible fuss about absolutely nothing, Eleanor. Forget it. I don't know why on earth we got started on all this. I'm meant to be comforting you, not telling you my small problems. I'm absolutely fine. Really.' He turned away from her and looked across the small lawn towards the overblown, spilling herbaceous border. 'Just look at the colour of those dahlias — one of Catherine's triumphs.' He turned back and smiled down at Eleanor. 'I have much to be thankful for, you see. Many small joys. Closer to God in a garden and all that.'

They walked on across the grass and towards the flowerbed. The bright yellow of the dahlias was indeed startling, Eleanor thought; almost too bright against the mass of hazy purples and greens that made up most of the background. The tall spikes of the lupins were bent over towards them, dry and brown, and when she reached out a hand to touch one she could hear as well as feel the dry seeds moving in the myriad hanging pods.

'I should have cut those off weeks ago,' said Andrew. 'We often get a second flowering from them if I deadhead them in time. Not as big as the first one, but pretty all the same. There just seems so much else to do.'

'Well, at least they've done what they've spent all year working towards,' said Eleanor, pulling a pod from the spike and opening it. 'I always feel rather sorry for the roses as I deadhead them day after day. Every attempt at reproducing snipped off by my secateurs before they can make their little babies. Frustrating their natural urges. Funny old business, gardening, really, when you come to think about it. Everything desperately budding, eating, reproducing, just so that they can start it all over again the next season. Every plant competing to get the water, the food, the air, the sun. Selfishness wherever you look. And all that cruelty. Insects boring holes in each other and munching their way out. Ghastly.' She emptied the small, round seeds into her palm and watched them as they rolled off and onto the grass as she tipped her hand upside down. She threw the empty pod back towards the bed and dusted her hands against each other.

'You are in a melancholy old mood, Eleanor, you really are,' Andrew laughed. 'Cruelty or not, it's very beautiful, isn't it?'

'Yes, it is. Very beautiful,' she smiled in return.

They turned away from the flowerbed and made their way back towards the French windows of the sitting room.

Just before they went inside, Eleanor said quietly: 'And you've got your beliefs, haven't you? I mean, you've never really talked about any of that to me, Andrew, but that really is something to envy. I envy you that. Knowing there's a reason for it all, some sort of point. I wish I had that. That must be a strength to you, surely? Whenever I go into an empty church, and just sit in a pew, or look at the statues or the paintings, or light a candle, I feel such a strong sense of – well, something. But I never like to explore it because I know it'll just disappear in a little puff of realism. But you can explore it. You have someone to turn to.'

'Yes. Yes, indeed.'

But she knew, even without looking at him, that the shutters had come down again.

As they walked back into the house through the French windows they met Catherine carrying a tray of coffee and biscuits into the drawing room.

'Come and sit down, Eleanor,' she said, smiling. 'Leave George out in the garden, will you? A cup of coffee will do you good. Take that chair there, dear,' she went on, gesturing with one shoulder at an armchair on one side of the fireplace as she put the tray down on a small table behind the sofa.

Eleanor knew it was Andrew's chair that was being

offered to her and that she was expected to protest and fuss until persuaded to sit in it, but she took it without comment to avoid giving Catherine too much satisfaction. She's loving this, she thought. She's loving knowing there's something wrong. It's making her feel smug and safe and she's going to be solicitous and wonderfully kind and understanding and vicar's-wifeish about it all. It made Eleanor feel even more determined not to reveal any more than she already had to either of them.

'I am so sorry I woke you so horribly early this morning,' she said. 'And I do hope you didn't mind me using the phone?'

'Of course not,' Catherine said. 'You know you can use it any time. Any time at all. Here . . .'

She crossed over to the armchair and passed a cup of coffee to Eleanor and then knelt on the floor next to the chair and looked up at her. Oh, very little-girly, thought Eleanor. Very charming and unassuming and sweet. Here it comes. Any minute.

'Is everything all right? You sounded a bit—'

'Fine,' said Eleanor, bringing the cup and saucer up to beneath her chin. 'Fine now, thanks. Just one of those things. Nothing to worry about. But it's lovely to have a break. I'll stay over the weekend if I may and then I'll leave you in peace on Monday and make my way home.' She took a sip of coffee then put the cup down again and smiled.

'Huh!' she said very quietly.

'What?' asked Catherine, looking up eagerly as if still hopeful there might be an interesting revelation.

'Oh, sorry — nothing,' said Eleanor, still smiling. You don't have sex, she was thinking. You're sitting there all smug and self-satisfied in your boring little dress and what you don't know is that I know you don't like sex. You're a cold fish, Catherine, for all your warm sympathy and wifely duties. You don't give my brother his rights, my girl. We may not do it often, but at least John and I—

'Oh Christ!' she said out loud, slopping the coffee into its saucer as her lap jolted with the sudden movement of her hand to her mouth.

'What is it?' asked Andrew, rushing to her chair from the window.

'It's nothing,' she said, bringing her voice quickly under control again. 'I just remembered something. It's not important.'

But the image of John on top of her that had come so suddenly unbidden into her mind was harder to restrain: even as she spoke she still saw the flushed sweatiness of his neck and the familiar grey head bobbing up and down with the rhythm of his movement. And, more clearly than anything else, she saw his face; it was reddening and tensing, the eyes focusing on somewhere and nowhere at the same time, the muscles of his cheeks and mouth pulling themselves into a mindless grimace that was animal in its intensity. He was coming.

And now she knew she wasn't the only one who had seen it.

Chapter Nine

Once again it was exactly two o'clock when Eleanor woke. For the third night running it was as if a silent but undeniable alarm clock had summoned her from sleep at precisely the same time. She was wide awake before she knew what the grumbling, tearing agony inside her was all about; it took a few seconds to dig into it and unearth the seething jealousy that had erupted and dragged her into consciousness. A flame burnt in her groin: she squirmed and dug at it with her clenched, entwined hands, turning her head to the side and squeezing her eyes shut as if she could push it away while she wasn't looking. But it burnt on, feeling scalding hot between her thighs, and insisting on her attention. Images of John caressing Barbara, his face twisted and flushed with desire, leapt into her mind and fed the flame, and she cried out loud with the unbearable mixture of sexual excitement and sheer miserable unhappiness that the visions produced. She opened her legs and pressed her hands harder up and into herself, indulging the need to push the irresistible physical sensation to its inevitable climax, moaning and juddering unwillingly into some sort of relief.

Then she felt ashamed: dirty and humiliated, in a way she hadn't since first discovering such secret pleasures as a child. Sex had been of little importance in her life, and she was astonished and horrified to discover the extent to which, uninvited, it had invaded her body and proved its continuing dominance. Now that it had been rekindled by the idea of someone else enjoying what she had thought to be exclusively hers, she realised how powerful a hold her physical needs still had over her, and she hated herself for finding excitement in the terrible, unavoidable images that forced themselves on her unwilling imagination. Regret preyed on her, tormenting her. Why hadn't she enjoyed the delights of the marriage bed more often? How could she have turned away so many times: times when she knew John was hinting at his need for sex? How could she have resisted the touch of his hand on her breast, or the feeling of his body sliding onto hers in comfortable, familiar, unthreatening lovemaking? Now she ached for it; her arms in the chastity of her double bed flailed and slid over the sheets as they instinctively searched for his chest to grasp and squeeze; she spread her legs and wept at the emptiness between them. Too late, she cried to herself. It's too late – I'm a stupid old woman. I loathe myself. I loathe him. I hate him: I hate them: I hate them together: but I want him. I want him so much I shall die. I shall pull out my hair as madwomen do; I shall cut myself; tear pieces of flesh from my groin; bite myself.

She sat up suddenly and put her head in her hands,

unable to lie down with her thoughts any longer, desperate for distraction. A crack in the curtains let in a sliver of moonlight, and she lifted her head and by the thin, white light looked round at her bedroom. She frowned as she tried to remember how she had felt when she was that other woman: the woman who had lived in ignorance, in innocence. The woman who had minded about things like furniture and fabric, who had chosen with such care everything in the room in front of her. The woman who had thought it mattered what colour the walls were; who had chattered to Ruth about the weather, holidays, John's whereabouts. *John's whereabouts!* She shook her head at the foolishness of that alternate being: how naïve she seemed now. Eleanor knew she could never inhabit the same world as she had; that, although she had to live in the same body, she was a different person in every way, and could never again look around her from the comfort of the bed without dying a little. Eleanor before the knowledge, she thought to herself, before the lifting of the veil, before the snake. Before the woman. A universe apart. Divided for ever from her present self by an unbridgeable chasm of awareness.

But what if she'd walked on by the side of that chasm without ever having looked down? If she hadn't found out, would it still have been there? Would it still have been true? If the Eleanor of a week ago had gone on existing, would the world have been different? Did her knowledge make it happen? If she could go back, walk past the yellow tie and ignore it, could she still make everything be as it had appeared? She almost felt that a strong enough effort of will could spin the part of her mind that mirrored the world so that it would reflect on the other side, that the brightness of its vision could be reversed into a misty new beginning that would show yesterday's reality, not the horror of today's truth.

But it couldn't, didn't, wouldn't happen. However hard she tried to turn away from the horror that insisted on confronting her she couldn't ignore it, and the urgent desire to know more began to dominate her thoughts. She needed to find out everything; the only way she could imagine getting through the day was to be allowed to spend her time picking over this sore that was infecting the whole of her body and mind; to pull at it, scratch it and fiddle with it until it revealed every last bit of putrid unpleasantness. She knew the healing process of allowing it to cover itself over with a skin of normality mustn't be allowed to begin until everything lurking inside had been dug out and destroyed.

She had planned to visit that woman again, but knew she was unable to face it. The images of her with John had become so horrendous and all-pervasive that she feared she would be unable to look at her without attacking her, or sending herself into a humiliating fit of weeping or ranting. So should she confront John? Was it today she should tell him? Would the satisfaction of revealing that she knew expiate this terrible jealousy that was dominating her?

A terrible fear clutched at her at the very thought. Supposing he left her. Supposing her confronting him just meant that he spent more time with his whore. Supposing he was pleased to have it all out in the open:

he might be relieved that she had found out; grateful to be free to go to her. No. It was far too risky. She couldn't bear it. Her physical longing for him had become so great that she couldn't countenance the idea of life without him, couldn't survive the thought of having to lie alone for the next twenty years picturing his hands on the other's body, his mouth on hers. She had always thought herself strong and independent; now she could see how much it was an illusion. Knowing he would always return at the weekends had been her anchor.

She felt no love for him, just gnawing, consuming need. The burning rage that screamed for revenge was as powerful as ever. She must be patient. Find out everything she could and then plan, carefully, how to get him away from her. She would have to suspend all decisions until she was calmer and more in control.

She picked up the hand mirror from the bedside table, put it onto her lap and looked into it in disgust. Her skin drooped down in heavy folds that were deadly pale in the moonlight that was reflected up off the sheets. 'John,' she whispered slowly, 'John, I loathe you. John, I need you. How can I hate you and need you at the same time? What am I to do? Who will help me?'

The girl. That was the only way she could find out more; the girl that she had somehow, extraordinarily, found some sort of sympathy – even empathy – with. Her stepdaughter. Somehow she must get in touch with her and carefully go over as much of her young life as she could, matching the girl's account of what she could remember with what Eleanor herself had been doing, saying, thinking at the time; watching for any clues that might help towards any kind of explanation or illumination. She couldn't begin to understand why, but the thought of this brought her some kind of temporary peace. Her stepdaughter. She would get in touch with her stepdaughter. It gave her a quiet satisfaction to start working out how she could contact her without alerting John, to deceive him as he had deceived her for so long. And she knew suddenly something more: that she would invite her down here. To the house.

It felt right. It pleased her to know instinctively how much he would hate it; how much it would upset him if he knew. To have his two lives intermingling behind his back, for Eleanor to be unravelling his secrets, discussing him with the daughter he had so carefully hidden. How dare they have kept this creature hidden from her? Brought her up together, changed her nappies, rocked her to sleep while Eleanor sat alone in the house, innocently pottering about or tidying his things or doing work for his business. How dare they?

To get the girl down here would add another piece to the mysterious jigsaw she found herself unwillingly putting together. Even as she hated the picture that was assembling itself only too clearly as she fitted each new little chunk into place, she was well aware that nothing could stop her now until it was finished; she wouldn't be able to rest until every little corner was complete, and not a single jagged hole was left unfilled, or one knobbly, convoluted spare piece left unaccounted for.

She would give the girl lunch. The thought of having

something to plan for, to work for, seemed comforting, and she put her mind onto the soothing area of menu planning. She had a brief moment of fear at the thought that she had no idea what a girl of nineteen would eat – especially this one, tied more closely to her by events than any child she had ever met, but at the same time utterly unknown. She might be vegetarian, or only eat fish, or never eat wheat, or – no, this was ridiculous. Eleanor must calm herself and think clearly; push aside the old insecurity she always felt when having to deal with children. Their direct looks and replies uncushioned by social convention always made her uneasy, and she would often find herself awkward and gushing in her dealings with them. But the girl wasn't a baby: she could speak for herself, for goodness' sake. When she managed to get hold of her, she would ask her. What could be simpler than that? She would cook something simple but elegant, the kind of understated good food that she felt sure was beyond the capacity, or even the knowledge, of that woman. This thought made her jump. She hadn't realised that she had felt herself to be in any direct competition with – Barbara (much as she loathed to speak the name, even in her head, the sound of it was now imbued with so much disgust that she used it as an insult instead of a description) until this moment. The jealousy had been obvious and unbearable, the anger and resentment fiercer than she would have believed possible, but up until now she had had no idea that she felt any need to compete. She smiled to herself, feeling for the first time a tiny chance of redemption in the challenge of bettering her husband's lover in this small matter of a meal for the daughter. If battle lines are to be drawn across the dining table, she thought, there's no question who will win.

•∞•

At eleven o'clock the phone rang. Convinced it was John, Eleanor looked up in fear from her seat on the kitchen stool but then ran quickly to answer it before she could let herself think too much about how she would handle it, instinctively trusting that the old Eleanor who had answered his calls thousands of times over the years would somehow take over and talk to him without giving anything away. She was thrown at the sound of a different voice than the one she was expecting. A voice she couldn't identify for a moment, but one that, once recognised, filled her with a nauseous terror. It was she. The whore.

'Yes, what do you want?'

'It's Barbara.' There was a pause. 'I'm the—'

'I know who you are, for God's sake. What do you want? You haven't told him, have you? You haven't been stupid enough to—'

'No, no, of course not. I wouldn't want to, can't you see that? I don't know what he'd do if ... But I'm frightened. I don't know what to do. He's bound to find out, isn't he? And then what's going to happen? He hates any – he just won't stand any trouble. What shall I do?'

Eleanor was so taken aback by the appeal to her from

the other woman that she answered without thinking, comforting the object of her jealous fury automatically.

'It's all right. You don't have to be frightened. Why did you ring me?'

'I'm sorry. I don't know what else to do.'

'Where's Susan? She's not listening to all this, is she?'

'No. No, of course not. She's gone out. She's gone up to the job centre. She told me that you'd been to see her. She thinks you're her aunt, doesn't suspect. But what if she says something in front of John?'

'Stop being frightened. It's important he doesn't find out. You've lied to Susan and to yourself for long enough, woman. What's so different now? Don't be so pathetic. Just go on being the two-faced liar you've been for so long and you can't go wrong.'

'I haven't lied. I—'

'Of course you have. Haven't you let Susan think you're married? That you're his wife? That he stayed at weekends with – what did you call me? – her aunt? Her daft, unwell aunt? You knew the truth all the time. You knew he was married, that you were wrecking a marriage. You knew you were taking someone else's husband – didn't you? You bitch.' Eleanor winced regretfully at the sound of her own insult, and silently vowed from now on to keep her anger discreetly leashed until she felt quite sure she could control it and use it to its best advantage. There was a silence on the other end of the telephone, and Eleanor realised she had hit on something important.

She went on, angrily, impatient to know more, and irritated by the feeble insecurity of the woman she knew to be listening, 'What did he tell you about me? Come on, woman, you're in no position to hold anything back from me, for goodness' sake, not after what you've done. What did he say about me, his wife? HIS WIFE!'

'Well, he — he always said that, you know, that you'd both not — that, oh dear, that you'd been very unhappy. That you didn't — I'm sorry, I'm not very good at talking on the telephone, I didn't — oh I don't know what to say.' The woman was crying now, her voice disappearing in a mumbled blur as quickly as Eleanor's had been rising in intensity. 'He always told me it was over, that he just felt sorry for you.'

Eleanor grimaced at the words but ignored them and ploughed on bravely, determined to dig out as much information as possible while she had the chance: 'But you knew we were still married?'

There was another silence, and Eleanor gripped tightly onto the receiver and clenched the muscles of her abdomen in her efforts to stop herself from yelling in impatience and frustration.

'Didn't you?' she said at last, in as near to a calm voice as she could manage.

'Yes, I did. But he always said, you know, that it was . . . oh dear.'

'*What*, for Christ's sake? What did he always say?' She couldn't stop her voice rising again in fury, hating herself for being in the miserable position of having to beg this woman for information that she knew could only hurt her.

'That it was, I mean that your marriage was — oh what

did he call it? He had a word for it that he always used when I asked him. Because I did ask him, you see, Mrs Hamilton. I did often ask him. I don't want you to think that I—'

Eleanor interrupted her, aware as she did so that she was allowing her voice to slip into the patient, patronising tone she used when addressing her cleaning lady or a shop girl. 'Look, I'm really trying very hard to be what they call civilised about this. I'd be very grateful, though, if you would do your best to answer my question and tell me exactly what my husband said to you about my relationship with him.'

'He used to say that it was a — a formality. And that when you were better he'd get a—'

'Better!' Eleanor snorted. 'What the hell do you mean by that? Am I ill? Did he say I was ill? What do you mean, when I was better?'

'I — I mean . . . oh dear, I mean . . .'

Eleanor could sense that tears were once more hovering not far beneath the surface, and interrupted the hesitant stuttering in impatient anger: 'For God's sake, pull yourself together, you silly woman. I'm the one who's been deceived, for Christ's sake. I'm the one whose life has been turned upside down, who has been consistently lied to and humiliated for twenty years. You've got it easy. Pull yourself together and get back to your washing or however you spend your time.'

Eleanor was amazed to hear the nastiness and spite coming out of her own mouth, and she drew in her breath in an attempt to calm herself. 'I'm sorry. I know you're having a tough time too. I just haven't got used to the idea of— I just can't begin to accept it all. Something will sort itself out. I'll make it sort itself out. But for now I just have to keep going. And he mustn't know until I decide that I'm ready to tell him. I don't want you to let him know that I know — that's very important, do you understand?'

'Yes. I do.'

'Good. Just go on behaving as you always did. You've been denying my existence and living a lie for all these years quite happily, so I shouldn't think it'll be much problem to you to go on doing it just a bit longer. Will it? You must be pretty good at lying by now ... Mrs Hamilton. Is that what you call yourself?'

After a moment's pause, Eleanor went on, aware once more that if she were to attempt to use this woman as the key to unlocking the truth of the past she must somehow restrain her natural inclination to abuse her and must preserve some kind of communication with her. 'Don't try to think about anything until we've both had more time to get used to things. To find out everything there is to know. I won't give anything away to Susan, I can promise you that. I don't want to.' Eleanor knew it was partly her own shame at the idea of the deception that she had unwittingly suffered for so many years that would prevent her even considering telling the child the truth of their relationship. It was enough of a challenge to face this girl: to have to see the pity or hatred she knew would inevitably appear in her eyes if she found out that this 'aunt' was in reality her father's secret wife was unimaginable. 'I shall remain her aunt for the time being. But I would like to see her; to talk to her, to look at her. I expect you can understand that. I'm sure you can't imagine what it's like to suddenly discover that your husband has a child. It isn't something one comes across every day, you know – oh, and a mistress, of course. That's another little surprise I hadn't foreseen.'

Even as she was saying it, Eleanor knew this new tone of bitterness was not going to get her anywhere; that she must drop the sarcasm that was creeping into her voice if she were to keep this frightened rabbit of a woman in her control. She tilted her head back and looked up at the ceiling as if appealing to someone, something to acknowledge what she was having to endure, while she went on, calmly: 'And I'm glad you rang. I think it's important that we talk to each other. And I believe you that you thought our relationship was – what did you say? – a formality. I can't forgive you, but perhaps I can begin to try and understand.' She felt she was teetering on the edge of apologising for the way she had spoken, but knew it would be a step too far and one she was not prepared to take. 'I'd like Susan to come down here, to the house. It'll be perfectly acceptable to her to be allowed to come and see her batty aunt after all these years. She's old enough now to come and see her, especially after the batty aunt's unexpected night-time visit. Don't you think? I'll explain to her why I don't want her father to know, so you don't have to worry about that. How ill am I, by the way? Completely crazy, or just a little physically incapacitated? Should I hire a wheelchair and have it sitting somewhere in the background, maybe? Or an oxygen cylinder?'

There was no reply, and Eleanor quickly went on, 'Don't worry, I'm not serious. And I'll – I'll try to call you after I've seen her. Just to make sure you know exactly what we've talked about, so that we can keep our stories the same.' She laughed, and went on, 'Quite a game, isn't it?'

'Yes, it is.'

'And for God's sake don't call me Mrs Hamilton. I have to say, that seems particularly unsuitable given the circumstances.'

'Yes. Thank you, Eleanor, I'll wait to hear from you later, then.'

Oh you stupid cow, thought Eleanor. Even to hear my name in your mouth, in your stupid, irritating accent is unbearable. What am I doing, discussing my life with you as if you had any real importance? *But she does,* the maddening voice that kept coming to her now, unbidden, whispered in her head; *Oh, she does, baby.*

'Wait a minute – how am I going to contact Susan? What's your number?'

As she wrote it down, Eleanor annoyed herself by feeling a little sting of surprise at hearing the same exchange numbers as those of the phone in the London flat, but she kept the calmness in her voice as she said a polite goodbye and replaced the receiver. 'What do you expect, you idiot?' she muttered to herself. 'It's in the same building.' But even as she said it, she was, yet again, attacked unexpectedly by a hot flush of disbelief.

The thought of the two flats, two lives, two wives, and the fact that a part of her was now accepting it as true made her sway on her feet in giddy incredulity. *What?* she thought. *What is all this? This can't be real. I must be imagining all this: this just isn't my life, this is someone else's, I'm—*

But she stopped herself, and took a deep breath to steady her trembling legs and clear her head. It's real. It's real, she repeated in her head.

Chapter Ten

When Ruth telephoned her from the office at nine o'clock on Tuesday morning it was all Eleanor could do at first to stop herself shouting abuse, but she was far too uncertain of the direction of the girl's loyalty to risk alerting her in any way to her discovery. She felt sure her voice was strained and awkward as she attempted to reply normally to Ruth's friendly chatter, but was pleased to hear no hint of suspicion in the other's voice, and as the conversation progressed she began to relax and even feel a little pride in her own performance. It pleased her to feel that she had chosen not to reveal her hand, that it was her decision alone and utterly in her power as to when she would confront them all with her knowledge. She could see now that the feeling of despair that had swamped her on realising that she was unable to unburden herself to John about this, the most serious crisis of her life, had another side to it. Never before had she tackled an issue of such gravity and complexity on her own; never since her marriage had she relied totally on her own resources to guide her. It had always been an automatic response to any problem to talk it through with her husband, and although there had been many times over the years when it had been her counsel that had prevailed, it felt extraordinarily unfamiliar to be handling complex decisions and choices without the backing of a partner. It was frightening and lonely, but she could feel it also promised the possibility of some measure of satisfaction that might help to take the edge off the biting pain that was now her constant companion.

The mixture of longing and horror she felt at knowing she would have to see John at the end of the week had been hanging over her since coming back from Andrew's the previous morning. Even the thought of trying to appear normal during the regular evening phone call had been terrifying her, but as she talked on to Ruth she began to see the possibility of acquiring skills in lying far more quickly than she would have dreamt possible. She even found herself smiling at the nicety of her deceit as the girl asked about her health and she replied enthusiastically about how well she felt and how lucky she was to live away from town with all its pollution and noise. She became confident enough to consider enquiring about John's whereabouts, but decided her voice might just not maintain its miraculous innocence when forced to speak his name aloud.

'So I'll see you soon, Ruth,' she said instead, suddenly determined to wind up the conversation as soon as possible. 'Was there anything special you rang for?'

'No, not really, Mrs Hamilton. Just a chat. Although

I think Mr Havers wondered if you were coming in this week. I know the design team have some more ideas to talk through with you when you've—'

'I can't possibly think about that now, Ruth.' There was a fractional pause, and Eleanor's mind trawled desperately for an excuse for the brusqueness of her dismissive reply as she quickly went on: 'I mean it's just not a good time at the moment, with the – er – you know – all the—'

'Of course not. Sorry, Mrs Hamilton, I forgot. I know you're very busy. I'm sure it's—'

'—all the – well, my brother's not been too well and I had to go and visit him over the weekend. I expect my – er – my husband mentioned it, didn't he?'

'No, no he didn't. Oh I am sorry. I do hope it's nothing serious.'

Damn, thought Eleanor, damn it. I needn't have told her. Now will she talk to him about it? Will it make him think again about why I went off so suddenly to Andrew's and question me and get suspicious? Oh damn, why didn't I keep my mouth shut?

'No, not at all, thank you, Ruth. But I just might have to go down again, you see, so I can't really commit myself to anything this week. You see.'

'Of course, Mrs Hamilton. They'll just have to wait, won't they? They certainly won't want to sign anything off until they've talked to you. You know how much they rely on your advice. But I'm sure they've got plenty to be going on with.'

'All right, Ruth. Tell them I'll be in touch when I

can,' Eleanor answered, railing inwardly at the two-faced flattery of the girl she was chatting to so warmly, ''Bye.'

''Bye, Mrs Hamilton.'

As she put down the phone the last two words echoed horribly round her head and she started with the shock of yet another terrible thought. Jesus Christ! What does she call *her*? Does the little bitch call her by *my* name? How does she list us in her database or Rotadex or whatever it's called? Do we share a card, the Mrs Hamiltons (x2) card? Or do we have one each? And – God Almighty – she'll come first. Barbara before Eleanor. Has Ruth ever dialled my number by mistake, and chattered to me about some invented nonsense when she really wanted to talk to his lover? Or has she got through to the bitch by mistake when she meant to ring me with an excuse for one of John's late arrivals or cancelled homecomings? But of course that way round it wouldn't matter, would it? They must have had a few laughs about it: *Oh dear! Silly me, Mrs Hamilton – I've got the wrong one again!* Or, no, more likely – *Barbara.* People of that class are far more likely to use Christian names to each other; they'll be mates, pals, in on the joke together. *Silly me, Barbara,* she'll say. *I've got the wrong one again! I meant to ring old Nellie!* And then Barbara will have a really good giggle about it. She must have a silly, cheap giggle, like a schoolgirl.

Eleanor sprang up from her chair and marched quickly towards the kitchen French windows, desperate for a gulp of fresh air to clear the poisonous thoughts that were fast becoming ever more inventive. The way her mind would insist on returning to themes and ideas that couldn't possibly be realistically explored and that could only exist as mad extrapolations from the thin base of facts available to her, was utterly exhausting. However often she pulled her thoughts away from them, the frantic musings would begin once again against her will, and hundreds of times a day she would find herself deep into some agonising fantasy without remembering how she got into it.

The sound of the front door slamming distracted her and made her stop where she was, halfway across the room. Before she even began to wonder who it might be, her reaction was to panic at the thought that she might have no clothes on, or be in her underwear, or nightclothes. She had no recall of how she had got up that morning, and whether she had bathed, or dressed, or brushed her hair. In the split second it took for her to glance down, she was relieved to see that she had somehow put on one of her straight navy skirts and a white blouse. Tights and shoes appeared to be on her legs and feet, and a quick dash over to the cooker hood gave her the opportunity to check in its shiny steel surface that her hair looked as if it had been brushed and a small smear of pink lipstick could clearly be seen on the blurred, distorted mouth reflected back at her. How amazing, she thought, that my body has done all that without my being aware of it. Even when confronted with the evidence that she had indeed removed a nightdress, opened cupboards, dressed and sat at her dressing table to make up her face and do her hair she could still find no memory at all of having done so. She said a silent thank you to her own body for carrying on so bravely without her, and turned towards the door, assuming what she hoped was a suitably noncommittal expression as she waited to identify the approaching footsteps.

When Carla walked into the room, Eleanor nearly cried with the relief of something normal, regular and unthreatening taking place. The cleaner's familiar figure, removing a short, green raincoat as she came in, revealing a comforting pink floral blouse and bright blue calf-length cotton slacks, was reassuring merely by its existence. Eleanor had been spending so much time in the cloistered confines of her own head that any evidence of external reality gave her a welcome anchor in the sea of dark, swirling uncertainty that threatened to engulf her.

'Good morning, Mrs Hamilton,' Carla threw over her shoulder as she went to the small kitchen cupboard to fetch a pale pink nylon housecoat from among the forest of broom, vacuum and floor-mop handles. The bright colours she always wore, combined with the throaty remnants of an accent that remained after two decades or more of working for the Hamiltons, brought a whiff of Spanish beaches and vibrant blossoms to the quiet Englishness of the country kitchen. 'Did you have a good trip?'

'What? Oh, to my brother's. Yes, thank you, Carla, I did. Good morning.'

'Shall I make you a coffee, Mrs Hamilton? I'm going to start in here this morning.'

'Yes, please, Carla. A coffee would be lovely.'

Eleanor sat down at the kitchen table and watched as Carla took the glass coffee jug and filled it half full from the cold tap before pouring it into the well at the top of the percolator. Eleanor made as if to speak, wanting to tell her for the hundredth time to run the water for a few minutes first, knowing that now the coffee would have that slightly musty taste that it always did when made with water that had sat in the pipes overnight, but she hadn't the energy or the interest. Musty coffee was the least of her problems, and the comforting friendliness that had been implied in the offer of a hot drink was far too precious to crush with such practicalities.

'Sorry to be late today, Mrs Hamilton. The kids – they drive me mad. Get off to school, I said, get off to school. But they don't listen to me, Mrs Hamilton, they just don't listen to me.'

So that's what the coffee was all about, thought Eleanor, a small peace offering. Little does she know it was entirely unnecessary. Little does she know I have no idea of simple basics such as who I am this morning, let alone complexities like what time it is or when she should have arrived for work. She probably worried all the way here about my ticking her off. What a waste of her anxiety; she could have turned up at three in the morning wearing a baseball outfit and have convinced me it was perfectly normal. Or skipped work all week and I would have thought nothing of it.

'Don't worry, Carla, it doesn't matter.'

Carla was pouring some dark shiny beans into the small electric grinder, but stopped to look round at her, clearly surprised by something Eleanor had said, or in the way she had said it. She was holding the packet in one hand,

and Eleanor briefly considered pointing out that she was using the strong after-dinner beans instead of the breakfast ones, but didn't have the energy.

Carla turned back, covered the beans and switched on the machine, appearing to wait until the unpleasantly grating noise was at its loudest before calling over her shoulder, 'Are you OK, Mrs Hamilton?'

'Yes, yes, I'm fine. Why?'

'No, you don't seem fine to me. You're not OK, Mrs Hamilton, you're not too well. I can see that.'

What on earth does she see? thought Eleanor. She's right, of course, but how can she possibly know? I'm not doing anything odd, am I? She glanced down at herself once more, panicking that her earlier check had ignored some vital strangeness in her appearance that was giving away the not-too-wellness that Carla had so correctly spotted. Perhaps her shoes were on the wrong feet, or her makeup askew, or her knickers round her ankles like some mad old woman. But again her quick inventory revealed nothing amiss and she sat back again in her chair to wait for the coffee, noting inwardly that the grounds had been poured into the filter in a little pyramid, and that without the top being smoothed across with a spoon, the water would run down the sides and through the machine without properly brewing the coffee. And now Carla was putting the glass jug back in place under the spout without warming it first with hot water, the way Eleanor liked to. Musty, weak, lukewarm, after-dinner coffee, she thought.

'How do you mean, Carla? Don't I look well?'

Carla crossed her arms and leant back against the hardtop as she looked down at Eleanor, tilting her head to one side and screwing up her eyes a little.

'You're quiet, Mrs Hamilton.'

'Quiet? What, am I usually noisy? Not known much for being a particularly loud person, am I, Carla?' laughed Eleanor, hearing in the superior tone of her own voice the implication that Carla's judgement was amusing in its ridiculous presumptiveness.

'You're not saying things you always say.'

All at once Eleanor knew exactly what she meant. Her acceptance, without criticism, of the woman's lateness; the fact that she was sitting quietly at the kitchen table watching her, instead of striding about the house pointing out what needed to be cleaned, or working on designs at her desk with a brisk summary of the day's chores called out to Carla as soon as she came in — these were what amounted to the strangeness that had given her away. Even the held-back criticisms of her coffee-making: how many would there have been had she let them out — the water, the beans, the grounds, the unwarmed jug? At least four times she would have pulled Carla up and found fault with her.

'Carla — am I an awful bitch?'

In her astonishment the woman turned round so suddenly where she stood at the sink that Eleanor thought she might fall, and half rose from her chair as if to catch her. But Carla steadied herself and dropped her hands by her sides, one clutching the pink rubber gloves she had been about to put on.

'What did you say, Mrs Hamilton?'

'I'm sorry, I didn't mean to startle you. I just felt I may have been a little — well, I suppose I just wanted to know if I've always been a bit — critical. If I always criticise you, Carla.'

Carla moved slowly over to the table and sat down in a chair opposite Eleanor, laying the gloves onto the pine surface, never taking her eyes off the other's face, and still frowning in disbelief at what she was hearing.

'Is there something wrong, Mrs Hamilton? Am I doing something wrong? Are you not happy with me?'

'No, no it's nothing like that. Really. Not at all. In fact I don't know what I'd do without you, Carla. I've had a bit of a shock, you see, and I'm — you're absolutely right, you spotted it at once, of course — I'm not quite myself. And I'm seeing some things very differently. I really do appreciate all you do for us, Carla. I'm sorry if I always snap at you.'

'Do you want to go and have a nice lie down, Mrs Hamilton? And I'll bring your coffee up to you?'

Eleanor laughed, but this time there was no hint of anything other than gentle amusement in its tone. 'Yes, you're probably right. I'm a bit crazy. Never mind. Just ignore me. How's your family? How are the children?'

'Very naughty, Mrs Hamilton. Alex — he is always in trouble at school, you know. But he's clever. He's a clever boy, but he gets himself into trouble. Maria is OK, but she doesn't work too hard, you know. She has her A levels — remember I told you, Mrs Hamilton, she does her A levels next year, in Spanish and geography? But

I'm not sure if she's going to do OK or not. I'm not too sure.'

'Carla, I have a girl coming to see me for lunch, probably next week. What do you think she'd like to eat? What does Maria like best? What's her favourite?'

'You like me to cook her something special? Should I cook for you my chicken with tomatoes and peppers?'

'No, that's very sweet of you, but I'll do it. What do they like? Children — young people. What do they all like?'

'Pasta, I guess, Mrs Hamilton. They all love spaghetti, don't they?'

'Yes, that's a very good idea. Or tagliatelle. I'll do some tagliatelle with a cream sauce. No one could not like that, could they?'

Eleanor crept towards the bed with the large scout knife held firmly in one trembling hand. She half squatted, half knelt, and the strain on her thigh muscles made them ache with tension. She could hear John's breathing, regular but with a small fluttering snore in every intaken breath, and knew he was unlikely to wake as long as she was careful not to make any sound that couldn't be taken for part of the usual routine noises. In normal circumstances he was a heavy sleeper: Eleanor could turn over in bed without having to think twice about waking him; she could read with the light on or go to the bathroom, but if the slightest change in routine took place and any variation in the creaks, rustles and sighs that were part of their regular weekend nights impinged on his semi-consciousness then he would sit bolt upright and be immediately fully awake.

So every bump and whine of a floorboard had to be explicable on her journey towards the side of the bed. After collecting the knife from the pocket of his Barbour that hung in the downstairs cloakroom, she had made her way casually up the stairs as if returning from fetching a glass of water in the kitchen, or a newspaper from the drawing room, knowing he was bound to be asleep, but taking no chances of his inner ear sensing the difference in sound that a stealthy approach would have from a confident one.

She had made for the bathroom, where she closed herself in and stood over the basin, gripping its side with one hand to steady her balance, unsure of the reliability of her legs as they threatened to turn to jelly now that she had reached this temporary haven, and holding up the knife with the other hand, staring at it in fascination in the mirror. It looked utterly innocent in its closed state: a child's toy. She released her grip on the basin and stood up straight, waiting for a moment to test her stability, then brought her hands together and began to pull with her nail at the side of the largest blade. It was half out when she heard John clear his throat next door, and, as she started a little in fright, the blade snapped back into its case with what seemed to her to be a clearly audible click. She quickly turned on a tap to give his subconscious a continuing reason for her absence from the bed, and pulled once more at the blade until it sprang fully out to stand to attention, ready for duty. It glittered in the spotlight above the basin as she stared at it once more in the mirror. As she kept looking at it, she twisted it slowly in her hand so that the blade thinned into a fine silver hair, then widened again into flat, flashing threat. As she watched, blood appeared on its tip and dripped slowly down its length. She grimaced, then looked quickly away from it and down at the water swirling round the blue enamel, letting the image wash away with it down the plug hole, until she could look up again and see clean, cool, untainted steel. She turned off the tap and put out the light.

She was surprised to find that, as she neared her side of the bed, she felt no uncertainty about what she was about to do. In fact she was now quite calm and clear-headed: almost looking forward to the next few minutes, which, whatever the extent of her success, would be extraordinary to say the least. A tiny smile lifted one side of her mouth as she congratulated herself on the brilliance of her route across from the bathroom; having no wish to risk even a half-glance from John should he wake, she was continuing to move in a hunched, spidery creep, keeping well below the level of his eye line, but creating noises comfortingly compatible with a normal upright walk.

At the side of the bed she stopped and listened again, keeping her own breathing even and normal in spite of the desire to pant it out in gasps after the strain of the journey. She planned a swift, decisive pulling back of the covers, done in exactly the same way she would have as if opening up the bed to get in it herself, but with just that little extra swish of movement that would uncover John's sleeping form as far as was necessary for the procedure to come. Procedure: she giggled a little silently to herself. Yes, she liked that term. It had a satisfyingly medical ring to it, as if the horror about to take place was necessary; ordained; a cleansing ritual that was for the good of the party concerned, and not within her power to withhold or bestow of her own volition.

The covers whisked back silently and easily, and without disturbing him. She stood up and looked down at him for a moment, then climbed carefully onto her side of the bed so that she was kneeling next to him, facing up towards the pillows. She changed her body weight onto one hip and curled her legs up to one side, so that, with one hand still holding the open knife, she was able to reach across with the other one and delicately take hold of one white-fringed end of his pyjama cord and begin to pull it infinitesimally slowly and carefully out of its simple bow. The word babbitt was ringing round her head while she continued the precarious operation. No, that couldn't be right – Babbitt was the character in that American book, wasn't he? It can't be babbitt. Bobbitt – was that it? Yes, Bobbitt. Bobbitting. And again she giggled.

The bow had undone easily, and now she flipped back one side of the striped material and studied what lay beneath. It looked so innocent, so *young*. It had been many years since she had looked at it directly, and it made John seem suddenly like a little boy. She half expected him to reach down and cup it in one hand, and suck his thumb with the other while he went back to sleep. She thought of how many, many times this funny little thing had been inside her and made her cry out with pleasure, of how shy of it she had been for the first few months of their relationship, how terrifying it had seemed those first times it had stood to salute her in its desire. Now she saw it as an old friend, an old friend she had taken for granted for many years and whom she now saw afresh and appreciatively.

No, none of that sentimental nonsense, she thought to herself, and suddenly reached out and grabbed it, holding the tip with two fingers and a thumb as she drew it up and away from its hairy surroundings, as if she were a nurse about to shave her patient. She wasn't at all surprised that John didn't wake. Somehow she had known he wouldn't, and even as she made to put the knife to the pale pink flesh, she had no doubt he wouldn't stir.

But every time she made a cut, it healed over. As fast as she could begin to saw through the skin and muscle, it closed itself back into unmarked, untouched wholeness. She persevered, but after a few minutes it became clear that any attempt was doomed and that she might as well give up and go to sleep. She threw the knife across the room, where it found its own way through the door, down the stairs and back into the coat pocket, then she pulled the covers back over them both and closed her eyes.

She opened them again and looked across at Carla, who had finished cleaning the sink and was collecting the vacuum cleaner from the cupboard. How long had she been daydreaming? Had it taken as long in reality as it had in her projected thoughts? She felt a mixture of relief and frustration at the lack of her fantasy's consummation:

it wasn't the first time she had been through the scenario, and always something prevented the final carrying through of the terrible task. Each time she came back to reality she felt melancholy and unfulfilled, but more than a little aware that she was grateful to find that even her fantasies were to an extent censored by an instinctive humanity and curtailed by a moral fence that would allow her to go only so far before pulling her up short against the wire.

She'd considered the other, more common, form of recrimination, of course; the other standard response to infidelity and jealousy: the cutting of the clothes. But that too she knew would bring her no satisfaction, even in her imagination. What pleasure could there be in destroying the suits that she herself had helped him to choose? What revenge in chopping off the sleeves of shirts that she had spent so many evenings ironing, or in recent years sent to the laundry, or packed carefully into suitcases? These were old friends; no way would they let her mutilate them. Her ordered domesticity was ranged against her: so far she couldn't imagine any act of revenge that would assuage her bitter jealousy. Every violent physical outburst that she imagined brought no relief. She would just have to bide her time.

Chapter Eleven

'Hello, Susan, this is your aunt.'

Good, good. So far. Very smooth. Not a wobble on the word aunt. Not too gushing and not too cool on the phrase as a whole. Keep going.

'Pardon?'

'Your aunt. From—'

'Oh, I'm sorry – of course I know who you are. I didn't think for a moment. Yes, how are you?'

'I'm very well, thank you, Susan. How are you?'

'I'm doing nicely, thank you.'

'I thought the least I could do since my very odd encounter with you the other evening would be to treat you to a meal. Would you like to come out here to the country? It would be lovely to see you and I could give you lunch.'

'That's very nice of you Mrs – em, Aunt – sorry, I don't know what to call you!'

'No,' laughed Eleanor, a little more wryly than might have been expected in the circumstances, 'of course you don't. Eleanor. Call me Eleanor.'

'Oh, right, yes. Thanks then, Aunt Eleanor, that would be very nice.'

'What's your diary like?'

There was no reply, and Eleanor tried again, aware how stupidly she had put it. If the girl went to the job centre as Ba— as she had been told, then there wasn't much question what her diary would be like, was there?

'I mean, is there any particular—'

'No, any day would be good.'

'How about next Tuesday, then?'

'Yes, that's great. But are you sure you want— I think – I think I'd better check with my mother. I don't really know if she'd want me to. I'm not quite sure – it's always been a bit of a funny area. *You* have, I mean. Sorry, I didn't mean to say that.'

Eleanor felt intensely annoyed at the reference to the woman that she was finding it increasingly objectionable to have to think about. Over the last few days since their extraordinary meeting her disgust and dislike, even hatred, of the newly discovered rival had grown dramatically. The jealousy, bitterness and shock had congealed into a sticky phlegm of loathing for the other woman, sometimes threatening to choke Eleanor as she lay awake on her night-time vigils. She could only clear it by either pushing the thoughts of her so far away as to be once more part of something unreal and unbelievable, or by fantasising acts of wonderfully satisfying revenge. These had tended to override the scenarios involving direct retribution on her husband. For the moment, at least, the daydreams gave her more peace by eliminating the other woman and leaving John a lonely, crumbling, abandoned wreck, utterly aware of his folly and begging Eleanor to take him back. In these dreams he loved her again, passionately, physically and unquenchably, and she would slowly let herself be wooed back into his arms. So it was unbearably irritating to hear Barbara spoken of as a person not only alive and well, but also someone to be reckoned with and applied to for permission to let this girl come to lunch.

'Yes, of course, Susan. I understand. I'm sure your mother won't mind. Do tell her how much I'd like you to come. Oh, and tell her I've still a few things to sort out with her, will you? I'll give her a ring sometime,' she added, hoping that a hint of menace would be conveyed to the other woman in the relaying of the apparently innocent message.

'OK, yes I will. Shall I phone you back, then, when I've spoken to her?'

'All right, Susan. Yes, give me a ring back when you know. Tuesday, we'll say then, shall we? And ring me back to confirm it's all right. Oh, and it might be as well not to mention this to your father. I'm sure your mother will explain.'

But before Tuesday there was the weekend to get through. As it approached Eleanor became increasingly nervous. She had managed to pick her way delicately through three phone calls from John, keeping her voice relatively calm and letting the strangeness of her dash to Andrew's and the general coolness of her demeanour be explained by a simple change of mood. Moodiness had inevitably occurred during the long marriage, and had been variously attributed by John to time of the month, migraine, menopause or just plain female silliness. As she felt his exaggeratedly patient response to her over the phone, Eleanor for once thanked God for the normally irritating explanation of 'woman's trouble', which helpfully covered all inexplicable behaviour.

But a face-to-face meeting was a different thing altogether, and she began to dread the two days fast approaching when she would have to act, lie and cover up as she had never had to before. Her plans veered wildly between confronting him with everything she knew and having it out once and for all, or sticking to her original idea of waiting until she knew more from Susan of what had been going on before she tackled him. She knew the latter was the better route, but a tiny part of her still fantasised that the whole horrible situation was an illusion; that somehow, when challenged with her discovery he would immediately be able to convince her that none of it was true. The possibility, however remote and irrational, of being able to return to normal, of being able to sleep without nightmares, was so seductive that she feared she might be tempted into blurting it all out, just to force him into a denial that she could somehow make herself believe.

'Eleanor? Darling, it's me.'

She still marvelled that he sounded so normal; that the voice of an adulterous liar was indistinguishable from that of a loving, faithful husband. But then of course that's what the voice had *always* been. It was only her awareness that had changed, not the man. She never had heard the voice of the loving husband – or not for at least twenty years, in any case. Funny that.

'Hello, darling. How are you doing?'

'Fine. I should be home about the usual time. I'm leaving at six.'

Oh God, oh dear God, help me.

'OK, good. I'll get supper on for eightish, then shall I?'

Feed him? Do I have to cook for him and feed him? Can I cook for him? Will my body go on physically working for him now he's not who I thought he was? Now I'm living in a parallel universe?

A quick picture of herself emptying a small green bottle with a skull and crossbones stamped on the side into a chicken casserole flashed into her mind and made her laugh out loud.

'Yes, about eight should be fine. What are you laughing at?'

'Oh, nothing. Just George throwing his chew around. Looks funny, that's all.'

Brilliant. You brilliant woman. Where the hell did that come from? Maybe the weekend's not going to be so bad after all.

·∞·

But it was bad. It was terrible. As his car pulled into the drive, Eleanor moved back the pretty chintz curtains in the kitchen to look out of the window. The bright gaiety of the vivid pattern of sunflowers on the crisp white cotton made a mocking frame in the foreground as she watched him sadly. Was he thinking of *her* as he got out of the car and slammed the door? Does he long for the weekend to be over so he can go back to the flat, kiss his daughter and climb into bed with— NO!

Perhaps it's all my fault, she thought as she saw him lock the car and walk slowly towards the front door. I've been cold and unloving and he's stuck by me while he could have gone off to – to her. They probably do it every night. Her big breasts squash down onto his chest, and she hugs him and kisses him and tells him how much she loves him. We just kiss on the cheek, and say things like 'Hello, darling, how are you? How was your day?' And then we don't really want to know, anyway. Perhaps I'll tell him I love him tonight; perhaps I'll astonish him with my warmth and passion and he'll discover me all over again.

Eleanor let the curtain fall back over the window and turned into the room. She moved automatically over to the fridge and took out a cold bottle of tonic water and a lemon, then carried them over to the hardtop. She opened the drawer beneath and took out a knife, sighing a little at the confusing lurch of excitement the sight of the sharp blade gave her as she pulled a small chopping board over from the sink and began to slice the lemon. She watched the knife sawing into the yellow juiciness of the fruit and sensed an echo of some of her more unpleasant daydreams.

'Oh, don't be so silly,' she muttered to herself. 'Anyway, it's that wretched curved serrated one for grapefruit. God knows how it always manages to be the only one in the drawer. You can't murder someone with a grapefruit knife.'

Shaking away the image of a smile-shaped jagged cut in John's throat, she walked over to the cupboard by the door and fetched two cut-glass tumblers, brought them back to the hardtop and popped a slice of lemon in each. She could hear the front door closing as she carried the glasses over to the fridge and balanced them in one arm as she opened the heavily suctioned freezer door and grappled for the ice cubes she had earlier decanted into a bowl. She dropped them into the glasses, swearing a little as one of the freezing cold cubes stuck briefly to the skin of her hand, then shouldered the freezer door shut, picked up the bottle of tonic from the side and walked towards the sitting room, trying hard to ignore the uncomfortable drumming of her heart against her ribs.

'G and T?' she asked as casually as she could manage as she moved through the doorway and into the room, aware of John's large figure settling itself into the armchair by the fire, but avoiding looking at it too directly by concentrating intensely on the bottle and glasses.

'Mmm? Yes, yes please, darling. Great. How are you?'

His voice sounded different! She could swear it sounded different. It had to be guilt. Guilt and fear. There was a trembling shiftiness in it that she had never heard before. She took her courage in her cold, damp, glass-clutching hands and looked across at him, certain she would be confronted by a vision of anguished regret, but saw instead the thinning top of John's head, bent over a newspaper. She waited, sure he would look up at her and throw himself on his knees to beg forgiveness, but as she stood there, clutching her half-prepared drinks, he carried on reading, seemingly utterly unaware of her immobile presence.

She crossed over to the small table behind the sofa and put the glasses and bottle down on the polished surface, feeling recklessly wicked at not bothering to find coasters or a magazine to put them on, letting the watery condensation settle onto the wood and ooze out satisfyingly. She pictured three ring-marks forming on the perfect marquetry and found it oddly comforting.

'I'm fine,' she answered at last, noticing that her voice, too, sounded oddly different. Perhaps it was just the way she was hearing everything, she thought, perhaps she had a sort of distorting filter that had grown in her ear like a cancer caused by the trauma of the past week. If not, then why did he go on reading, instead of looking up at her in astonishment and asking what the hell the matter was? She must sound normal, after all – and no doubt he did, too. Don't make a comment about anything, nor take anything at face value until you have some sort of corroborating evidence, she silently instructed herself. Your senses can no longer be trusted. Just like your husband.

She poured a stiff measure of gin into each glass, topped them up with tonic and handed one to John before sitting opposite him on one end of the sofa. He took his automatically, not looking up from his paper or acknowledging her in any way, and she took the chance to look more closely at this new species she now found squatting in her happy home. The faithless, two-timing husband. Sitting, sipping his drink. Settling himself comfortably like a cuckoo recently hatched into a sparrow's nest, spoiling and polluting it with the wrongness of its presence, but forcing the poor beleaguered sparrow into accepting and nurturing it.

She was pleased to find that the sexual frenzy she had been experiencing every night appeared to be under control; the reality of his body in the chair opposite her was somehow far less magnetically attractive than it had appeared in her fantasies. She felt sure that — as long as she could keep her imagination in check — she would be able to stay as cool to him physically for the duration of the weekend as she would have been in normal circumstances. Her plan for declarations of love and displays of passion would have to wait until she was far more experienced in handling this double game.

He looked up and saw her watching him. She took a quick drink and cleared her throat.

'What?' he said, a little irritably she thought, but then she pulled herself up as she remembered the unreliability of her own evidence.

'What do you mean, what? I was just — I was just thinking you looked a bit tired, that's all.'

'I am. Bloody tired. Bloody awful week.'

Oh poor dear, she thought. Poor old thing; all those meetings and discussions and architects' plans and a mistress to make love to and a daughter to lie to — let alone the phone calls to the old bag in Surrey. It must be exhausting for you. Poor old thing.

'Yes, I've had a bit of a rough week too.' Oh I *like* it! she smiled to herself. I love the gentle irony, the wonderfully

British understatement of it all. A bit rough! Ha! What a shame I've no one to share it with. You'd love that, John, you really would. You'd laugh at that one. You'd look at me in admiration and have a good laugh. Old Eleanor's got a sense of humour after all.

'Oh really? That's – em, that's . . .' But he had drifted off back into his paper again, crossing his legs and burrowing further into the squashy seat of the chair as he lifted the open pages high enough to be able to rest his elbows on the arms, blocking her view of his face completely.

She took another gulp of her gin and stood up.

'I'll put a light under the veg. Fifteen minutes or so do you?'

But he didn't answer, and she raised her eyebrows and tipped her head on one side as she looked over at him, secure now in the knowledge that he was utterly unaware of her discovery. She turned and walked across the hall to the kitchen, feeling a little more in control of things again, and ready to tackle the evening ahead.

The smell of roast chicken brought her up short. She could see the bird through the small glass panel in the front of the oven door, glistening and golden, surrounded by neatly shaped small roast potatoes. John's favourite. Or was it? Had that been yet another lie? He probably loathed it. Too ordinary; unadventurous. Boring.

She probably cooks marvellously inventive dishes: clever little veal escalopes with smart little reduced sauces; decorated raised pies filled with game. And she serves them dressed in a see-through nightie; or black lace underwear; or nothing. Naked. Do you want to keep your man interested? Serve him Sole Véronique and put on your best saucy basque and his favourite perfume. Turn down the lights and put on the music. Here we see Barbara, wearing a gorgeous black chiffon négligé and tucking into a beautifully presented coq au vin (oh nice one, Eleanor, she smiled to herself, good cheap joke, very suitable). See how invitingly Barbara leans forward and coyly looks under her lashes, meat juices dripping down her chin. See how—

Oh, don't be ridiculous! she shouted silently at herself. Have you seen the woman, for God's sake? She cooks frozen dinners and fried sausages. She wears curlers and flowery pinnies. She sleeps in a long nylon nightdress. I hope. Oh God, let her sleep in a long nylon nightdress; let the days when he touched her be over.

She tipped the remainder of the gin and tonic down her throat, moved to the stove and lit the gas under a pan of sprouts. She stood there a moment, then felt suddenly, desperately in need of another gin. But the gin was in the drawing room. For her to help herself to a second gin would be so extraordinary as to risk setting alarm bells ringing in John's so far happily innocent head. And there was no way she could be certain of getting in there and pouring one without his noticing; it was far too risky to rely on his apparently dedicated interest in the day's news lasting long enough to act as cover. She would just have to do without.

But she couldn't. She watched the bubbles begin to

appear round the edges of the saucepan and thought about the fridge, mentally scanning its contents for signs of alcohol. The red wine waiting on the table would have to be left untouched; it was part of the regular Friday-night ritual that John opened the wine as Eleanor brought the food to the table; to open it early and take a glassful from it would be asking for trouble. But the fridge trawl was worth pursuing: she had a feeling there was some sort of bottle at the back of the middle shelf that had been in there for some time.

She opened the fridge and quickly found it. It was a Sauternes. A bottle of Sauternes that a friend had brought over last year just before Christmas for them to drink with the Christmas pudding. But they never had, and it had sat in the fridge ever since. Perfect. John would never miss it, and she could have a good glassful while the sprouts cooked and she made the gravy. She had a small moment of panic while trying to find the corkscrew, worried that it might be sitting on the drinks' table in the drawing room, but then found it in the cutlery drawer and quickly opened the bottle. It made an uncomfortably loud plop as the cork came out, but after a second's breathless pause to wait for quizzical remarks from next door, she relaxed and poured a large glass of the cool, golden liquid. It was heavy and sweet, and Eleanor could feel the makings of a headache arranging themselves in the back of her neck as she took a large swig, but she simply muttered a 'What the hell!' to herself and took another one.

By the time the sprouts were cooked the glass was finished. The warmth and slight dizziness that was making its way in waves up from her belly into her head was relaxing her, and she calmly poured out another large glass as she let the water bubble on, and took generous gulps from it as she half-heartedly took the chicken out of the oven. She watched the steam rising from it in fascination as she poured a third glass, then speared the chicken with two forks and transferred it a little clumsily to a serving dish. The bird wobbled and slithered and threatened to slide off the edge of the plate, but she prodded it back as she giggled a little and began at last to make the gravy.

Oh hell! she said to herself. I forgot to pour off the fat. Never mind. Bugger it. She giggled again at her own language, and stirred the flour into the fatty juices, marvelling again as she admired the beauty of the globules of shiny grease as they floated among the lumps of half-mixed flour.

·∞·

'Ready darling!' she called out in what she hoped was a suitably normal and wifely sort of voice. *Trilled*, she thought. That's what I did. That's what the perfect wife does from the kitchen when the meal's ready. She *trills* out to her husband. Perhaps even a 'Coo-ee, darling! Supper's on the table. Come and get it, honey!' No, no, she frowned, I'm getting confused. That's America. Honey is America. That's Mary Tyler Moore in *The Dick Van — Dick Van . . . Thingummy Show*. *Dick Van Dyke. Dick Van Dyke*. That's good, she went on, giggling again at her own silliness. Dick and Dyke in one name. I must remember to use that at a dinner party. Why hasn't anyone spotted that before? That's brilliant. Really funny and – and modern. A good modern joke. I think that'd go down really well. Surprise them. That Eleanor's got a marvellous sense of humour, you know. So up to date. All Dick jokes are good. Very funny. And Dick is good. Of course dick is good, it's lovely. Particularly when it belongs to someone else. I must ring Barbara and chat to her about it. Must ask her if she's happy with his dick or if she'd like it changed in some way. Does she get enough of it? Should I make him rest more at weekends so he's got a bit more energy in the week? Well, how's a girl to know these things if she doesn't ask? It's very important that we girls get together and talk about these things. Very important. A dick's a dick for a' that. What do you mean, you batty woman? Barbara, we need to talk about John's dick . . .

'What are you smiling at?'

John had paused in the doorway and was watching her, the folded newspaper clutched in one hand and his glasses in the other. 'Is it ready or not? I thought I heard you call?'

'Yes, yes, dear, it's ready,' smiled Eleanor, humming a little as she drained the sprouts into a colander over the sink. 'Whoops!' she laughed as several of them bounced and jumped over the edge and fell on the floor. 'Never mind. S'prising sprouts! An uprising of sprouts! Do you want to open the wine? It's all ready. And start carving. Please, dear.'

John put the paper and his glasses down on the hardtop and moved over to the table, where the chicken stood steaming on its serving dish.

'Where's the corkscrew?' he asked.

'Ooops, my mistake,' giggled Eleanor as she quickly thumped the colander, full of sprouts, down into the sink and grabbed the corkscrew off the draining board.

'Just a tick,' she said as she turned her back and surreptitiously unwound the cork from the metal spiral, then took it over to the table and handed it to John with an enthusiastic grin.

'That was lucky!' she said.

'What was?'

'That I . . . that I found the corkscrew so quickly.'

John pushed the metal tip into the red foil covering the wine and turned it vigorously. Eleanor went on watching him, then suddenly laughed.

'Corkscrew,' she said out loud.

'What?'

'Sorry, just thinking what a funny word it is, that's all. Hasn't it ever struck you?'

John gave a sort of noncommittal grunt and Eleanor sighed as she walked back over to the stove to decant the gravy. He picked up the carving knife and fork and began to attack the chicken, then stopped and looked across at her.

'No plates.'

'What, John?'

'There are no plates.'

'Well, fiddle-de-dee, nor there are!'

He watched her as she took two plates from the cupboard beneath the dresser and carried them over to the table.

'Cold?' he said.

'No, I'm fine. I'm rather hot. Unusually hot, I—'

'No, the plates. Aren't you going to warm them?'

'Oh, I see. I thought you meant me.'

'I know. No, I meant the plates.'

'I thought you meant you thought I was cold. That's really funny. Don't you think? Poor plates, did you think they were cold?'

'Eleanor, what are you on about? For heaven' sake, do you want to heat the plates or not? Why are you being so silly tonight? What is the matter with you?'

'No, I don't want to heat the plates. I can't think of anything as boring as having to heat the plates. What the hell, John, let's go mad. Let's eat off cold plates. Let's be really bold and different.'

'Oh, for God's sake! Very well, let's eat congealing gravy and cold food. I'm really too tired to cope with your mood tonight, Eleanor. Let's just eat and be done with it.'

Chapter Twelve

Saturday morning brought a splitting headache and a terrifying moment of panic at the thought of what might have been given away over the soggy sprouts and fatty gravy of the night before. Eleanor sat up in bed to reach for the glass of water on the bedside table, but had to stop in mid-movement to tip her head forward into her hands as sickly waves of pain hit hard behind her forehead. She belched a little, smelling the remains of greasy chicken and rotting vegetables in her stomach as the breath hit her nostrils, then kept her eyes closed within the cool safety of her palms as she picked over the slowly surfacing memories of what had taken place. She was relieved to find she could remember everything, and was soon able to reassure herself that, apart from a memory of John's irritation increasing as the evening wore on, nothing irrevocable or dangerous had taken place during or after the meal.

She had gone up to bed first, aware, even in her unusually tipsy state, that if she didn't force herself to leave John's presence and shut up, she would soon say or do something she would regret. Her jokes had become wilder and more peculiar, and although John seemed relatively unfazed by her odd behaviour, she sensed that the moment when she leant suddenly over the table and asked forcefully if he would have preferred coq au vin was coming perilously close to initiating some sort of crisis.

She lifted her head from her hands and gingerly opened her eyes. Next to her the bed was empty, and she let herself flop down across it sideways, sighing as she released her weight onto the crumpled sheets and snuggling down a little under the blankets. She lifted one hand to her head, rubbing the temple in small circles very gently and carefully, as if too strong a pressure would break through the skin and leave her fingers buried deep in her skull, muddling around in the thoughts and emotions swirling inside. Her eyes were very close to the white landscape of the sheets; her nose could pick up faint traces of sweat left on their surface, and as she studied the hills and valleys created by the now departed weight of John's body a new and peculiar thought floated into her mind.

What if she had known all along? It suddenly seemed perfectly possible that she could have retrospectively kidded herself that she had lived in ignorance of John's double life. Whenever she had heard of people carrying on affairs for years behind their partners' backs she had scoffed in disbelief. No one, she had always insisted, could live for more than a few months with someone without being immediately aware if the other was being unfaithful. The idea that someone could maintain two separate families and keep them so independent as to preserve one of the cheatees in a state of innocence was so implausible that she had always refused to believe it could happen. When she had read of such things she had assumed that the cheated wife – for it never seemed to be the husband – had in effect known all along, and was either protecting her own embarrassment by pretending that she hadn't, or was managing to fool herself that she had never known. So how could she know if she herself was burying the prior knowledge of John's other life? She felt suddenly filled with despair at her own lack of certainty about anything: even about her own mind.

She moved the hand from the side of her head and stroked it across the sheets, aware of her breast moving a little beneath her nightdress as she did so.

'John,' she whispered, letting her nipple rub against her upper arm as she continued to move her hand backwards and forwards, 'did I know what you were up to? Am I mad? Do I not even know myself what I know?'

The full horror of the implications of this thought began to crowd in on her as she went on stroking the sheets, moving her hand faster and letting her nails scratch irritatingly over the cloth.

Perhaps we've discussed it all; come to an arrangement; decided we can make it work, she thought. Perhaps I've forgotten and blocked it out in some moment of psychological crisis. Buried it inside and covered it with illusions of a traditionally happy – or fairly happy – marriage. Oh God – now how will I confront you? 'Well, of course, Eleanor,' you'll say, 'don't you remember, dear? We went through all that a couple of months ago.

Nothing new there, old girl. Pull yourself together and think back.'

She turned her head down into the bedclothes and closed her eyes, shutting out all other sensations as she concentrated on breathing in the faint smell of male body that still clung to the sheets. She was dismayed to feel her body's urgent desire for him rekindling itself.

'John, I need you. I'll forgive you. I'll forgive all of it if you'll love me again.'

'Eleanor?' The shout came as if in answer to her thoughts, and she had to stop herself calling out too eagerly in reply.

'Yes?'

'Cup of tea?'

She pressed her lips together tightly and winced as the shock of the innocent, familiar offer brought her in a split second near to tears. She knew she would gulp and judder if she attempted any reply, so kept silent and concentrated instead on preventing herself from crying.

'Eleanor? Tea?'

She took a deep breath, opened her eyes and rubbed her face hard with her hand, then sat up quickly and called back at the same time, attempting to surprise her body into sounding normal before it had time to allow her true feelings to break through into her voice.

'Yes, lovely.'

And as she said it she was suddenly aware that, quite for certain and without any possibility of doubt, she had not, ever, in any way, known anything prior to the previous week about her husband's extraordinary secret.

·∞·

This realisation gave her strength, and armed with the knowledge that she was not after all as crazy as she had begun to fear, she controlled the rest of Saturday with a calmness and apparent normality that gave her quiet satisfaction. By the time Sunday lunchtime was approaching she was beginning to congratulate herself on another terrifying milestone having been passed uneventfully, when something happened that she later kicked herself for having failed to foresee, and which threatened to bring the situation to a head far earlier than she had planned.

After lunch they strolled in the garden a little. It was cloudy, and the occasional gusts of wind that blew across the lawn carried a crisp chill that made a sharp reminder of winter to come, but every now and then the sun flickered weakly through a tiny break in the woolly greyness and touched the reddening leaves of the large oak tree with dots of shivering yellow-gold. Eleanor crossed her arms in front of her chest and hunched her shoulders, bending her head down as she walked, aware out of the corner of her eye of John's brown-brogued feet striding perfectly in step with her a yard or so to the side.

'The leaves are turning,' she said, thinking how trite it sounded, and wondering if she was irritating him.

'Mmm.'

'Still, it's been a marvellous summer. Really can't complain,' she went on, wondering if he would be leaving later that day, or early in the morning.

John didn't answer, and they carried on walking, Eleanor trying to curb the desire to say something, anything, to fill the silence. It was not unusual for their post-Sunday-lunch walk to be taken without either of them talking at all for the entire half-hour or so, and she knew it was only because of her changed circumstances that she felt the compulsion to speak. A horrible feeling that John might be about to say something revelatory was making her very nervous, and although each time she glanced up into his face she could see no sign at all of anything unusual or strained in his expression, she surprised herself by knowing how desperately she wanted to preserve the status quo, at least for the time being. She realised now that over the years she had always felt a small stab of loneliness as John had made to leave for London at the end of every weekend, and the thought of that loneliness being suddenly multiplied a thousandfold by a departure that would be not just for four or five nights, but for ever, was chilling. Her future so far was still bounded by the regular calendar of John's comings and goings. Her reaction to him might be totally different – her emotions for him shredded and skewed by her terrible knowledge – but there was no question that he was the central force in her life, and at any point in the wild swings of her feelings for him, from ravaging desire to burning hatred, it was impossible to imagine it without him. It was ironic that she had thought the only danger of the weekend was that she might be tempted into revealing her discovery: now she felt the tables turned, and dreaded that John might be considering telling all and forcing a realistic appraisal of the marriage and of the future.

The telephone rang and John looked up. She was

relieved to see that, even raised fully into the light and turned towards her, he seemed as vague and bored as he normally did during their walks together. The large, strong nose was still as powerful as ever profiled against the sky, but the sagging contours of his neck beneath the line of his chin, and the patches of pink revealed on his scalp where the grey strands of hair had blown out of place made his face look soft and pulpy; almost old-womanish.

'I'll go,' she said, and made to walk towards the house.

'No, don't worry,' he said, putting a hand on her arm, 'I'll go. I've had enough of a stroll, anyway. Getting quite chilly. The leaves are turning, I see.'

'Yes, I just— Oh, never mind. OK, I'll just walk once more round the pergola and I'll come in too. Give a shout if it's for me, or tell them I'll call back.'

But when, after a couple of minutes, she walked into the drawing room through the French windows, quiet on her rubber-soled shoes, she wished she had gone back earlier. The sight of John's back, hunched over the receiver, and the sound of his quiet whispering, filled her with terror. It can't be, she thought, it just can't be. The bitch promised. She wouldn't dare – surely.

She stood completely still and tried to make out the meaning of John's indistinct words, not daring to move near enough to be able to hear more than the occasional muffled syllable. He suddenly turned, aware of her presence, and Eleanor was astonished to recognise in his face a look that told her in a flash that he was as terrified as she was. He stuttered an unrecognisable sound or two into the receiver before letting his voice peter out into silence. The two of them stared at each other for a second, mutually mesmerised by their fear, then John suddenly cleared his throat and turned away again, speaking now in a voice of normal volume, but with an uncharacteristic quiver still hovering behind the words.

'OK, then, I'll speak to you soon. Thanks for calling . . . Yes, of course . . . Goodbye.'

He put the receiver down and cleared his throat again, then turned back to Eleanor. 'Simon. From the office,' he said.

'Oh, right,' Eleanor answered, finding difficulty in speaking through the pulsing in her throat. 'What did he want?'

'Figures.'

'What?'

'Just some figures. For January.'

How badly he lies, she thought. How he's managed to keep me in the dark all these years when he lies as badly as this I can't imagine.

'Why would he suddenly want figures on a Sunday afternoon?' she asked, enjoying watching John struggle as she came back at him unexpectedly.

'For the – um . . . Oh Eleanor, really, you don't want to know all this. It really isn't your department. For heaven's sake, why are you so suddenly interested in my business affairs? You wouldn't understand them anyway, so there's really no point in my—'

'What?' she said. '*What* did you say? How dare you? For one thing, you know perfectly well I would understand.

There's no need to keep up the little woman thing here, John, when there's only you and me here. I don't mind at the office; I've got used to the amusing little jokes about not worrying my pretty little head with statistics, letting me come up with pretty patterns and colour schemes and leaving the business up to the men and all that. I'm happy to go along with that if it pleases you. But you don't have to do it here – you don't have to fool yourself it's true. I deserve more than that, surely. And I see little enough of you, for God's sake. I think I've a perfect right to question why your office staff should ring you on a Sunday, one of only two days I see you each week, to ask you some pathetic question about figures.'

Eleanor was amazed and delighted to find herself arguing in such familiar style and with so natural a reference to John's weekday absences. John sighed, exaggeratedly, clearly sure that his clumsy cover-up had been believed; relaxing in the luxury of the old criticisms from his wife.

'Sorry, darling, you're quite right. He really shouldn't have rung, and I didn't mean to be patronising. Sorry, old girl. No offence, eh?'

She felt like hitting him, but instead brushed her hair back with her hand and decided to let him temporarily off the hook – or at least reel it out a little so he was no longer aware of having been caught on it in the first place.

'No offence,' she smiled. 'Are you staying tonight, by the way?'

'No, I think I'd better get back. I've an early meeting and

some work to catch up on in the flat before then. Don't worry about food, I'll eat something in London.'

I'll bet you will, she thought.

·∞·

As soon as John had gone upstairs to collect his things together, she rushed over to the phone and dialled 1471. 'You were called today at fifteen oh five hours,' began the impersonal recorded voice, stilted and precise in the refined tones of a fifties BBC announcer, going on to reveal a London number as being the source of the recent call. 'To return the call, press three,' the voice went on. Without stopping to think, Eleanor quickly pressed three. A bell rang out at the other end and she held her breath and listened, half aware of John moving about in the bedroom over her head, ready to cut the call off in an instant as soon as she had confirmed the identity of the caller.

'Hello?'

It wasn't her. Eleanor felt her tension and dread evaporate in a flash as she recognised Susan's light, young voice. She hesitated a moment, the muscles of her arm halted in rigid immobility by the sound of the unexpected voice just as she had automatically begun to replace the receiver.

'Hello?' Susan asked again, a hint of tears in her voice.

'Susan, it's me. Eleanor. Aunt Eleanor.'

'Oh my God!' the girl replied. 'I rang a moment ago, and I—'

'I know you did.'

'Oh no, did he— I mean, how do you know? Did he tell you? Have I done something terrible? I'm so, so sorry. I just didn't think. I've hardly ever rung this number before and I just didn't think. We have it for emergencies and things at weekends, but he always told me not to ring. Because he always said you didn't like people phoning, you see.'

Eleanor sighed, more in irritation than surprise; so accustomed now to extraordinary revelations that she found herself not at all shocked to hear of yet more lies and complexity in her husband's other life.

'I just feel gutted,' Susan went on. 'I'm so stupid. I did it just—'

'Susan, it's all right. No, he didn't tell me. He didn't tell me anything. He's not angry. It's all right, you haven't spoilt anything.'

Eleanor heard John move into the bathroom and knew he was in the last stages of his preparations, the use of the lavatory and washing of his hands being the regular prelude to his making his way out of the house and to the car.

'Look, Susan, I can't talk for long. Just tell me quickly – why did you ring? And what did you say to him? Will he know something has changed?'

'No, it's all right. When he answered I realised how stupid I'd been and I told him Mum was ill and that she'd asked me to get hold of him. I've done that before, you see. He'll tell me off later, for ringing when you were there, but he won't think anything's wrong. He'll just be really pissed off.'

'And why did you ring?' asked Eleanor, ignoring the temptation to comment on the girl's language.

'To say I can come on Tuesday. That's all. I'd love to come on Tuesday.'

There was a pause. Eleanor found herself oddly moved by Susan's acceptance. She sounded so normal, and so polite.

'Well, that is good news. I shall collect you. By car. If you haven't been before this can be quite a tricky place to find, and there aren't always taxis at the station. You haven't got a car, have you?'

'Shit no!' laughed Susan. 'Of course not! Neither has Mum. But she can't drive anyway. I can drive but I—'

'Susan, I think we'd better stop chatting now. I'll pick you up outside Baker's, the dry cleaners in Marylebone High Street, do you know it?'

'Sorry — I talk too much. Yes, of course I know it.'

'I'll pick you up outside there at eleven o'clock on Tuesday then. And you don't talk too much. Not at all. All right?'

'Yes. Thanks. Thanks, Aunt Eleanor, I'm looking forward to it. 'Bye.'

'Oh and Susan — you'd better tell your mother what you've said, hadn't you? About her being ill, I mean. Or when your father asks her, she'll—'

'I was just going to do that now. Do you think she'll mind? I mean, it's such a muddle, isn't it? She'll have to lie about being ill and asking me to phone.'

'Susan, I don't think she'll mind at all. I'm sure your mother will be able to cope with lying quite smoothly. Don't worry.'

'But wouldn't it just be easier if we told Dad that we'd met? I don't see why we have to—'

'No!' Eleanor had raised her voice, but quickly quietened it again as she continued, 'No, Susan. There are things you don't understand, you see. I'll explain everything to you soon, I promise, but – well, you know how complicated families and relationships and things can be. It's just easier at the moment if your father doesn't know about my funny night-time visit. Look, I must go now. See you on Tuesday, all right?'

'All right. See you then. 'Bye.'

''Bye.'

Just as she put the phone down John came down the stairs, carrying the familiar black leather overnight bag and briefcase that regularly made the twice-weekly trip up and down the A3 with their owner.

'Who was that?' he asked as he put them down outside the drawing-room door and walked towards her.

'Just Andrew,' Eleanor answered, hoping she wasn't opening up a re-examination of the reasons for her recent trip by having chosen her brother's name as a hasty excuse.

'Oh. OK, is he? I mean, you're not thinking of going down again or anything?'

'No, he's fine. Not at the moment I'm not, anyway. Although I might take a few days down there again soon. I still don't feel quite myself somehow.'

'No, I can see that.'

Oh can you? thought Eleanor. Aren't you a caring, perceptive little husband then?

'Well, maybe that's a good idea,' John went on, 'bit of fresh air and so on.'

'We've plenty of fresh air here, John. We have just as big a garden here. I don't go for the air, you know.'

'Sorry, sorry. No need to be prickly, Eleanor. You know perfectly well what I mean. However lovely your garden is — and yes, I know you do hours of work in it — the air of the green belt just isn't quite the same as that of deepest Gloucestershire. All right? I was not casting aspersions on the beauty or size of your—'

'Oh for God's sake, don't be so bloody pompous, John. Go and get in the car. You don't want to find yourself in the traffic,' said Eleanor, pleased to be again maintaining a naturalness in her tone, while secretly assuaging a tiny fraction of her anger by indulging in a marital row. She marvelled at her own capacity to translate the vicious, searing words of rage that stormed her mind as she looked at him, into these innocent little stabs of attack.

She followed him as he fetched his coat from one of the hooks in the back hall and walked towards the front door, collecting his bags as he went. His hair was still dark where it moved over his collar at the back of his neck, and as he bent and looked down to grasp the handle of his briefcase it lifted horizontally in a little spiky fringe, reminding Eleanor of the neck ruff of some tropical bird she had seen at the zoo. The skin beneath was pale and unlined but had the same pulpy look she'd noticed in the garden. As he straightened up the hair slid over it again and the collar was once more set against the ruddiness of the rest of his neck. He turned to look at her and she saw the white, dry hair at his temples and in front of his ears, contrasting startlingly with the still black eyebrows. You're growing old, John, she thought. No matter how many mistresses you have, no matter how virile they make you feel, you're growing old. Just like me.

He bent to kiss her on the cheek, and she thought of Judas. He smelt of wood smoke from the bonfire they had walked past in the garden, and as he put a hand briefly onto her upper arm and squeezed it, she felt a wave of sensuality rush up her body towards her head, where it mingled with the feelings of anger and betrayal already filling it. She wondered again at her ability to hate and want him at the same time, and patted him briskly on the chest to stop herself reaching out and grabbing him in a storm of weeping, desperate need.

'OK, darling,' she said, moving a little away from him and opening the front door, 'see you during the week, I expect.'

'Are you coming up?'

'Yes, I should think so. I might come up Wednesday or so. Spend a night at the flat and get a few things done.'

So I suppose he plans his week nights around me? Eleanor thought. How complicated his life must be. When does he decide which home to sleep in? And with which woman? I suppose he's planning right now: a couple of nights with her, and then one with me, and then—

She cut her thoughts short to raise a hand to wave goodbye.

''Bye, darling!' she called in what she hoped was a charmingly wifely sort of tone. 'See you on Wednesday!'

Chapter Thirteen

'Have you ever thought of cutting your hair, Susan?'

'Well, I do cut it. I mean, it'd be far longer than this if I didn't.'

'Yes, of course. How silly of me,' Eleanor answered, smiling at Susan over the half-eaten plates of pasta. 'I didn't mean that you'd never cut it. Obviously. I just wondered if you'd ever thought of having it shorter? You have such a neat face — a good shape. It's heart-shaped, really, isn't it?'

'Is it?' Susan laughed. 'Well, I've never heard it called that. I hate it, anyway. My face.'

'Oh you don't! You mustn't. You've got the kind of face they use for modelling, you know. It's just that — well, it's none of my business, but I'm not sure you make the most of it.'

Susan looked genuinely puzzled. She turned towards Eleanor, a forkful of tagliatelle halfway to her mouth, and frowned slightly, apparently about to say something.

'What?' asked Eleanor. 'What were you going to say?'

'I've got a crap face. Why d'you say that about mod-elling? Models are beautiful.'

'No, it's bone structure, you see. That's what counts. Not that you'd want to be a model anyway, Susan. You could have a far more interesting life. But you do have wonderful bones.'

Susan giggled and stuffed the pasta into her mouth, leaning over her plate as a stray noodle slipped from the fork and dangled over her chin. 'Well, I think you've got a pretty funny idea about models, that's all I can say.'

'Yes, you're probably right. But I'd still love to see you with shorter hair. And with less makeup.'

'What's wrong with my makeup?'

Eleanor sensed she'd gone too far, and quickly leant forward and put a hand over Susan's.

'Nothing. I'm old-fashioned, I expect. I'm just not used to all that shading and things – don't pay any attention. You're a jolly pretty girl, anyway.'

'Thanks.'

Eleanor watched her as she went on eating. She was indeed pretty, but it was frustrating to see her young, fresh skin buried beneath the thick foundation, and the over-layered wispy cut of her hair made it look lank and thin and dragged her face down. A good, blunt cut would thicken it up and let it curve round her strong jaw line. And a delicate, pale makeup base with soft, smoky eye shadow would accentuate the gamine quality that Eleanor could see lurking beneath the deceptively modern mask. A cross between Juliette Greco and Dora Carrington – but in nineties style.

'Is the pasta all right?' she asked, pleased to see the girl scraping the last remnants of sauce off her plate with the side of her fork.

'Yes, it's really nice, thanks.'

'Have some salad.'

'Thanks.'

'What does your— I mean, what do you eat at home? What's your favourite?'

Oh God, she thought, I sound like some terrible newspaper quiz, or a list of questions to a TV star: *'What's your favourite food? Which is your favourite colour?'*

'Well, I eat out with my friends mostly. But Mum's a really good cook. Casseroles and roasts and things. And I like pasta. But we don't usually have it like this.'

Eleanor stood up and reached over to clear Susan's plate. 'I've made some baked apples, Susan. You don't have to eat any if you don't want, of course, but—'

'No, that sounds great. Thanks. Shall I help you clear the plates?'

'Don't worry – there's so little. Don't move. So what do you eat when you go out? Isn't it awfully expensive?'

'McDonald's. Chinese. Stuff like that. Dad gives me money. He and Mum like to eat together anyway, so he doesn't mind me going out. So he gives me money for it. You see.'

'Yes, I see.'

Eleanor looked down at the top of Susan's head as she stretched to pick up the empty pasta dish. She felt an extraordinary pang of pity, picturing the girl clutching a five-pound note, hurrying out of the flat in Marylebone in search of a tasteless hamburger or bag of chips while her father toyed with his mistress in peace. How dare they? she thought. How dare they bring a child into the world and not give her everything they would want for themselves? No – not for themselves: no doubt that pathetic, common little bitch of a lover thinks her daughter is gorgeous. Long, lank layers of hair and cheap earrings are just up her street. But John: John has no excuse. She glanced down at Susan's tight lilac sweater and black jogging pants and at her gilt earrings: three small hoops in the thin, curled edge of one ear and two rings and a stud in the other. Now the pity she was feeling changed to anger that John could allow his own daughter to grow up with so little style. Hasn't he any pride in her? You're the equivalent of his whirly ceilings, my girl. He knows you're ugly and wasted but he just doesn't care. Has more important things to invest his time and money in.

She carried the plates over to the sink and rinsed them off before bending over to stack them in the dishwasher. As she straightened again and moved towards the oven to get the apples she caught sight once again of Susan's slight figure hunched over the kitchen table. She paused for a moment and stood quite still. She could feel an extraordinary and exciting idea beginning to tingle at the back of her head, but before it could crystallise into something clear enough for her to understand, the moment was broken by Susan suddenly shifting in her chair and leaning back with a small sigh. Eleanor reached for a blue-edged tea towel, aware that the thought was continuing to form itself gradually into a coherent idea as she opened the oven and carefully took out the dish that held the large, shiny apples. They had split a little on the tops, exposing the fluffy whiteness of the fruit against the wrinkled green skin, the stuffing of dates, honey and raisins oozing upwards out of the centres and down the sides and mixing with the buttery juice that surrounded them. The beauty of the glistening roundness of them gave her a pang of nostalgia for something she couldn't identify, and she frowned as she turned to put the dish down on the hardtop, releasing it quickly with a little thump as the heat of its edges began to burn into her hands through the towel. Susan turned quickly at the sound and smiled up at her.

'That smells great. What did you say it was?'

'Baked apples, Susan. Just baked apples – nothing fancy. Haven't you had them before?'

'No. No I haven't. I like apples, but I haven't had them hot like that. God – look at the steam!'

'They're very old-fashioned. I used to have them as a child. But they're quite tasty. Very easy to do. Do you do any cooking?'

'No, I'm not really bothered.'

Eleanor nodded and pulled two white bowls towards her.

'So, do you want to try some?'

'Oh yes. It looks great.'

Susan pushed her chair back and stood up. She walked the couple of paces over to the hardtop and leant onto it, crossing her arms on the surface and watching Eleanor intently as she carefully lifted a plump apple into a bowl and spooned the golden sticky liquid over it.

'This is really nice of you, you know,' she said. 'You didn't have to do all this work.'

'Would you like cream with it, or ice cream? I've got some Häagen-Dazs if you'd like that.'

'Ice cream. And — no, that'd be silly, wouldn't it?'

'What?'

'Can I have cream as well? Or would that be silly?'

Eleanor smiled again and put a hand onto Susan's for a moment.

'Of course it's not silly. You have whatever you want, Susan. I've bought all this to give you a good lunch, so we'll both be happy if you eat the cream *and* the ice cream, won't we?'

'Yeah, I guess so. That's good then. I love cream.'

'So do I.'

.∽.

Eleanor watched with enormous satisfaction as Susan finished her apple and then ate a second helping of ice cream. She knew now exactly what she had to do, and she continued to construct her plan, slowly and methodically, as she finished clearing away the remains of the meal and clicked the dishwasher door shut.

'Shall we walk round the garden?' she asked, unsure if she might be suggesting something unbearably boring.

Susan pushed her chair back and stood up. 'Yeah, OK, if you like. Thanks again for the lunch — it was great.'

'I'll get your jacket. I put it in the cloakroom.'

'The cloakroom!' Susan laughed. 'Sounds like at school.'

'Yes, I suppose it does,' smiled Eleanor. 'But they're jolly useful things to have, even if you don't find them in many houses nowadays. I hate to think where I'd put my muddy boots and gardening gloves and things like that.'

Susan followed her as she made her way out of the kitchen and down the back passage, stretching her arms above her head and grunting with the effort. 'Yeah, well most of my friends' houses haven't got gardens, let alone special rooms to put the gloves in.'

'No, of course not. I'm very lucky – and very spoilt. Don't think I don't know it. But your flat is very comfortable too, isn't it?'

'It's OK. I wish we had big rooms like this, though.'

'Well, the drawing room's quite large, isn't it? And with the balcony – that's a lovely room, isn't it?'

'How do you know?' Susan asked her, turning to look at her in genuine puzzlement. 'How do you know how big our lounge is, and about the balcony?'

'I took a quick look round before I burst into your bedroom,' Eleanor answered calmly, relieved at how quickly and smoothly she had covered her mistake. 'Now, let's find your jacket.'

Susan looked round in fascination at the muddle of walking sticks, tennis rackets, boots, flower vases, climbing shoes and dog bowls that were collected on the grass-matting floor of the long thin room. Waxed jackets, fishing rods, loden coats and assorted heavy cardigans and raincoats hung on hooks along the wall, almost obscuring the small handbasin that nestled among them. Eleanor pulled Susan's anorak from the nearest peg and held it out to her, but then hesitated.

'It's really quite damp out there — spitting a bit I think. I'll lend you a longer coat or your trousers'll get soaked.'

'No, it's OK — I don't mind.'

'Well I do. You'll be freezing. Here — don't be silly.'

She smiled and lifted a well-worn Burberry mac from a hook and held it out to Susan, quickly hanging the anorak in its place before she could protest again. She watched as the girl put it on, and then took her own coat and a thick scarf from the nearest hook and ushered her back out into the passage.

Eleanor held open the back door and gestured for Susan to go past her into the garden. For a moment Eleanor stood still, the doorknob in her hand, watching, thinking how well the creaminess of the raincoat fabric suited her. She had been right when she talked about modelling: the girl had a natural elegance and beauty that was quite charming. She closed the door and took a few quick steps to catch up, then the two of them walked side by side along the gravel path that edged the lawn.

'Are you cold?' asked Eleanor.

'No, not really.'

'Yes you are, I can see you are,' laughed Eleanor. 'You're freezing, aren't you?'

'Well, I am a bit,' Susan laughed back.

'You're a townee, that's your problem. Here, look at me,' she said, and she stopped walking and touched Susan's shoulder gently so that she turned to face her. Eleanor lifted her hands to the girl's collar, turning it up and tucking it snugly together at the front. She took the scarf from round her own neck and wound it gently round Susan's, then stood back again and smiled.

'Better?'

'Yes, much, thanks.'

'You look quite stylish. Rather chic. The colour of that brown scarf is lovely with your hair. I've always thought it looks rather dreary on me.'

They walked on past the end of the lawn and under the pergola, whose skeletal frame was barely covered by the fast-fading climbers that twined along its wooden stakes.

'You should see this in the summer,' said Eleanor. 'It's really beautiful.'

Susan didn't answer, and Eleanor went on, 'Covered in roses and clematis. It smells marvellous when you walk along underneath it. We planted it about ten years ago and it's amazing how quickly it's grown.'

As soon as she had spoken she realised her mistake, and searched desperately for another subject to cover her tracks and divert Susan from the obvious question. But it was too late.

'Who's "we", Aunt Eleanor? If you don't mind me asking? Was that with your husband, then, or —'

'Oh well, yes, sort of Susan I mean — but we don't want to talk about that, do we? I'm afraid that's going to be another thing you're just going to have to let me keep rather to myself. I've had a very — well, let's just say there have been many unhappinesses in my life and I — I'd rather not talk about some things. Sorry, I'm being impossible, I know. I can only say that I promise I'll talk to you about anything and everything one day, if you still want me to. But for the moment just let me be a rather batty, eccentric old aunt. All right?'

'Of course.'

'And, talking of aunts, do stop calling me Aunt Eleanor. It makes me feel ancient. Just call me Eleanor, will you? Now, let's go through the gate at the end of the garden there and we can have a good long walk to work off our lunch.'

·∽·

By the time Eleanor and Susan returned to the house Susan's nose was pink with the cold and Eleanor's fingers were beginning to go numb. After hanging their coats up they made their way back towards the kitchen, but Eleanor caught Susan by the arm and pulled her into the large, light drawing room on the other side of the hall. 'Come in here,' she said. 'We'll light a fire and warm ourselves up.'

There was a tray of biscuits and crumpets ready on the low stool in front of the fire, and once Eleanor had used the gas poker to get the fire blazing, she settled Susan into one of the two armchairs that faced the fireplace, and disappeared into the kitchen to make tea.

'Have you ever toasted crumpets in front of a real fire?' she called as she went.

'No,' answered Susan.

'You'll love them,' Eleanor shouted back. 'I bet you love butter too, don't you, as well as cream?'

'Pardon?'

'I said, I expect you like butter, don't you?'

'Yeah – I do. But it's so fattening. I eat Flora, mostly.'

How crass I am, thought Eleanor as she poured a little hot water into the empty teapot and swirled it around. The girl's probably never seen a crumpet, let alone toasted one. She probably lives on crisps and Coke while she's drifting around Marylebone keeping out of the way while John and the bitch – 'LA LA! Di dum di dum!' she suddenly sang out loud. 'Not going to get into any of that, now, am I? Pom pom pi tom. Keep it happy and bright. Keep it happy and bri-hight!'

'Are you calling me, Eleanor?'

'No, dear. Just singing to myself. Won't be long!'

Now should it be Earl Grey or Lapsang? Or will she hate that? Do I make Indian for now and wait till she trusts me more before I introduce her to China tea? Or do I go all out now and start the process of – of what? What is it? How do I label it in my head? Her re-education? Grooming? No, no that sounds like some dreary finishing school. Enlightening. That's good. Very modern. I shall think of it as her enlightening.

Eleanor emptied the hot water into the sink and held the warm pot between her cupped hands for a moment, enjoying the familiarity of the smooth, round china against her palms. She put it down with a little sigh and reached for the tin of Lapsang Souchong.

All out, she thought. I go all out, straight away. Operation enlightenment.

·∾·

Susan looked into the little pile of coal and logs that was

just beginning to smoke in the hearth, and then at the tray of tea things on the stool. For the first time since she had arrived, she felt ill at ease, and tried to work out why. There was something in the room that worried her, something wrong; something that didn't make sense. She glanced up at the mantelpiece, scanning the objects on it from left to right in search of the cause of her sudden change of mood, but the display of Staffordshire china dogs, carriage clock, candlesticks and small silver boxes told her nothing. There were several white invitation cards slotted between them, and she stood up to get close enough to read them, knowing they couldn't have been the cause of her discomfort, but intrigued to know what kind of social life this strange aunt might have.

'What are you doing, Susan?'

Eleanor's voice was almost sharp, and Susan turned round quickly, guilty at having been found with one of the cards in her hand.

'Oh, sorry, Eleanor. I just wanted to see. They looked so — so sort of official. I just wondered what they were. Sorry.'

'They're just invitations, of course. To drinks and things. I didn't mean to snap — I just thought of something, and I— Do sit down, dear. You're awfully close to that fire, and it's going to flame any second now.'

Susan put the card back on the mantelpiece and sat down again as Eleanor carried the teapot and milk jug over to the tray. Susan still felt uneasy, and knew that Eleanor could sense her change of mood, but she lent forward and tried to cover it with a smile as Eleanor spoke.

'Mind you don't touch this – it's boiling. Now, do you like milk, or shall I get you some lemon?'

'No, milk, please. And two sugars.'

Eleanor poured the dark golden liquid into one of the cups, and gestured towards the plate of crumpets with one elbow.

'Now, take one of those crumpets and spear it onto that long-handled fork thing. There's a little bit of flame there now, enough to start toasting, I think.'

When Susan had eaten two crumpets and a slice of fruit cake, she sat back in her chair and stretched her arms in front of her. 'That was lovely,' she said. 'Really nice. China tea's my favourite. And I don't usually eat tea. I love crumpets, but I never seem to cook them enough in the toaster, they end up a bit white and squidgy.'

Oh well, thought Eleanor, I suppose John's tastes are bound to have filtered down to the child a little; found their way through the common, plastic little sieve that is Barbara. Maybe my task won't be so great after all.

'It's a bit of old-fashioned fun, isn't it?' she said. 'Toasting them in front of the fire. I don't think I'd want to do it every day for breakfast though.'

She paused for a moment, watching Susan as she looked into the fire, charmed at the tiny orange flickers reflected in the girl's dark eyes, but still uncomfortably aware that something unspoken had disturbed the girl since the time she had gone out to the kitchen for the tea.

'Do you think you might like to come again, Susan?' she

asked. 'I'd love to show you a bit more of the house, and some of the lovely old paintings and things I've got.'

She suddenly had a vision of the three of them. John, Susan and herself. Seated just where she was now. Around the fire. Laughing, chatting. Toasting crumpets. Two parents and a child. Is this what she wanted? Her plan – the enlightening – had been so hastily assembled by her subconscious that she hadn't yet mentally taken it to its logical conclusion. Even before the addition of the child into the equation – before the thrilling possibilities of tormenting Barbara through the seduction of her daughter had occurred to her – she had never faced the question of what she wanted her future to be; of what result she hoped would eventually emerge from the mess of lies and misery in which she was enmeshed. She had pushed aside so many times decisions about if, when and how to confront John with her knowledge that she had lost the habit of thinking about it coherently at all. The attacks of physically tormenting jealousy – lessening now a little in their frequency, if not in their intensity – left her grappling desperately with rage and longing; torn between the desire to hurt, maim – even kill – the object of her furious desire, and to embrace him, hold him, smother him and make love to him again and again and again. After each little storm abated she never got any further than to turn away exhausted and put off the decision to another time.

It's going to worry you, Barbara, isn't it? It's going to be frightening. When she starts to notice the way you speak. The way you look; the cringing way you approach everything; the apologetic, cringing way you live. When she sees the beautiful things I have, what I can show her, give her. Barbara. Barbara. She'll see it, Barbara. She'll learn to look down on you; to pity you; for the way you are, for the things you like, for the way you behave. And then. And then I shall tell her. Tell her what you really are. How it's worse than that. How your disgusting little veneer hides something even more revolting. How beneath the common, pathetic little surface you're a whore. A husband stealer. A liar. And that's when she'll start to hate you.

'Susan, how would you like to come and see me regularly? I mean, perhaps each week or so? I've really enjoyed our afternoon and there are so many things I'd love to show you. Things we could do together too. I mean – theatre, or concerts. Do you enjoy going to the theatre, for instance?'

'I've only been a couple of times. With the school. And at Christmas, I think. I like the movies, of course. And I've been to a few concerts. Wembley. And – oh I don't know, I can't remember.'

'Well, I'd love to take you to the theatre. I'll find something I think you'd like. And you must let me do a little shopping, too. Buy you a few things.'

'No, you mustn't do that. I don't need anything. I'm fine.'

'I know that. I know you don't, but that doesn't mean there isn't anything you want, does it? Think of it like a story – when a rich old lady turns up and buys the heroine beautiful clothes and jewels. A sort of fairy godmother. A godmother to show you just how beautiful the world can be; how magic some of its music is. How special it feels to have silk next to your skin, or to drink ice-cold champagne while you listen to Mozart.'

Susan laughed and put her teacup down on its saucer. 'Well, you're not old, for a start. And you're certainly not a fairy. Or not like the ones you imagine. But you do sound a bit like a story. This doesn't seem real, somehow.'

But Eleanor could see, in the tiny gleam of excitement flickering in the girl's eyes as she turned them towards her, that a little flame of aspiration had been lit in Susan's soul, and that nothing and nobody would now be able to put it out.

Eleanor drove Susan to the station and saw her onto the London train. When she returned she went straight to the mantelpiece and checked the card that she had found in the girl's hand. It was an invitation to a local drinks; nothing to worry about there. Across the top 'Mr and Mrs Hamilton' had been written by hand in ink.

'Well, if I was married to his brother, then presumably there must have been – or still is – a Mr Hamilton. And even if one assumes he's dead, the people inviting me might not have known. Nothing too serious there, I think,' she said out loud.

But she still couldn't quite relax. She was convinced there had been something different about Susan when she had come back into the room with the tea. She had looked a little guilty; a little unsure. Eleanor glanced around the room. She had taken great trouble before Susan's arrival to remove any obvious evidence of John's inhabitation, not wanting to risk any awkward questions from the girl on encountering obvious signs of a man around the place, and she could see nothing that could cause suspicion.

But had she tried sitting on the stool in front of the fire, she might have noticed, from the different viewpoint it gave across the room, the framed wedding photograph hanging on the wall in the corner.

Chapter Fourteen

J ohn sat in his armchair opposite Barbara trying to read the newspaper. It wasn't often that he worried. His policy in life of taking the line of least resistance had stood him in good stead, and his barked-out orders at work and controlled testiness at home hid nothing more than a desire to be left in peace and avoid problems. He couldn't bear people fussing about things – any hint of argument or emotional scene made him want to run for cover – and it was unsurprising to those who knew him that his favourite tasks were those that could be tackled alone in his office, and that his favourite moments of relaxation were spent buried in newspapers or books. But occasionally he would be forced by events to stand back and take an objective view of his life, and what he saw would fill him with sweaty horror. For a man who liked simple arrangements and problem-free domesticity the extraordinarily dangerous and complex setup that he had slipped into almost without noticing was a potential nightmare.

It had all seemed so easy at first. His marriage had

been more than satisfactory at the beginning: Eleanor had proved herself to be an efficient and intelligent wife – an asset to the company as much as to his home life – but it hadn't taken long to discover that physically her needs were very different from his. He had assumed it was just exciting sex that he missed, like so many men of his generation seemed to, and the occasional fling with a secretary or girl picked up in a bar kept him quite satisfied in that department for many years, but after the first few sessions with Barbara he had been surprised to find himself missing her relaxed, spontaneous warmth and affection as much as the unexpected proficiency of her technique.

The invitations to well-cooked, homely suppers were irresistible. Countless evenings spent alone in his flat, or out with colleagues in pubs or restaurants where he had been expected to make small talk about sport or politics, had left him vulnerable to the charms of cosy, undemanding domesticity, and Barbara provided it willingly. The feeling of being so obviously adored was new and very seductive, and Barbara was so quick to sense his needs that she made the evenings spent with her little havens of comfort and relaxation that soon became indispensable. Sometimes they would spend evenings in her small flat in Paddington, but the thought of Eleanor telephoning and finding him out made John nervous, and more and more frequently he would invite Barbara to cook and sleep in his flat.

In spite of her careful tidying and clearing in the mornings, he knew Barbara's presence would not go undetected for ever, and when she was made redundant from her office job and forced to leave her flat, the decision to rent her one two floors below John's had been natural and sensible. He couldn't see that either woman was hurt by the arrangement, and often congratulated himself on keeping his marriage so problem free by having his other needs catered for during the week.

He had astonished himself by suggesting to her that she had a child. He had worried that she was getting bored; that the long days and weekends spent on her own might leave her vulnerable to predatory males roaming about London looking for comfort just as he had been, and it suddenly seemed such a simple idea to provide her with the perfect, time-consuming distraction that he knew she secretly longed for.

She had never clearly expressed a desire for a baby, but had given herself away many times by the way she would talk of pregnancy and childbirth, and by becoming just a little too emotionally involved in television programmes where children were featured. He knew she never mentioned the possibility, not because she didn't want them herself, but because she thought he didn't, and that her every effort was to make his London life run smoothly and comfortingly in the way he liked it.

But it wasn't purely for her sake that he had suggested it. If he thought back, John admitted to himself that the idea of a son – kept well out of his way by Barbara except for the times he might feel like brief forays into fatherhood – was rather pleasing. The ability to return at weekends to the child-free zone in Surrey would make the perfect balance.

But of course it hadn't worked out as he had imagined it at all. The child had been a girl, and in spite of Barbara's tireless efforts to keep her from irritating John, she had disrupted the easy harmony of his London life far more than he had imagined. The noisy messiness of babyhood had led into the impossible demands of childhood and then the sulkiness of teens. And since leaving the local college the girl couldn't even find a job. He did his best to remain aloof from her moods and tantrums, but a certain involvement was becoming increasingly unavoidable.

Now he knew there was something wrong, something upsetting Barbara, and he reluctantly put down the paper and looked at her over his glasses. 'Where's Susan?' he asked, crossing his legs.

'Out. With her friends.'

'Uh. She's out a lot lately, isn't she? No problem is there? Not having a problem again, is she?'

'No. No, of course not, John. She's fine. She's grown up now, you know. You don't need to worry about her.'

'So you keep saying. But I've never liked that crowd she mixes with, you know that.' He pushed his glasses onto the bridge of his nose and looked back down at his newspaper. Barbara watched him, a mixture of love and terror in her heart. She couldn't understand why she was finding this all so difficult. It wasn't as if she had never lied before; for years she had lied to the child about her father; about his mysterious weekends with 'Aunt Eleanor'. Not to mention the biggest lie of all: the way they had let Susan think that they were married, that she was legitimate, that this was John's family; his only family. But all that had happened by default over a long time and so gradually that there had never appeared to be a conscious decision to lie. It had *felt* true, too. The real truth had felt like the unreal part. Eleanor had become a shadowy, aunt-like figure in Barbara's consciousness many years ago, and John had been her own husband as surely as Susan had been their legitimate, one and only beloved daughter.

But this was different. She wasn't used to lying to John, and she was finding it an unpleasant and frightening experience. She had always enjoyed the moment he came home from work; his tiredness making him rub his eyes and kick off his shoes like a little boy. There was nothing she liked better than to slip his jacket off his shoulders, put her arms around his neck and kiss his sweet, rumpled face as he grunted and protested, then sit him down in his armchair and let him complain to her about his day, while she rubbed his feet or rested her head on his knee. She had never felt even the slightest twinge of jealousy when she had thought of Eleanor, who had become merely an apocryphal figure, entering the house only via John's descriptions of meetings with her during the day, or phone calls he had received, or simply complaints about her that he had felt like voicing.

Barbara had always wondered at the desire of women like Eleanor to go to work, to need more in their lives than the care of a house and family. The stories John brought home of Eleanor's meetings with his designers or architects amazed her, and she was genuinely puzzled by the amount of energy it seemed to her such a woman must possess. Any qualms about her situation that she had had in the first few months of her relationship with John were quickly put to rest once she gave any real thought to the third party in the triangle. Any woman, she reasoned, who could happily let her husband stay up in town all week and not miss him, who demanded more in her life than being his wife and the mistress of a beautiful home, was a human being so far removed from anything she could begin to sympathise with that she felt no guilt at all at fulfilling the role she saw the other as voluntarily relinquishing. How could she love him, she reasoned, like I do?

Ever since their first meeting in the wine merchant's round the corner from the flat she had known she would love him completely and for ever. The charm with which he had teased her about the bottle of Blue Nun she had been buying for her sister's birthday tea had caught her breath, and the extraordinary invitation to pop round to his flat to taste what he called real wine had been irresistible. It might have been only sex he had been after, but she was so used to that being the only route open to her to secure a brief hour or so of superficially warm human contact that she had felt no guilt or shyness at giving him quickly what he wanted. The lessons learnt through years of sex with a startling number of previous bed partners had paid off, and she was able to make that first evening physically exciting and unusual enough to guarantee a return visit. What she hadn't expected was the childlike surrender with which he soon began to depend on the nurturing devotion which she expressed in supplying not only his sexual but also his everyday bodily and emotional needs, from home-cooked meals to perfectly ironed shirts and from patient listening to unquestioning, uncritical love.

I have everything I could possibly want, she often thought. This wonderful man who needs me and desires me, and his daughter, born out of love. Let E. (as she always thought of her) have her job and her staff and her committees and her good works. I'll do what she should be doing and look after the man who provides her with everything she has.

Barbara had come to feel almost noble about it, as if, by her silence and her devotion and her acceptance of the lack of any real legal or social standing she was unselfishly keeping the other two afloat. Her own time was so happily, and fully, spent in caring for John and Susan and in shopping, cooking and cleaning that she found it impossible to imagine wanting anything more.

The feeling of unease in dealing with John was new and horrible. Her love for him was unequivocal and uncritical, and it was the sense of it being just so wrong that such a trusting, clever man should be misled that worried her far more than any anger he might feel towards her on its discovery. She was used to his anger; seeing his bad temper as a challenge more than a threat; a chance to soothe him and coax him back into good spirits.

Susan had been going to E.'s two or three times a week for several weeks now, and she hated not being able to talk to John about it. The girl was changing; there was no doubt about it. There was an arrogance in her manner that hadn't been there before, and a dismissive attitude to her mother that made Barbara feel almost tearful. Susan had always had a corner that Barbara had been unable to penetrate; the resigned-looking girl who had gone out in the evenings with her friends when John's moods had made her feel in the way had always been difficult to know, but up till now Barbara had convinced herself that this was something common to all young girls, and that the solitariness and secrecy were perfectly normal. This new lack of communication was different. And she was terrified that at any moment John would notice some of the clothes that the woman had been buying her, or smell the new scent she'd persuaded her to wear. The short hair had been easy enough – Susan was always experimenting with her looks, and John had even said he liked it.

'Are you ready for your tea, John? I've made a beef stew.'

John stretched his arms in front of him, letting the newspaper drop onto his lap, and yawned and pulled off his glasses as he looked up at her. 'I certainly am. I'm starving and exhausted.' He cocked his head on one side and smiled. 'Come here, you silly thing. What are you looking so worried about? Dumplings not risen? I'll soon sort that out.'

As she pushed the newspaper onto the floor and moved to sit on his lap, letting her heavy breasts rest against his chest the way he liked it, Barbara thought herself the luckiest woman in the world.

When Susan finally came home she went straight to her

room and shut the door behind her, letting Barbara's cry of welcome echo unanswered along the hallway. She walked over to the long mirror hanging on the wall next to her wardrobe and studied herself, a little taken aback by the image that confronted her – as she always was these days – but not displeased. She was getting used to the shorter hair, and enjoyed the way it swung gently around the bottom edge of her jaw in a thick, glossy curve as she moved her head, but the change of makeup still took her a little by surprise. She had become so used to the thick, black eyeliner and heavy foundation that the subtle, smudgy brown around her eyes and the pale porcelain-like texture of her skin still looked startlingly minimal and undefined when she caught sight of herself. The first thing she had done after the session with the makeup artist that Eleanor had set up for her was to rush home and reapply her old look, but on catching sight of herself reflected in a shop window later that day she had been surprised by the garishness of the image and had resolved at that moment to give the new, subtle makeup a chance. After a few days of following the chart that she had been given and experimenting with the products that Eleanor had insisted on buying her she had to admit that she was beginning to like it. She also liked the admiring glances she was getting, and was amazed to discover what power she could exert by a small swing of the hips or shake of the bouncy hair.

She stood still for a few seconds and listened. She could just pick up the muffled sound of the ten o'clock news, and knew that the two of them would be safely shut in the sitting room for at least the next twenty minutes, so she crossed to the bed and perched on the edge of it while she dialled Eleanor's number.

'Hello? Eleanor? I just wanted to thank you. Again. I love this new suit – it's beautiful. And lunch was – delicious.' She was picking her words carefully, consciously avoiding those that Eleanor had asked her not to use, and pleased that she'd just in time remembered not to call the food 'nice'. She still found it extraordinary, and not a little silly, that her aunt minded so much about particular words and ways of doing things, but felt that to go along with her wishes was the least she could do to repay the older woman's generosity. What did surprise her was how irritating she was beginning to find it when her mother used the very words and phrases that Eleanor was teaching her to avoid. She had never thought much about how her parents spoke or behaved, taking it all pretty much for granted, but her new awareness was forcing her to notice the difference between the two of them, and it made her feel strangely uneasy. Her father – when he spoke to her, which wasn't often – talked like Eleanor, and her mother talked like – well, like – what was that word that Eleanor kept using, which made Susan laugh? Common. Her mother talked in a way that was common.

'It was a very enjoyable day, Susan,' Eleanor's distinctly uncommon voice answered down the phone. 'And I appreciate your politeness, but I'm the one who should be thanking you for indulging me. It gives me great pleasure to buy you things and make the most of your prettiness and charm. But you know that, I'm sure. Now what did you really think of the scallops? You can be completely honest, you know – I won't be offended.'

'No, I know – and I really did like them. Honestly. And the desser— pudding. It was great. It's fun, isn't it? This going out together and you telling me things. And I'm going to teach you a bit about music, Eleanor. You're absolutely hopeless about modern music, you know. There has been a bit since the sixties. What does "house" mean to you?'

'I have heard of it, Susan. I'm not as completely out of touch as you like to think. House music. Yes – it's disco music, isn't it? What they play to dance to. What I would call disco music, isn't it? So there.'

Eleanor heard Susan laugh down the phone, and smiled to herself. It was something quite new to her, this feeling of comradeship with someone so much younger than she was, and she had recently begun to acknowledge just how fond she was becoming of this stepdaughter she had never known she had. She had foreseen that the mission to re-educate the girl, with its intended devastating payoff, would bring her satisfaction; what she hadn't realised was that it would bring her so much emotional pleasure at the same time. She was becoming more proprietorial as each day went by, and found herself resenting it each time the girl had to return to what she saw as the bad influence of her mother.

The retraining of Susan was taking up a large proportion of her time: between her visits she spent hours planning the next shopping trip or museum visit, carefully mixing pleasure with culture so as not to frighten off her prodigy with too much obvious education. She found this time spent in preparation surprisingly soothing, using it as a barrier to fend off the thoughts about John that still permanently hovered threateningly at the edges of her mind. It was helping physically, too. Whenever the familiar pangs of jealousy began to invade her body she turned her mind quickly to ideas for the next outing, and found the burning misery that invaded her very bones would ebb slowly as she pictured Susan in a new outfit or gazing at a painting in the Tate. She was impatient between meetings for the chance to carry on with her project, using the excuse of waiting for the completion of Susan's reprogramming to deflect the ever present, screaming question: *when*. When to tell him. When to confront him. And harder than anything else: what to hope for thereafter.

'Now, that's from reading a newspaper every day; another thing I'm determined to get you to do. You'd be surprised just how much you can keep abreast of things by reading one paper thoroughly every day.'

'Oh I can't, Eleanor. I can't bear newspapers.'

'Of course you can. You just need me to show you how interesting they really are – and I don't mean the gossip in the tabloids either—'

'I know you don't. I'm not quite that stupid,' Susan interrupted.

'You certainly aren't, Susan. Don't you dare say for one moment that I think you're stupid. You're an extremely clever, talented and attractive girl. Why else do you think

I'm so fond of you? Why else do you suppose I enjoy being with you so much and giving you things?'

There was a little pause before Susan answered.

'Do you really mean that?' she asked quietly.

'Of course I do. You're a delight.' There was another short silence, then Eleanor took a deep breath and spoke hesitatingly, almost nervously. 'I have something rather extraordinary to ask you, Susan. You mustn't take offence and I hope you'll shout at me, if that's what you feel like doing, but at least listen for a moment. I want you to—'

Suddenly there was a gentle little knock on Susan's door, and at the same time it opened and Barbara's head peeped round it, a flushed pink on her cheeks and a nervous anxiety in her small eyes. 'Oh sorry, dear, I didn't know you were on the phone. Your dad wants to see you. He says he hardly ever sees you. Will you come and sit with us, dear? Who are you talking to?'

Susan knew exactly what the rosiness in her mother's face signified and it sickened her. The images that had confronted her on the many occasions when she had crept unheard into the sitting room or bedroom were blistered on her mind's eye, and the ensuing evidence in her mother's face had become only too well known to her.

'What's it got to do with you who I'm talking to? And why should he suddenly care about seeing me? Tell him to piss off.'

On the other end of the telephone line Eleanor heard, acknowledged and smiled.

'Oh Susan, really, you mustn't speak to me like that.

What has got into you, dear? Come and say hello to your father right now and don't be so cheeky. You know what he'd do if he heard you talking like that, don't you?'

'I'll come when I want. Now leave me alone, I'm on the phone.'

Eleanor could just hear the closing of the door and the rustle of bedclothes as Susan settled her body back down onto the bed, but took care not to let the intense pleasure she was feeling creep into her voice as she spoke loudly into the receiver in order to get the girl's attention.

'Susan! Your mother's quite right; you really mustn't speak to her like that. You mustn't speak to anyone like that. There are far more gracious ways of expressing your frustrations, you know. "Piss off" is a phrase I shall hope to persuade you to abandon in the future.'

Susan laughed out loud and rolled over onto her back.

'Now, Eleanor, what's this mysterious thing you want to ask me?'

'You'll think me completely crazy.'

'I'm sure I won't. I trust you, you know that. You wouldn't ask me anything wrong, I know that. Go on – ask me.'

'Well – oh dear, this feels ridiculous suddenly. I – I'll just say it, that's the best thing, and then you can completely ignore it and never mention it and that'll be a good way of letting me down gently. I wondered if you'd ever consider – ever think about – changing your name?'

There was a silence on the other end, and Eleanor held

her breath and could feel her heart rate make a sudden and rather startling increase.

'Change it?'

'Yes. Yes, you know – use another name.'

'What, my surname, do you mean? Why?'

'No, not your surname. Of course not your surname, that's what you were born with and it's your real name and it suits you,' (and me, she thought wryly). 'No, I meant your Christian name. It just doesn't seem – oh dear, this sounds rather rude, but I don't mean it to be – it doesn't seem to quite go with your personality, or with the way you look. Especially now.'

'What a weird idea. I—'

'Don't say another thing, Susan. You're quite right, it's weird. Just forget I ever mentioned it.'

'No, wait a minute. I didn't say it was— Well, so what would I change it to?'

'I wondered about Sophie. It begins with the same letter, so you wouldn't have to worry about initials on things and all that. And it just seems more elegant for you – more beautiful. More charming.'

'It's a bit poncy, isn't it?'

'How do you mean?'

'Well, you know.'

'Sloaney? Is that an expression you'd use? Is that what you mean?'

'Yeah, I suppose so. Something like that.'

'Just forget it, Susan. It's only a bit of fun. A daft idea of mine. Now I've got exciting plans for next week, so don't be late.'

'Can I ask you something now, Eleanor? As weird as you asked me?'

'Of course. Anything.'

'Was my dad a twin?'

Eleanor felt a jolt of fear shoot through her. What did this mean?

'No, Susan. Why?'

'Oh, nothing. It's not important. I just wondered.'

.∞.

But they were both left with unanswered questions, and both of them thought long and hard about why they had been asked. As Susan sat watching television with John and Barbara later in the evening, she found herself mentally playing with the idea of being a Sophie. A Sophie Hamilton. It sounded rather good. Was it going to be like the makeup, which had seemed so wrong at first, but which now gave her intense pleasure every time she caught sight of herself in a mirror?

'Didn't you hear me, Susan?'

Her mother's voice crashed into her daydream, the word 'Susan' as spoken in the question overlapping uncannily with an imagined 'Sophie' in her thoughts.

'Pardon? I mean what? What did you say?'

'I said do you want anything to eat? Or a hot drink before bed?'

'No, I don't. Thanks.'

Her mother's gaze returned to the television screen and Susan watched them both for a moment before she spoke, resting her head on her knees and thinking hard.

'Mum,' she said at last, 'who thought of my name? Who thought of calling me Susan?'

'What a funny question! I really can't remember. I expect it was both of us. John, do you remember how we came up with Susan's name? I remember we talked about it for a long time, but I'm really not sure how we decided.'

'It was you, Barbara,' John answered, grunting as he reached forward to put his empty glass down on the coffee table in front of him. 'Don't you remember? I wanted something a bit more Victorian-sounding, like Emma or Sophie or one of those sort of things. But you were so keen we decided to go with Susan. It was you.'

'Oh well, there you are, Susan. You've me to thank, dear.'

'Yes,' said Susan quietly. 'Yeah, I see. It figures.'

'What a funny girl you are!' her mother laughed. 'You sound quite miserable about it. What does get into your head sometimes, I shall never know, Susan. Now why don't you get yourself to bed, dear? You'll be exhausted in the morning.'

But Susan lifted her head from her knees and looked at her with such cold scorn in her eyes that Barbara looked quickly away and down at her hands, cringing inwardly at the humiliation she somehow sensed she had been led into unwittingly.

Chapter Fifteen

John sat back in his chair, his face the colour of cold porridge and his eyes sunken back into his head in shock. His mouth was slightly open, and a tiny bubble of saliva hovered between his lips at one side, shimmering in the light from the window as it trembled in time with the minute twitching of one cheek.

'Did you really think I could be so stupid?' said Eleanor. 'Did you really think you could have gone on with your ludicrous, dirty little double life without my having not only known about it all these years but allowed it? Condoned it as something to keep you out of my way; out of my bed for as much of the time as possible?'

'Eleanor – no!' John whispered. 'No, don't – I can't bear it. I could only keep on with it because I thought I was able to do it without hurting you, without you knowing anything about it. I can't bear to think that— Oh God, I just can't bear to think that you knew; that you've put up with it all this time. So patiently. So uncomplainingly. Can't you see that I would have given anything, anything to get out? To be with you all the time. To be rid of that silly tart and her bastard daughter.'

'Oh now, John, come on. That's not very gracious, is it? The silly tart — well, yes, possibly. I have to say I can't quite concur with your taste there, but—'

'Oh, but it's not my taste, darling. It's truly not. One stupid mistake and I've paid for it all these years. You're the only woman I've ever loved or wanted. You must know that. I adore you. I want you. I need you.'

'—but the daughter: well, there, John, I may say something that will surprise you. Sophie — I assume you've noticed that she now calls herself Sophie?'

'Yes, yes of course I have. But — was that you? You mean that was you? Is that why she's become so — different. Elegant. Well spoken?'

'Of course. And I have decided, John, that we shall adopt her. I am well on the way towards making her the daughter we never had. We shall bring her up as our own, and the—'

'Oh yes, darling! Yes! You angel!'

John had flung himself onto his knees now and was making as if to kiss the hem of Eleanor's skirt when she realised she was wearing trousers. Damn! she thought, and quickly changed herself into a rather attractive chiffon evening dress with a ballerina-length skirt. Perfect height off the floor for kissing. Now, where was she? Oh yes, John had just flung himself at her feet, and she was about to graciously allow him to re-enter her life and carry her off to the bedroom. But the mood was broken, and the picture stubbornly refused to rematerialise in her head.

She abandoned the image and tried another one. The quiet, humble wife. Expecting nothing, asking for nothing. The simple and unquestioning acceptance of her husband's infidelity so unbearably moving that she saw John sitting at the table where they had just finished dinner with tears in his eyes, leaning forward in the candlelight and grasping her hand.

'You are the most wonderful wife a man could ever wish to have. May I dare to hope that you will stay with me? That we can spend the rest of our lives together? Oh, my darling, forgive me, forgive me. Let me love you as you deserve to be loved.'

'There's nothing to forgive, John. I'm the one who was at fault. I didn't give you what you needed. I've been too busy with my committees and my charities and all the design work I did for you. I've not been there enough for you.'

'Oh darling, don't say that! You're so caring; so sweet and selfless. All the people you help — all the kindness you show to everyone. I've been so selfish. So unbearably selfish.'

'I think it might be better, John, if we said goodbye. You owe your child your time and love. She needs you. And Barbara. I have to let you go.' (Yes, that's good, thought Eleanor. I like that, that's very good.)

'No, darling!' John had leapt to his feet, a look of horror and despair on his face. 'No, don't leave me! Don't ever leave me! I can't live without you — can't you see?' (Oh dear, no. That's getting even a little *too* much Mills and Boon, thought Eleanor. Try that one again.)

'No, darling!' John had leapt to his feet (yes, all right so far), a look of horror − (OK, and − and what? Maybe not despair. Maybe just suffusing love. Yes, yes that's better −) a look of suffusing love on his face. 'Eleanor,' he said seriously, 'you must never leave me. Don't you understand that if you leave me I shall die? Life without you is unthinkable. I can't live without you (careful, you're slipping back). I never want to live without you. I love you. (Oh yes, oh yes!) I love you, I love you, I love you.'

Eleanor rolled over in bed and sighed. The endless daydreams were coming closer and closer together now. She could feel herself fast approaching the moment when one of them would become reality. So near. She was so near now to being ready. John, Eleanor and Sophie. That was her future now, she could see it clearly. A loving threesome until the time when Sophie would marry. And marry well, of course, she would see to that. Barbara could be paid off, or shipped out or given work somewhere far away − whatever is done with discarded mistresses. Eleanor wiggled her shoulders in delight. That was a good phrase. She would use that one again. Discarded mistress. Like an old pair of socks. Worn out. Threadbare. Smelly.

She suddenly sat up in bed as a startling and exciting thought took hold of her unexpectedly. Today. It would be today. She was ready.

·∞·

John felt impatient and irritable. The annoying scene with Susan − or Sophie, as the ridiculous girl had insisted on being called for the last couple of weeks − had jangled him. What was he supposed to do, for God's sake? He couldn't work flat out at the office all day and then be expected to sort out all the girl's problems as well, could he? In any case, it was quite evident she didn't want to be sorted out. She seemed perfectly happy to him, and even though he could see she was communicating less and less with him and Barbara, he had to admit it made life far more peaceful when she wasn't pottering in and out of the sitting room demanding attention as she had in the old days. If it wasn't for Barbara's obvious anxiety, which made him feel he should be doing something about it, he'd be quite happy to leave well alone. Last night's little argument was becoming typical: her mother insisting she come in and greet him when he arrived home, and the two of them then finding they had really very little to say to each other, resulting in the inevitable recriminations and insults which merely served to widen the gap between them. He really must have another word with Barbara about letting the girl go through this difficult period on her own. A little more space would be good for all of them.

He was driving a little too fast, he knew that, but the satisfaction of feeling the easy response of the BMW's engine to his demand for just that bit more thrust than usual was irresistible, and he used the feeling of power to counteract the impotence he felt in his musings about Su— Sophie. He would arrive home a little earlier than usual, too, and with any luck catch Barbara on her own and bury his head in her breasts and let the strains of the day dissolve in her accepting, warm caresses. He shifted in his seat as the image began to excite him, and he pressed his foot a little further down on the accelerator as he crossed Marylebone High Street.

·∽·

There was no way that the driver of the blue Sierra could have known about, or avoided, the large BMW that shot out of the side turning. The young man twisted his head in a reflex of terror as his instinct warned him in a millisecond of the approaching crash, but even as his brain began to send the signal to his foot to slam on his brakes, it was too late, and the impact of the combined forces of the two cars drove the steering wheel deep into his chest. The impetus was enough to send it crushingly into his ribs, which in turn bent themselves inwards, far enough into his chest to puncture fatally the heart that had been working so efficiently for twenty-one years. The nose of his car was buried in the side of the BMW, and the two horns combined in a blaring wail as the artery leaked relentlessly into his chest, filling it slowly but inexorably: drowning him in his own blood. His head rested on the steering wheel; the pink nape of his neck exposed where the hair lifted forward over the clean whiteness of his shirt collar.

John was still. The driver's door was crushed in on him sideways, and he too had his forehead resting forward onto the steering wheel. But he was breathing. Just.

·∽·

Eleanor was getting out of the bath when the phone rang.

All day, since the momentous decision taken in bed that morning, she had been carefully planning every move, and the bath was to be the prelude to slow, careful dressing and a drive up to the London flat. She would almost certainly get there before John returned from the office and she would invite Sophie to join her, revelling in the girl's surprise at finding her dear aunt just two floors above her, watching her amazement at seeing how different the same flat could look when cared for with taste and style.

And then – the great moment of confrontation; Sophie at her side. Two elegant women offering him the chance to start again, to be forgiven, to make it up to them. And later: John's hands on her breasts, his mouth whispering in her ear, his hips pressing against hers. And below, two floors below, the woman sitting alone, knowing she has lost him for ever.

She hummed a little as she wrapped herself in a towel and meandered over to the telephone, catching a glimpse of her pink-cheeked face as she passed the bedroom mirror and throwing it an acknowledging smile. As she moved to pick up the receiver she felt nothing but optimistic confidence, even cockiness, and answered it with a brightness that was soon to echo horribly inside her head. In the terrible minutes that followed she couldn't believe that she hadn't known, that the ringing of the telephone hadn't somehow conveyed to her the sinister truth in its apparently innocent sound, that nothing had warned her that her life was about to be turned upside down for the second time.

By the time she reached the hospital she was numb with the shock. Images cartwheeled through her head as she walked towards the accident and emergency department, the indefinite details she had received from the brief police call not giving her enough information to formulate any clear picture of what she might expect to find. It was serious; very serious. That much had been made only too clear. But he was alive – probably. Oh God, no – not probably; that was too cruel. He had been alive when the policeman had rung. They wouldn't have lied to her. But he could have gone, slipped away, while she was on her— No, he mustn't, he couldn't die. She wouldn't let herself even think it.

She made her way quickly through the rows of chairs towards the desk and took a deep breath in an attempt to steady her impatience as she waited for the large black woman in front of her to finish her request for someone to attend to her cut hand. *Get out of my way, you stupid woman*, she mentally screamed at her. *Can't you see I've a matter of life and death here? Take your pathetic little injury and move out of my way.*

'I'm here about my husband. John Hamilton. The police phoned me and . . . I'm sorry—' Eleanor had to stop as a gulping sob shook her voice uncontrollably and choked her attempt to continue.

'Sorry?'

'John Hamilton,' she went on, shaking her head to surprise her body into being able to speak without succumbing again to the lump of horror rising in her throat. 'He's been involved in a – he's been involved in an accident. I'm his wife.'

'Just a minute, please. Could you take a seat for a moment, Mrs Hamilton, and I'll fetch someone to help you?'

'For God's sake — don't you understand, you stupid girl? My husband may be dying and I—'

'Just calm yourself for a moment, please. I know you're upset — just please take a seat. The sooner I can find someone to help you, the sooner we can get you to your husband. Sit yourself down in the first row there and I'll be back to call you in just a tick. I promise.'

Eleanor reluctantly perched on the edge of the steel and canvas chair and watched as the girl lifted a telephone on the desk and turned slightly away from her as she spoke into it with what she was relieved to see appeared to be urgency. The girl glanced up and towards her as she continued to speak, but then frowned in what looked like puzzlement as she stopped in mid-sentence and listened, swivelling her body even further away as she did so, until Eleanor could see little but the curve of her cheek where it blended in profile into the outline of the receiver.

'Oh God, no! Don't let him be dead! Oh, dear God, dear God, dear God, don't let him be dead!' she whispered to herself as she went on watching the girl's back intently, terrified that if she even blinked she might lose this moment of suspension and let the world drop in an imploding mess of horror. The girl turned back towards her now, and was speaking again into the telephone so quietly that Eleanor could make out nothing of what was said, but conveying through her continuing frown something that Eleanor could make no sense of, but which filled her with terrible fear. Something was horribly wrong.

She could stand it no longer, and leapt up from the chair and moved to the desk, only just managing to stop herself grasping the girl by the shoulders and wrenching the information from her.

'What? For God's sake, what is it? Tell me – please, tell me. What's going on?'

The girl put down the receiver and stood up, then spoke as she walked round to the front of the desk and took Eleanor gently by the arm.

'May I ask you to come with me, please? Dr Simons would just like a word with you.'

'For Christ's sake, let me see my husband! Where is he? I need to see my husband!'

'Of course you do. Just come with me, please.'

She led her along a corridor and into a small, bright room that opened off it. Eleanor vaguely noticed the phrase 'Family Room' that was stencilled onto the cream paint of the door as she passed through it, but was relieved to find it empty apart from a few nondescript pieces of furniture that her mind was too overwhelmed to take in. She stayed standing as the girl gestured to her to sit down, then brought her hands to the sides of her head in a fierce clench of despair as panic threatened to make her fall. After what seemed to be just a couple of seconds, a young man in a white crumpled coat appeared round the door and walked quickly towards Eleanor with his hand outstretched and a cheerful smile on his face. Ignoring the hand and the smile, Eleanor grabbed him by the upper arm, fiercely, and spoke closely into his face in a guttural whisper full of anger and fear.

'For God's sake, young man, take me to my husband. He's been involved in a serious—'

'Just a moment, Mrs Hamilton,' the doctor answered, gently removing Eleanor's hand from his arm and stepping slightly away. 'Forgive me – believe me, I do know how anxious you are, naturally, and I am going to do my utmost to help you. Your husband is in no immediate danger, and I will, of course, take you to him in just a moment, but . . .'

He hesitated, while Eleanor's emotions wheeled and plummeted in a giddy mixture of relief at hearing John was alive and out of danger, and sickness at seeing the anxiety and uncertainty on the man's face.

'Yes? Yes, what is it?'

'I have a small problem, which I'm sure can be cleared up in just a few moments and which no doubt you can put straight for me. It's not at all an uncommon problem that we encounter. Well, let me come straight to the point. We, er – we already have Mr Hamilton's wife here in the hospital, at his bedside in intensive care. I just wanted to avoid any – well, you can see what I mean, I'm sure.'

'Yes.'

'We not infrequently have a former wife appearing at the same time as— But I just want to avoid any possible embarrassment. Are you Mr Hamilton's first wife?'

'I am his wife.'

'Yes, yes of course. Well, as long as you know that the other – that Mrs Hamilton is at your husband's bedside. I just wanted to be sure. Shall I take you to see him, now?'

•∞•

It was hard for Eleanor to tell which upset her more as she approached the bed: the sight of the tubes, wires and bits of metal protruding from John's head, linking him to mysterious machines that whirred and clicked on the trolley at the bedside, or that of the small, bent figure sitting on the chair. Eleanor turned to the doctor, still at her side, and spoke calmly and proprietorially.

'How is he? What happened? What is the prognosis?'

She astonished herself by acknowledging even as she said the last word that she revelled in the thought that Barbara might not know what it meant.

'Mr Hamilton has had a very serious road accident, I'm afraid.'

'He ran into another car, Eleanor. It's terrible – it's just so terrible . . .'

As Barbara turned to look up at her, Eleanor felt a wave of nausea wash over her at the sight of the woman's bloated, puffy eyes and mottled skin. She lowered her gaze to the woman's hand, red-knuckled and sore-looking where it grasped a soggy, mucous-filled tissue.

'Shut up,' she said quietly. 'I'm trying to talk to the doctor about my husband.'

'Mrs Hamilton, please . . .' the young doctor went on. 'Yes, your husband was involved in a very serious road accident and I'm afraid he's extremely unwell. We do have him stabilised, and, as I said, at the moment he is in no immediate danger, but – well, at the moment all we can do is watch very carefully and wait. I'm afraid there are head injuries involved, and one can never be sure with such things exactly what—'

'What sort of head injuries? You can tell me – I'm not stupid – tell me what's going on. What's going to happen to him? Is he going to die?'

'Mrs Hamilton, please. Your husband is in deep coma at the moment, and as this has persisted for several hours now I am unable to give you at this stage an optimistic assessment. At this stage his eyes are closed, as you have seen, and he has no sleep/awake pattern of any kind, which is why I describe his condition as of now as being in coma. It's very hard to say at this point exactly how your husband's condition is going to progress. He has a relatively minor fracture of the skull, but what is more worrying is the bad shaking up his head took in the impetus of the crash. The brain scan shows evidence of serious damage to the brain surface as a whole, but so far there is no possible way of us knowing just how badly, or how permanently, his brain function has been affected.'

He was speaking in a low, conspiratorial tone which pleased her, leading her to assume that he now realised she was the correct Mrs Hamilton and that the other woman was to be ignored and sidelined in the ensuing discussion.

'The next few hours are vital. We have to watch carefully for any swelling in the brain; this, obviously, is critical. As the skull is a rigid box it can't expand at all, and if the brain swells it may be forced down into the base of the skull. This can compress the vital brain centres and – well, I'm sure I don't need to explain to you that of course anything like that taking place would mean—'

'Of course you don't. Thank you, I understand.'

'I have, of course, explained all this very carefully to – to Mrs Hamilton, here.' He gestured a little half-heartedly towards Barbara, who had turned back towards the bed with her head bowed and her shoulders hunched forwards.

'Oh. I see. Well, in future, Dr – sorry, Dr . . . ?'

'Simons.'

'In future, Dr Simons, I'd be grateful if you would confine any discussion of my husband's condition to me. This woman is no relation to him, and anything she needs or does not need to know can be conveyed to her by me.'

Barbara didn't even look up, but muttered quietly down into her chest, 'That's fine, doctor. Just do as she says. I don't care. That's fine.'

'I'm afraid in any case I shall have to ask you both to come with me now and leave the team to continue monitoring John's progress. I shall keep you fully informed of any changes whatsoever, but the best thing for everyone now is for you to let us get on with our job. I'll find a nurse to come and get you a cup of tea.'

Chapter Sixteen

The two women sat opposite each other in the family room, two cups of tea on the small table between them. There was silence, broken only occasionally by the sound of Barbara sniffing, blowing her nose or gasping a little as she wiped her eyes with the sticky tissue. Eleanor gazed at her in revulsion, maintaining her own quietly calm state by recognising just how close she herself was to disintegrating into an emotional heap exactly like the woman opposite, but determined to keep herself as remote as possible from a kinship of any kind with Barbara. Any scrap of tolerance, even pity, that she had begun to feel for her over the last few weeks had disappeared as suddenly and devastatingly as had her recently found sense of purpose and optimism. The shock of the accident and of seeing John in such horrific and terrifying circumstances seemed to have temporarily wiped all feeling from her conscious mind except that of overriding, ferociously strong hatred. Hatred not only for Barbara herself, but for all the unknown forces she now felt had been determined to mess up her life from the start. She could feel no hope of any kind about anything at all.

'Eleanor. What shall we do? What can we do?' The distraught woman looked up and caught Eleanor's cold gaze piteously.

'Nothing, of course. We shall wait. Or, at least, I shall wait. I don't really see any need for you to be here. I shall contact you as necessary. I think it's right that John has only his real family here now. Have you contacted Sophie?'

'Oh poor, poor Susan. Yes, I have. So she gets you to call her Sophie, too, does she? Poor little thing. So sweet. But I still think of her as Susan. I can't help it. She's on her way. She sounded so upset. Oh, poor little thing.' She began to cry again, and Eleanor turned away, frightened she might do something stupid like hit the woman if she had to go on looking at her.

'I shall tell Sophie, if you like. You really don't have to stay. I can tell her. I can look after her. We're very close, you know.'

'Yes, I know. I'm very grateful. You've been very kind.'

'I don't want your gratitude. I didn't do it for you. I'm trying to save her.'

Barbara looked across at her with an expression of uncomprehending misery. 'Save her? What from?'

'Oh, never mind.'

'Please let me stay, Eleanor. I know we're in an awkward situation, but I couldn't bear not to be here. I just want to stay here and be near him. We've managed so well since –

well, since you found out the truth. I was so relieved, you know. I hated all the lying and you not knowing. I always said to John that we should sort things out. And it's been so – so sensible between us, hasn't it? I can stay, can't I?'

'I can't stop you.'

'That poor young man . . . Oh, it's so dreadful. You know he died, don't you?'

'Yes. We'll leave all that to the police, shall we? And the lawyers.'

'But he died – only twenty. It's so horrible. Poor young man. Poor, poor—'

'Barbara, you didn't know him. People die every day in road accidents. Let's just concentrate on John, shall we? Now, I have things to do. I have to ring someone from the office; let them know that—'

'It's all right, I've done it. I rang Ruth.'

'What?'

'Ruth. At home. She'll sort things out tomorrow. She always does. She was going to phone you, but I told her I'd already got the police to do that. She was very surprised, of course, to hear that we – that we knew each other, but she said to give you her best wishes and condolences.'

The scream of rage inside Eleanor's head was so loud it threatened to escape, but she pressed her eyes and mouth shut for a second until the spasm had passed.

·∞·

They sat on in silence for a bit. Eleanor reached forward and picked up the cup of tea nearest to her, but hesitated on seeing the brownish mottled scum that clung to the surface. She put it back down on the saucer and sat back in her chair. There was another long pause, then she spoke quietly, looking out of the window intently as if trying to decipher something just out of view.

'What did you want? What did you hope to gain?'

'What do you mean? Gain from what?'

'From taking my husband. From stealing another woman's husband.'

There was another silence, then Barbara buried her head into her chest and began to cry quietly. She said something impossible to identify amidst the muffled sobs.

'What? I can't understand you. Stop crying and answer me.'

'I said nothing,' Barbara murmured, sniffing and swallowing. 'I didn't want to get anything. I just wanted to love him and look after him. That's all I ever wanted.'

'I don't believe you. You wanted money, and security and a home. Didn't you? You trapped him. Didn't you?'

'I just wanted him. I wanted to make a home for him. That was all.'

'Huh!' Eleanor scoffed, then turned away from the window to look directly at the distraught, dishevelled creature in the chair opposite. 'How did you do it? Get pregnant, I mean? How did you trick him? Was he drunk and you threw yourself at him? Or did he pay you? Was he lonely one night and picked you up like a tart? Is that it?'

'No, Eleanor. It was nothing like that. Oh God – look, what's the point of all this? What's the point of hurting each other any more than we have already. I've done wrong, I know that. Oh God, I know that – can't you see? But it wasn't wrong that I cared for him and looked after him and loved him. You didn't seem to— Oh, never mind. We need each other now. Can't we at least — be kind to each other?'

'Tell me how you did it. I need to know. How did you trick him into letting you get pregnant? He never wanted children. It was the last thing he wanted. Our lives were planned so carefully — he wouldn't just have abandoned it all unless he'd been forced to. How did you do it? You can tell me. You might as well. It can't make any difference now.'

Barbara sighed, a deep, forlorn sigh full of unhappiness and resignation. It echoed with something disturbing; something nameless that Eleanor didn't like, and it filled her with a terrible foreboding that she couldn't understand. It was as if by continuing to question the reluctant woman she suddenly sensed that, far from easing her own relentless need for more knowledge, more truth, more secrets to be revealed, she might just instead be forcing open the lid of a terrible Pandora's box of unknown horrors.

They both went to speak at the same time, and even as Eleanor tried to stop her, Barbara had already begun to utter the words that struck into Eleanor's heart with a force of sickening intensity.

'Because he wanted it. He begged me to have his child, if you must know. I know it'll hurt you — I know you'd both decided not to have children, but he wanted one with me. He always said I was — was a motherly sort of person. That I was meant to be a mother. I don't see why I should try to protect you from that any more or why I should take any more of your insults. You let him go. You gave up on him. It wasn't my fault – or his. We'd been together for months first. It wasn't how you think. He wanted a child – a baby. And he wanted me to have it.'

'I don't believe you.' How many times had she said that? She couldn't go on simply denying everything this bitch said. She had to think. She had to remain in control. And she had to believe that the future she had been about to engineer that very morning was still a possibility. John, Eleanor and Sophie. Together. A picture of herself and Sophie pushing John in a wheelchair suddenly flashed into her mind. Surprisingly, it didn't look too bad. Not as upsetting as one might think. John looked almost serene. And she and Sophie looked peaceful, ministering – in control. Exactly. Maybe things weren't going to be so bad, after all.

'I don't want to talk about it any more. I'm sorry, Barbara, you're right. We should be civilised about this. I don't for a moment believe what you've just told me, but this isn't the time to argue. We're both extremely upset and may say something we'll regret. We have to think of John now. Stay if you want to.'

How very gracious of you, thought Barbara, allowing the anger she often felt grumbling underneath at the way Eleanor treated her to surface briefly. You patronising fart. But, she reasoned, as you say, this is no time to deal with our problems. Plenty of time for that later. All my energies must be concentrated on John now; on getting him better. If that means putting up with your insults and snobbishness, then so be it. I'll laugh about it with him later.

·∞·

By the time Sophie arrived Eleanor and Barbara had had several visits from the medical staff and had been allowed to see John twice more. The first time had been initiated in a flurry of excitement when the young doctor had come to inform them that John's eyes were now open, but a dash to intensive care had led to the disappointment of being told that there were still no discernible signs of awareness. They retired back to the family room to await Sophie, and the doctors and other staff continued to come and go, bringing little news but helping to allay their mounting panic with bulletins of 'no change'. A nurse brought fresh tea, and they both drank it, acknowledging a kind of truce in the wordless passing of milk and sugar across the small table. Eleanor couldn't help a little lurch of pride at the sight of Sophie as she walked in, so smart and pretty in her little cream dress and so polite and grateful to the nurse who escorted her. She walked straight over to Barbara and threw her arms around her, then turned in surprise as Eleanor greeted her.

'Oh! Eleanor! You're here. Oh, that's good. Oh, thank you for coming – I'm so glad you're here. Poor Dad – how is he, Mum? What's happened to him? Can I see him? They didn't really tell me. How is he?'

Eleanor looked across and felt a stab of self-pity as she took in the instinctive pairing of mother and daughter as they clung to each other. The subtle, but undeniable exclusion of her 'aunt' was unexpected, and she knew all at once that she had been picturing a very different scene as she had waited so impatiently for the child's arrival.

'He's not at all well, baby,' Barbara was saying. 'You'll have to be brave, Susie. Dad's not too well.'

'Oh for heaven's sake, don't patronise the girl!' Eleanor exploded. 'Be straight with her. She's perfectly old enough to be told exactly what's going on. Your father has been in a very bad accident, Sophie, and they don't know yet exactly what will—'

'Eleanor, if you don't mind, I'd like to talk to my daughter. Just let me talk to her, please. If you like we'll go out and talk somewhere else, but I'd be grateful if you'd let me tell her about her father in my own way.'

Sophie looked from one woman to the other in a daze of unhappiness. 'Oh, please,' she said, 'just tell me. Is Dad alive? You're not keeping it from me, are you? He is alive, isn't he? Oh, please?'

She began to cry, and Barbara pulled her onto the chair next to her as she cradled her and whispered urgently at her, 'Yes, baby. Of course he is. Dad's alive. And he's going to be all right. Just wait and—'

'For Christ's sake, Barbara! You're talking about my husband! He's nothing to do with you! He—'

Even as she stopped, Eleanor realised it was too late. Sophie had snapped her head up so suddenly on her words that Eleanor leapt towards her and grasped her shoulders as if afraid she would fall. The girl looked shocked, her expression a mixture of confusion and fear, but Eleanor could see enough terrified understanding going on behind

238

her eyes to know that there was to be no going back. The dreadful seed of knowledge had been planted, and whatever was said or done in the next few minutes, it would grow in Sophie's mind until it choked out all the lies that had been planted there.

'Oh Sophie. I'm sorry,' Eleanor said quietly. 'I'm so very sorry. I — we — didn't want you to know. Not yet. We thought it would be easier if— Oh Sophie, Sophie. I'm sorry.'

'What — what are you sorry— I mean, I don't understand. What do you mean, your husband? How can he be? What do you mean? Are you—'

'Dad was married before, Susie,' Barbara calmly interrupted. 'Eleanor was his first wife. We didn't want to upset you, as they were still very close, and Dad wanted to go on seeing her; making sure she was all right, you see. So Dad decided it would be better if you didn't know. So when he visited Eleanor every weekend we told you she was your aunt. That's all, sweetheart. It's nothing more than that.'

'So — were you married to Dad's brother first? Before Dad?'

Eleanor made as if to answer, but Barbara went on: 'No, Susie. Dad doesn't have a brother. Eleanor was just married to Dad.'

'But why on earth didn't you tell me? Half of my friends are living—'

'I know, dear. It seems silly now, but it started like that and just sort of went on. It's the way your father wanted it.'

239

'I see,' said Sophie, remembering the puzzling wedding photo as she said it. 'Yes, I see now.'

Eleanor was astonished at the smoothness with which Barbara lied. The neatly packaged picture of a happy little second marriage, perfectly normal, perfectly acceptable – everything above board and in the open – infuriated her, and she was about to counter the cosy scenario with another hefty dose of the truth when she felt Sophie staring at her. She looked so utterly . . . Eleanor searched for the right word to describe the heartbreaking expression: forlorn. Yes, that was it. A girl who, in a few short minutes, had made the two most devastating discoveries of her life. And suddenly Eleanor knew that her growing love for this confused child was at this moment far stronger and more important than the hitherto unsurpassable sense of outraged injustice and jealousy that had been dominating her for so long. For now, she would be quiet. She would accept the unbearable unfairness of this woman's ghastly lie, and allow herself to remain the first, discarded wife in Sophie's eyes for the time being. But only for the time being.

She sat back in her chair, crossed her arms over her chest and decided, once more, to bide her time.

•∾•

Over the following three days the three women found themselves settling into an uneasy, but workable routine. Sophie appeared to have accepted Barbara's version of the family setup, and seemed more concerned with the progress of her father's condition than with bothering to ask either of the others any further questions. They took it in turns to sit at John's bedside whenever a break between tests, treatment or routine nursing would allow, each hoping to be the one to see the first sign of some kind of recognition, or at least consciousness, in his inert form. Doctors came and went, gentle and careful in their detailed explanations of brain function, nerve damage, brain scans, physical trauma and all the other factors terrifyingly gathered together to create a cloud of uncertainty hovering above the damaged human being between them.

Eleanor liked to think she understood everything, and countered the explanations with questions gathered from late-night reading of a medical encyclopaedia hastily picked up from the library on one of her journeys between the hospital and flat. But in reality she understood no more and no less than either of the other two, and the extraordinary truth, that made its way slowly but inexorably into the consciousness of the three of them, was that nobody — not the consultant, the intensive care doctors and nurses, and certainly not Eleanor or Barbara, knew what John's future was likely to be. His body remained stabilised but unresponsive; his mind remained unknown.

By the third day John's physical condition was deemed to be safe enough for him to tolerate the move to a general ward and the three women continued to take it in turns to sit with him, massaging his hands, whispering into his ears, knowing that he was almost certainly totally unaware of every attempt made to reach him, but unable to resist a little indulgent twitch of hope deep inside every time one of them sat down to take her turn in the latest foray into the depths of his unconsciousness. His eyes remained open, and sometimes Eleanor would stand up and lean over the bed, trying to find the spot nearest to where John appeared to be looking directly at her, but frustratingly unable to catch the apparent focus of his gaze. Each time a doctor would tap a hammer onto a kneecap, shout his name, scratch the sole of a foot or push a pin into the skin on the back of his hand they would hold their breath in unbearable anticipation, every sense straining to catch a sound, a movement, a breath of response. And sometimes there was one – a twitch of a muscle, a jump of a foot, a flicker of an eyelid, and a hopefully beseeching gaze would be turned on the doctor, only to have it crushed by the explanation of reflex pattern responses and continuing basic unresponsiveness. And each time their hearts would sink a little lower and their hopes dim a little more. They talked little among themselves, merely acknowledging each other's presence as the change in shift took place, not liking to break the relatively peaceful flow of purposeful watchfulness that had established itself in the small side ward.

Eleanor returned to the London flat for a few hours in each twenty-four to grab a little sleep while Barbara or Sophie took a turn at the bedside. It was the first time she had slept there since the day of the discovery, and it was a relief to know that when she was there the 'other flat' was always empty. She worked hard to turn her imagination quickly away from any thoughts of cosy two- and threesomes that had taken place only a few yards below her for all those past years. She had just enough clothes stored there to keep her going for the immediate future, and the occasional call to Carla, who had been happy not only to look after the house but also to keep George at home with her, in Surrey reassured her that, for the time being at least, there was no need for her to leave London.

·∽·

It was startling how quickly all three of them adapted to the new routine of hospital, sleeping at one or other of the flats and of doing just enough shopping and cooking to maintain themselves. Sophie was considerate and loving to both women, spending some time alone with her father and some with either Eleanor or Barbara by the bedside or in the flat. It appeared to make perfect sense that her father's 'first wife' should use his London flat as a base for visiting him in the hospital, and all discussion of any depth had been pushed aside into an unacknowledged limbo. There the big questions that Eleanor and Barbara knew were seething to be faced could be stuffed away and ignored, allowed to fester and breed until such time as either of them could consider letting anything enter their consciousness other than the unthinking routine of sitting with John or robotically carrying on with the rest of their limited lives.

The occasional call to the office revealed that, as Barbara had said, Ruth had 'sorted things out' with her usual efficiency, putting insurance claims in train, dealing with accident investigators and helping with the day-to-day domestic issues of both London and Surrey. Eleanor hated to deal with the woman, but, terrified of losing control to Barbara, insisted on being the only one to speak to her. Martin Havers had smoothly taken over the running of the company, and Eleanor marvelled how little John appeared to be missed. Another little bit of leverage, she sometimes thought as she sat watching him. You always felt so important, didn't you? Well, just fancy. It's all running smoothly along without you. What do you think of that?

The doctors continued to be noncommittal and vague in their answers to the continual questioning that they received from the anxious women, but in the ever widening gaps between visits and in the resigned looks that accompanied them, Eleanor, in particular, sensed a hopelessness settling in that frightened her. A terrifying word was hovering at the edge of her consciousness, and she couldn't be sure if she had recently overheard its use in connection with John during one of the almost furtive, muttered discussions that the posse of medical visitors were wont to have around the bedside, or if she had projected it onto her awareness from some formerly glimpsed encounter. Vegetative. That was it. And what was the rest of the horrible phrase? Permanent. Christ, yes, that was it. Permanent Vegetative State.

Barbara's visits were full of bustle and activity. Unlike Eleanor, who tended to sit quietly brooding as she spent hours in a solitary vigil at John's side, Barbara would chatter and fiddle, smoothing his brow, singing him little snatches of cheap tunes or reading him stories from the *Daily Express*. Eleanor found the one-sided conversations increasingly irritating as she encountered them on arriving or leaving at the times of her visits, and she channelled her rising annoyance into a determination to do something; anything, to effect some change in the unending, heartrending routine. Direct questioning of the doctors still resulted in a refusal to predict the eventual outcome of John's condition, but she did manage to get one of them to admit that there was 'nothing more we can do for him'.

She was sitting in Dr Simons' office when the damning phrase was used, and she shook her head to rid herself of images of John's body shrivelling and decaying in the hospital bed, ignored by white-coated backs as they moved on to where something could still be done. She knew it was time to initiate action; to engineer some sort of confrontation by bringing into the open the horrifying phrase that still lurched around her head.

'He's vegetative, isn't he?' she asked. 'You can tell me. I've read about these things, of course. He's in a permanent vegetative state, isn't he?'

The doctor hesitated, and pressed his hands flat on the desk in front of him. He bit his lip and sucked in a small breath as he looked across at her. 'Well, that's an extremely rare condition, Mrs Hamilton, as I'm sure you know. These things that you read in the newspaper are — well, things are never quite as simple as we'd like them to be. One never wants to be too definite about these cases, and newspaper reports are inevitably sensationalised, of course. But, well, yes, since you ask, I have to say that the nearest and simplest description I can give you of your husband's condition at present is, indeed, that of persistent vegetative state. You'll notice, I'm sure, that we tend to say "persistent" rather than permanent. It's not a good idea to brand such things as permanent – at any stage really. There's so much we just don't know.'

'They switch them off, don't they?'

'I beg your pardon?'

'These vegetative people. Like the Hillsborough boy. They switch them off?'

'There have been occasions when nourishment has been withdrawn, Mrs Hamilton, yes. There's no question of "switching off" as you put it, because of course your husband is breathing on his own, as you know. But, there is absolutely no question of our considering anything like that, I assure you. These things are very difficult, and, as you know, we feel there isn't much more we can do here. But, since you've raised the matter, there are various neurological institutions where John may be able to get care more specific to his needs. I can easily put you in touch with the right people if you so wish. There will need to be approaches to the relevant authorities as regards funding and so on, but there are people here to help you with that. I don't know whether there is an insurance situation here, or—'

'Yes, of course, my husband was fully insured in every way. That isn't a problem. There is money to be used for treatment, if that is going to help. And you misunderstand me when I talk of switching off, or withdrawing nourishment, or however you put it. I would not condone such an outcome in any circumstances. I have unfinished business, you see. I have to tell you Dr Simons, that there is nothing that I will not do to give my husband every possible chance of recovering whatever function there may be . . .'

'Well, naturally, Mrs Hamilton, I know just how much you—'

'No, I don't think you understand. There is no question of my not being able to communicate with my husband. It is unthinkable. Quite unthinkable. It is essential — beyond anything you may be thinking; beyond all normal experiences in this kind of case — that I am able to talk to my husband in a way that can get through to him. There has to be a way; if he is alive, if he is breathing, that he can be made to be aware. I have something extremely important to tell him; something I was about to tell him on the day of the accident and which I cannot countenance going to my grave without his knowing.'

The doctor was well accustomed to coping with distraught relatives, but there was something in the way the woman spoke that he found extremely disturbing. Her expression was unfathomable: he wondered how it was possible for eyes that appeared to be dead of all emotion to be at the same time expressing such relentless purpose.

'Of course, Mrs Hamilton. Believe me, I do sympathise more than I can say with your situation. And, indeed, sometimes the most distressing aspect of a sudden accident such as this one is the realisation that things have been left unsaid, or words spoken that have been regretted. Or finding a little present or note from the injured relative, or something that one had meant to give them: all these things are very upsetting indeed.'

But on looking up at her again, he realised that she wasn't listening. The deadness of the eyes was still there, but they had acquired a focus that was turned in on themselves and removed from the room. His comforting words were not penetrating whatever wall of thought had been put up between the two of them, and Dr Simons realised that wherever Mrs Hamilton's mind had gone, nothing he could say could impinge on it in any way. He felt himself give an almost imperceptible shudder, and shifted in his seat and gave a little cough to cover it. Whatever she was thinking was stamped with a determination that was untouchable; and the young doctor felt an instinctive sense of relief that, whatever or whoever might be the beneficiary of the intensive contemplation taking place behind the inscrutably unemotional eyes, at least he could safely assume that it had nothing to do with him.

Chapter Seventeen

The hospital was set on the side of a hill, and as Eleanor and Sophie approached it along the old A40 it loured over them in a way that was strangely comforting. More parental than threatening, Eleanor thought as she pulled the car off the main road and into the forecourt: a benign mother hen watching her chicks scuttling under the safe warmth of her feathers. The lettering of the myriad signs directing doctors, visitors and patients to various departments of the building and grounds was oddly soothing too. Eleanor found herself wondering how so many hospitals, roads and public buildings appeared to co-ordinate the style of their notices into a coherent, familiar pattern, at once essentially British and well meaning but at the same time silently stern in their polite instructions. 'Visitors' Car Park', 'Stevens and Railton Wards Only', 'Cafeteria – No Parking', 'Medical Staff Only': all were spelt out in the same, straightforward black lettering on white, blue-framed backgrounds that held the unmistakable aura of nannying that made her feel in safe hands.

After the several telephone calls that had been necessary to arrange John's admittance and transfer she felt she had absorbed the feeling of the place and that she had a good idea of the type of institution she would find, but on seeing it for the first time she realised she had imagined something altogether on a smaller scale. The three large Edwardian sections of the building – a centre block and two wings – were linked by modern wood- and steel-covered walkways, and as she parked in a bay just outside one of these glass-lined corridors she began to experience a familiar feeling of discomfiture at the mix of old and new; the straightforward functionality of the structure immediately in front of her awkwardly at odds with the ornate mouldings and balustrades of the older parts.

She and Sophie had braced themselves for what they might find on Railton ward. Knowing that all the patients – or clients, as she noticed the staff described them – were in a similar condition to John, she was prepared for rows of inert, sightless figures lying in beds side by side in giant wards, or perhaps a chain of tiny separate rooms, each containing an unaware body, functioning as a physical entity, but with a mind as unresponsive and inanimate as the bed on which it lay. But nothing had prepared either of them for what they found, and Eleanor had to stop herself releasing an exclamation of confused shock as she stepped out of the lift on the first floor and met her initial sight of the inhabitants of the ward.

What immediately hit her was the apparent ordinariness of the scene in front of her. A television was on in the corner, and seven or eight wheelchairs faced towards it, their backs turned to Eleanor and Sophie, and the tops of the heads of their occupants clearly visible above the backs of the chairs. Before the two women could advance far enough into the room to be able to see the patients' faces, a nurse hurried over to meet them and ushered them quickly into a small side room.

'I don't understand,' said Eleanor to the nurse, who smiled at them as she closed the door. 'I thought this ward was all going to be— I mean, I thought they'd all be like my husband: vegetabl— I mean, not responding. Not aware of anything. Those people are all sitting up watching television.'

'One of the first things we do is to get our clients sitting as upright as possible. Dr Livens will talk you through all of this, of course. But as you'll see, the physical condition and position are our first priorities. Patients frequently come to us surprisingly undernourished, perhaps with pressure sores, bad muscle tone and so on. Naturally, before we can begin to assess any kind of opinion of the extent of the brain damage involved, we need to sort out all the physical problems. And the clients you saw in the ward outside are in varying stages of awareness, of course. I'm sure you'll get to meet most of them over the next few days. Watching television is perhaps not a fair description of the way they are reacting to it – some of them are totally unaware of it – but for their carers, and indeed for purposes of stimulation, the television is very useful.

'Your husband is here, Mrs Hamilton. He is comfortably settled into a side ward, and I'll take you to see him in a moment. One of the first things we shall do is to arrange for him to have his own wheelchair. Before any serious attempt is made to communicate with him we would like him to be seated: the brain is far more active and responsive in an upright body. And do please forget what you may have heard or read about constant stimulation. The old idea of talking, playing music, offering smells and so on twenty-four hours a day is no longer the way we work. Just as when a child is learning language, the periods of rest are as important as the times of learning. The brain can only take so much at a time. On the ward as a whole we have regular periods of rest; quiet periods as we call them.

'Your husband will be receiving the most up-to-date approaches to this kind of brain damage in the world, but obviously there is no instant, magic cure or treatment. Many people feel that once they have a relative in the hospital progress is going to be quick and dramatic. It's only fair to warn you that of course it never is like that. We have no way of knowing at this stage if there is any awareness inside your husband at all. There is absolutely no objective way of assessing that, unfortunately – no test at all can tell us. If only it could, it would make everything considerably simpler, of course. Is there anything else you or your daughter would like to know at this stage?'

Eleanor was about to correct her as to her relationship with Sophie, but the girl was already speaking.

'No, I don't think so. Except – do you think he's in any pain? Any discomfort? I can't bear to think that he might be hurting, and unable to tell us.'

'Please don't worry – Sophie, is it? We are extremely

experienced here in judging the physical condition of our clients, and in keeping them as comfortable as possible. There is no question that your father has suffered very extensive brain damage, and is unlikely to be experiencing much physical sensation of any kind at present.'

'There will be other visitors – do you have any kind of visiting hours?'

'Please feel free to come here whenever, and for as long as, you wish. The more we can all work together, the better it is for John. And we are happy to welcome anyone who you think would like to come and see him.'

'My mother will be wanting to come. This is . . .' She hesitated, and glanced across at Eleanor, who kept looking straight in front of her, '. . . well, sort of my other mother. Um – stepmother. It's a bit complicated.'

'Oh, I see,' smiled the nurse, looking utterly unembarrassed. 'Well, you're all more than welcome.'

Eleanor turned towards Sophie and reached her hand across to give the girl's knee a little pat of acknowledgement. 'Thank you,' she said quietly.

·∞·

After a few days of tests and assessments John was assigned a wheelchair. Eleanor found it quite unnerving to see him sitting up: on some occasions when the chair happened to be facing directly towards her as she entered the ward and his head was supported in an upright position she was quite startled by the effect of his appearing to look directly at her. She followed the nurses' example in speaking to him as if he could understand every word, and although at most times she felt rather foolish, as if she were addressing a dummy, there were moments when his gaze seemed so aware that she suddenly had the odd feeling that perhaps he was, indeed, taking in everything he heard.

The doctors would still give no indication of what John's future might hold, but Eleanor felt her optimism fading as every day passed with no hint of response. She and Barbara were managing quite efficiently to dovetail their visits so that they achieved the minimum possible overlap whilst still ensuring that one of them was with John at all the times when his eyes were open and he was in what they learnt to call a 'waking state'. Generally their timing was arranged so that they avoided having to see each other at all, and when Eleanor sat alone beside John's chair she was almost able, for the first time in months, to convince herself that she was the only woman in his life. She was surprised to find herself feeling more peaceful than she had for some time, and couldn't understand, when she gazed at the seemingly uninhabited face of her husband just why she wasn't more devastated. She felt moments of sheer panic at the thought that she might never again be able to talk to him, to tell him of what she knew, to watch as she surprised him with the extent of her knowledge and the patience with which she had borne it, but in the times in between she was experiencing a curious tranquillity.

One night, after another day of watching John's body undergo the assaults it needed to keep it alive, she suddenly knew exactly why it was that she was so calm. She was lying in bed, going over in her mind the events of the day. She had watched as the young physiotherapist had lifted John onto a padded table in a side room and encased his legs from knees to ankles in plaster to persuade them to straighten out of their painful-looking spasms. She had helped to pass his liquid feed slowly through the tube that took it directly into his body; she had combed his hair; wiped the dribble from his mouth; talked inconsequentially about everything and nothing. She had read him stories from the newspaper; pushed his chair in front of the television; helped to tuck him up in bed. And now she knew. It wasn't just that she was so much in control – that alone would have been oddly satisfying after the months of feeling at the mercy of everyone's desires but her own – it was more than that.

He couldn't be – ever, not at any time, day or night – in bed with *her*. He couldn't be . . . Eleanor wanted to say the f'ing word, just as everyone seemed to nowadays, but she couldn't. *Making love* was an impossibly wrong description of what he and the whore used to do together. *F'ing* was crude, unpleasant, animal – far better suited to what the two of them must have done together. But her mind refused to say it, even to herself. But she felt it. She felt the word, the thing that he and Barbara couldn't be doing. They couldn't be f'ing. They couldn't be kissing; fondling; petting; touching nipples and thighs and— Eleanor could see now how terrible had been the strain of never knowing, for so long, what John was doing when he wasn't with her, and of having always assumed, even subconsciously, that he was with Barbara. Doing things.

Now she knew exactly where he was and where he

would be, day and night, for what might just be a very long time indeed. She smiled to herself, turned over onto her side and pulled the covers tightly around her shoulders.

'Dad. Dad – I love you. Do you remember this scarf? You gave it to me last year. For my birthday. And then you shouted at me because I left it on the floor in the sitting room. You said you wished you hadn't wasted your money on me when I was so careless with things. And then I said it was a stupid scarf and I didn't want it anyway. Don't you remember? Come on, Dad, you must remember? Listen to me. And Mum picked it up and sent me to my room for being rude to you. Look, I'm wearing it now. You see – I do take care of things. I like it really. It's lovely, I— No it isn't. It's a stupid scarf. It's an ugly colour and it's old-fashioned and I hate it. Now – come on, have a shout at me again. Don't you want to shout at me now, Dad? Oh Dad – please have a shout at me. Oh Dad, no – please don't do that. Can't you just—'

But Sophie had to turn her head away and stop speaking as the sight of her father's drooling, slack mouth made her want to retch and cry at the same time. A nurse came over and put a hand on her shoulder, quickly wiping John's mouth with the other at the same time.

'Come on now, Sophie – you've been so strong. Don't give in now, honey. Don't let your father see you crying, now. He wouldn't want that, would he?'

'What difference does it make? He can't see anyway. He doesn't know if I'm crying or laughing. He doesn't even know I'm here. Why do you all go on pretending he can hear you? Why don't you just admit he's gone? That he can't hear us or see us or understand anything or— Oh God, I can't bear it.'

She stood up quickly and walked away from the wheelchair and across the room to the door. 'I'll just go out for a bit, Ellie. I'm sorry – I just can't . . .'

'That's OK, Sophie. You know you don't have to apologise. It's very, very tough on you, all this. Go out and have a bit of fresh air. Or get a drink from the machine. But just let me say one thing.'

Sophie turned to look at her from the doorway. 'What?'

'You're wrong when you say we all know your father can't hear us. Nobody knows that, Sophie. Just remember that. He might be able to hear every word we say.'

Sophie was glad to find the ground-floor waiting area empty. She chose a sandwich and a can of Coke from the self-service dispenser, pushed open the top of the can and took a quick sip, carried them over towards a chair and low table in the corner, hearing as she did so the sound of someone coming into the room behind her. As she went to put the food and drink down, the strap of her bag slipped off her shoulder and the weight of it fell onto her hand, jogging the can out of her grip and onto the floor, where it rolled across the carpet, spilling Coke as it went. She swore to herself and stooped to pick it up, half aware as she bent over of the tightness of her skirt across her hips. As she dabbed at the carpet with a paper napkin she heard a quiet wolf whistle behind her and an equally quiet but clearly audible throaty whisper in a male voice — 'Nice one!'

She straightened and turned round quickly in furious embarrassment, ready to counter the crude verbal assault with an equally crude put-down, but was stopped with her mouth open and the sound already half made in her throat by what she saw.

He was in a wheelchair.

She stuttered a little, her embarrassment now making up in awkwardness for what it had lost in anger, and then glanced around the room in an unsuccessful attempt to look as if that was why she had turned in the first place.

'What?' said the man in the chair. 'You were going to say something. What were you going to say?'

'I — I was— nothing.' She turned away and put the empty, sticky can down on the table.

'Can I buy you another drink?' the man went on.

'No thanks, I'm fine. Thanks anyway.'

She ate her sandwich in miserable discomfort, aware of the rustling of the cellophane in the quiet room as she took each piece from its wrapping. She felt horribly thirsty, and considered buying another Coke, but was unable to face whatever taunts might emerge from the wheelchair as she passed by it to and from the machine. She thought hard as to where she had seen a water fountain, and was about to get up and walk out, when the man spoke to her again, his North London accent clearly distinguishable now that he spoke out loud.

'Why did you stop what you were going to say? You were going to shout at me for whistling at you, weren't you? Why didn't you?'

Sophie could feel herself beginning to blush, and she rested her face in one hand and leant her elbow onto her knee so as to cover the redness in the side of her cheek as she turned to look at him. He was younger than she had realised on that first furious glance. He had dark hair that was long enough on the top to flop over his forehead, but shorter enough round the sides to show his large, reddish ears. His eyebrows were thick and as dark as his hair, and the blue T-shirt he was wearing under his leather jacket was loose around his neck, showing a hint of more dark growth at its base. Rather apelike, Sophie thought to herself. She glanced quickly at his hands to see if they looked as hairy as the rest of him, but the mild sense of disdain she had been feeling was replaced by a little jab of pity as she saw the twisted, bent spasm of one of his wrists that reminded her uncomfortably of her father's legs.

In the same split second that she looked at it, the young man moved his bent hand underneath the other, straight one, and Sophie felt even more awkward when she realised that he had been aware of her pitying glance.

'No I wasn't. I was just annoyed that I had dropped the drink. I wasn't going to—'

'Yes you were. And you know bloody well why you didn't. Because I'm not normal. Because you saw I was in a wheelchair.'

There was a pause while Sophie tried desperately to think what to say.

'You see, this is what we're going on about when we ask to be treated the same as you would treat a normal person. You all like to think you treat disabled people the same as if—'

'Now look — just a minute.' Sophie felt a sudden burst of anger, and could hear that she was talking too loud, but didn't care. 'Why the hell are you suddenly giving me a lecture? I was only trying to be polite. Yes, all right, of course I was going to say something. You didn't only whistle, you sort of leered at me under your breath. I didn't because — well, actually, because I didn't like to. You could be in pain, or a bit crazy or — anything. Couldn't you? It was perfectly reasonable of me not to treat you like a normal person, as you put it, because you're not. You're in a fucking wheelchair, for heaven's sake.'

There was a moment's silence, and Sophie began to regret her outburst as images of the young man keeling over in his chair or shuddering into a fit flashed into her head.

'I'm sorry,' she said. 'That was very rude of me. I shouldn't have said that. But you do make it incredibly difficult, you know. With all this equality thing, I mean.'

'Why do you say you're sorry? You don't really think I mind, do you? I know I'm in a fucking wheelchair — as you put it. And you make it *incredibly* difficult — *actually* — with your whistling thing, anyway.'

Sophie chose to ignore the mimicry of her relatively posh accent and the vocabulary that Eleanor had so carefully instilled and went on, 'What do you mean?'

'You know – with us not being allowed to whistle at you in the street any more and all that.'

'Oh, don't be so ridiculous. It's just common courtesy not to treat someone the way you were treating me. That's all. I'm not saying I never want to be whistled at.'

'Oh, right,' he answered, and raised his eyebrows the smallest bit.

'Well, that's just as bad,' Sophie said, smiling as her eyebrows raised themselves in return.

'What is?'

'That look you're giving me.'

'Oh, come on – grow up. Look, darling, if I'm giving you a look you can simply fuck off, right?'

Sophie laughed. 'Now who's being touchy? Yes, I know I can fuck off. But I'm having a sandwich in peace and I don't feel like moving. So please stop whistling, leering and looking. OK?'

'But you've finished your— Oh, what the hell. Sure,' he said, and turned away towards his table. He picked up a plastic cup with his straight hand and sipped at it, keeping his back towards Sophie. She watched him for a while, then startled herself by feeling a little twinge of sexual excitement as she looked at the way the small dark curls of his hair moved over the nape of his neck. She was amazed to find herself longing to reach out a hand and feel them with one finger, twisting and spiralling them around her flesh until they pulled tight and she could use them to jerk his head back until it forced his mouth open as it stretched against the tautness of his neck. She saw herself standing over him, controlling him, his eyes as wide open as his mouth as she held the hair tightly and bent over and covered his lips with her own and plunged her tongue inside the wet cavity of his open mouth.

'What's your name?' she heard herself saying.

'Bugger me – women's liberation. She's only asking my name.' He cocked his head on one side and smiled a little, but the mimicry of her accent returned as he went on. '*Simon*. And you must be *Amanda*.'

'Why the hell are you being so rude?' asked Sophie. 'I asked you a perfectly civil question.'

'It's just the fucking poncy way you say it. So kind of you to want to know.'

'Oh, shut up!'

'*Oh, do shut up Simon!*' he mimicked.

There was another silence for a moment, then Sophie suddenly burst out laughing.

'Sorry,' she said. 'I didn't mean to be poncy. But I'm afraid my name's Sophie.'

'Oh, it's not – not really?'

'Yes, really.'

'I nearly said Sophie before, instead of Amanda. It's not – not really?'

'Yes, it is. Well, it didn't . . . It was . . . No, it's— Yes it is. Sophie.'

'Fuck me. Well, mine's not really Simon. It's Robbie.'

'Robbie. You mean Robert?'

'No. I mean Robbie.'

Sophie reached out her hand and leant towards the chair. 'How do you do?'

'How do you do?' Robbie answered, taking her hand in

his and shaking it. 'At least I've got one that works, you see. And it's good at a lot more than shaking hands.'

As Sophie smiled back at him, she found herself wondering just what exactly Robbie's hand might be good at, and for the second time that morning surprised herself by realising how much she would like to find out.

Chapter Eighteen

'ay I have a word with you, Eleanor? And I think perhaps Barbara should be in on this too, if that's all right with you.'

Eleanor had always assumed occupational therapy to involve things like basket making and papier mâché but had learnt over the weeks John had been in the hospital just how wrong she was. Rae was one of the most extraordinary people she had ever met – small and gentle in appearance, but magnificently daunting in the way she controlled the OT department and in her firmness in dealing with matters that were as near to touching the very meaning of being that Eleanor had ever come across.

'I'm sure I can tell Barbara whatever it is that you have to say,' Eleanor suggested. 'I'll make sure she understands, if that's what's worrying you. It's really easier I think if I see you alone.'

'No – I have no worries at all about her understanding. She's a very bright woman and I have never had any reason to doubt that either of you is fully aware of the implications of everything that we tell you about John's condition. As you know, we've had every possible sort of family situation here to deal with and nothing can surprise or embarrass us now, Eleanor.'

'No, of course not. I didn't think for a second that—'

'And, indeed, the two of you appear to have such a very civilised relationship that you're an example to all of us who have "exes" to deal with.'

'Ah well, yes.' Eleanor looked down for a moment. 'I've always felt there's no point in making problems. We, um, we all get on pretty well.'

'In any event, I think it's time we had a get-together. Will you call Barbara or shall I catch her this evening when she comes in?'

·∞·

It had been some time since she and Barbara had been in the same room, and Eleanor had to work very hard not to let the old familiar feelings of contempt and fear overwhelm her so that she would be unable to take in what Rae was saying. She succeeded in maintaining a friendly and polite exterior, but noticed that she could only keep her mind on the woman's words by avoiding looking at Barbara, whose neat, irritating figure was perched on the edge of her chair, bent forward in supplicant concentration.

'You may remember,' Rae was saying, 'that when you first came here I mentioned briefly the new equipment that we use now as part of the attempt to find awareness in some of our clients. We have had some remarkable results and I have begun to use it on John during some of my sessions with him. He is physically fit enough now for me to attempt communication with him regularly.'

'Do you mean he may not be in permanent vegetable after all?' Barbara asked, her face strained with the effort of trying to prise every possible ounce of meaning from what the therapist was telling them.

'*Persistent* vegetative state, we prefer, Barbara, as you know. And even that is a very unsatisfactory term. How long is persistent? We have had several cases admitted here classed as irredeemably vegetative, which have since proved to be misdiagnosed. I myself have worked with several clients who have been diagnosed as PVS and with whom I have eventually managed to establish a clear dialogue. You may even have seen pieces about them in the paper,' she smiled, gesturing briefly at a large notice board on the wall behind her desk.

Eleanor looked up at the cuttings pinned to the board and saw among them a photograph of a young man sitting in a wheelchair with an elderly man and woman on either side.

'But how?' she asked. 'How do you establish a dialogue, as you call it?'

Rae opened a drawer in the desk and pulled out a small metal pad with a wire attached to it. 'Here,' she said, passing it to Eleanor. 'You see that the top piece of metal moves a tiny bit – rather like a foot pedal, but needing less pressure? Well, that's attached to a little bleeper, and I use the simple old method of one bleep for yes, two for no. You'd be surprised how little physical effort it needs to operate one of those. And of course it doesn't need to be the hand

– I've searched many patients for days and days, trying to find the slightest bit of movement, just a fraction of muscle that they can use under their own control: the side of the foot, perhaps, or underneath of a thigh – and you'd be amazed how many times there is awareness in there just waiting for the right way to express it.'

'And you think that John may be——'

'It's too soon to say anything for sure, Barbara, but I do seem to be getting responses that are correct slightly more often than I would expect for random chance. I want to continue to work with him for a while longer before I can say for sure that he is understanding me, but I thought it was time to tell you both how things were going. I'd also like you to watch me with the bleeper so that you can begin to use it with him yourselves.'

Eleanor pressed the metal flange gently with her fingers and felt it move with a small click.

·∞·

Later that evening, Eleanor watched as a young nurse made John's bed. Something worried her about the scene in the occupational therapy room and she tried to think back over everything that had been said and remember what it was that was echoing uncomfortably in her head. She could clearly see the bleeper in her mind's eye, the shiny metal catching the light as she had turned it in her hands, excited and nervous at the same time at the extraordinary possibility of being able, once more, to get through to her husband. But it wasn't that. There was something else.

She remembered. It was the cutting. The cutting on the notice board about the young man who had been taken for a vegetable and then discovered to have awareness and to be able to communicate. But it wasn't the story that had worried her. It was — what? What was it about the newspaper cutting that was niggling at her? She tried to take another good look at it, closing her eyes and resting her head on one hand to picture it more clearly. She could see the headline: something like, 'The Son We Thought We'd Lost For Ever — Man in Vegetative State for 8 Years Found to be Aware'. But it wasn't that.

'Are you all right, Eleanor?' the nurse asked, tucking the sheet underneath John's inert body.

'Oh yes, Katie, I'm fine. Just thinking, that's all,' Eleanor smiled at her.

·∽·

Sophie had taken to having a drink in the downstairs waiting area every time she visited her father. She valued the quiet time she was able to have there, relaxing in the absence of both Eleanor and Barbara. She still had to think twice to stop herself thinking of Eleanor as her aunt, and the shock of the retrospective discovery of a stepmother was still fresh enough to cause her enormous emotional confusion. The rare moments when she had to cope with both women at once were the hardest. She could sense the friction between the two of them, however carefully they covered it with their civilised, polite veneer of tolerance, and an excuse to leave the intense atmosphere of the ward was too tempting to pass up. She had no desire to question either of them as to details of their marriages, feeling she had quite enough to deal with in coping with her father's condition, and happy to push aside the complications of his previous life as being irrelevant to the present situation.

But it wasn't just the thought of escape that persuaded her to seek out the small room on the ground floor after every visit. She also hoped – without quite admitting it to herself – that she might just happen to bump into Robbie again. She had been surprised to find herself thinking about him in the days since their first meeting; rerunning, as she lay in bed or sat on the coach on the way to the hospital, the brief conversation they had had. As she went back over the things that had been said she would replace her own answers with alternatives that were far wittier and more amusing; change the clothes she had been wearing for sexier ones, and redo her hair and makeup in the way that she felt would have made her most attractive. She was puzzled by just how often she found herself going over it and by how much she kept hoping to see him again – wondering if the pity she had instinctively felt for him was fooling her into thinking she had experienced some sort of instantaneous emotional affinity with him. The ludicrous phrase 'love at first sight' kept popping into her head.

But for two and a half weeks there had been no sign of him and she began, reluctantly, to assume she would never see him again. She briefly considered asking the nurses on that floor if they knew who he was, but was too embarrassed at the idea of Robbie hearing that she had been asking about him to risk it, and at the same time unsure, in any case, as to what she would do with any information she might pick up. The whole subject felt so much like a fantasy that the idea of giving it any kind of reality by mentioning it out loud felt too preposterous to be possible; it seemed the words would dissolve like candyfloss in her mouth before she could say them.

But it didn't stop her dreaming. She came to the hospital three or four times a week, and three or four times a week she collected a Coke from the machine, carried it over to the same chair in the window and thought about the boy in the wheelchair. She imagined hearing the low wolf whistle behind her, and turning to find him smiling at her, reaching out his good arm towards her. She saw herself getting up and walking across to him, grasping his hand in hers and bringing it up to her cheek. Sometimes she would wheel him out into the grounds, or read a book to him while he gazed at her adoringly.

'I suppose this is some sort of madness,' she said out loud to herself one evening as she put the empty Coke can down on the table. 'Some sort of replacement or whatever they call it. I'm compensating for having a father whose mind has been sucked out of his head. Oh well,' she went on, as she stretched her arms above her head and looked at her reflection in the rain-spattered window, 'it's fun, anyway.'

She folded her arms over her chest as she went on looking at herself. The garden was dark outside and the curtains were open; the light from the standard lamp next to her chair outlined her figure with a fringe of yellow down one side against the blackness of the glass, and she turned her head a little to one side to let it shine onto her profile. She rubbed her nose with her index finger and sighed. 'It's not as if Dad ever talked that much to you, anyway, is it? Not as if he ever really seemed to like having you around, is it?'

Suddenly something moved in the garden and made her jump. For a split second she saw a shining Tinkerbell darting across the window, but at the same moment realised it was simply light reflected in the glass from something behind her. She turned round quickly to see the metal of Robbie's wheelchair gleaming as he moved it towards her.

'Oh!' she said. 'Sorry.'

'What for?'

'I – er – I jumped. I mean – I didn't know you were there.'

'I wasn't. I've only just come in. Who were you talking to? There's no one here.'

'Oh, nothing. I was just talking out loud, that's all. How are you?'

'Fine. Great, thanks.'

There was an awkward pause, and Sophie thought how different this meeting felt to the way it had been in her imagination. She tried desperately to think of some of the scenarios that had worked so well in one of her many day-dreams, but the phrases that had felt so right and flowed so easily were impossible to say in this uncomfortable reality. He even looked different. In the brief glimpse of his face she had had as she turned, she saw how wrongly she had remembered him. His nose was longer and his eyes less gentle than she had pictured them, and there was an uneasiness in his manner that surprised her.

'How are you?' he said at last, and Sophie looked back at him.

'Oh I'm fine, thanks.'

'Why are you here? Are you—'

'No, I'm just visiting. My father.'

'Oh, right. Is he HD or MS or what?'

'What? No, no I don't think so. I mean, I don't know what you're saying.'

'Huntington's. Or multiple sclerosis.'

'Oh I see. Yes, of course, I know what MS is. No, he's – um – he's BG.'

The boy frowned. 'BG? What's that?'

'Brain gone.'

'I see.' There was another pause and Robbie looked down for a moment. 'I haven't heard of that.'

'Well, no, you wouldn't have.'

Something in her tone made him look up again, and he laughed as he saw her smiling hugely at him. 'Were you joking?'

'Yes, of course I was. Or – no, I wasn't joking when I said – I mean, his brain has gone, but I don't think I'm meant to call it that. PVS, that's what they call it. Persistent vegetative state.'

'When they don't hear or speak?'

'Or understand, or look, or feel, or – or anything really. Yes, that's the one.'

'Christ. That's a bugger.'

'Exactly.'

He looked down at his lap and Sophie studied him for a moment, wondering how she could possibly have felt disappointed those few seconds ago. He's gorgeous, she thought. I want to rush over to him and kiss him.

'How did he get like that?' Robbie asked.

'Car accident.'

'Christ.'

'How did you get like – like that?'

'CP. Cerebral palsy. Born like it. I just come here every couple of weeks or so for physio. This wing is mostly for people like me – or the multiple sclerosis ones. Some live here and some come and go, like me.'

'Can they do anything? Make you better?'

'Not much. But I'm fine. Lead a normal life and all that. On the whole.'

'Do you want a drink?'

'Yeah, OK. I'll have a Coke.'

Sophie fetched a can from the machine and brought it over, using it as an excuse to sit in the chair next to his, and enjoying the brief touching of his hand as she passed it to him.

'Thanks.'

'It's a pleasure.'

'Oh – it's a pleasure is it, *Amanda*?' he said, dropping into the mimicry of her accent.

'Don't start that again. Anyway, I told you my name.'

'Yes, of course – *Sophie*.'

'Shut up.'

'OK. Sorry.'

He pinioned the can between his legs and opened it with one hand, then took a quick drink before going on: 'So, *Sophie*, do you want to go out?'

'What?'

'Do you want to go out?'

'What do you mean?'

'What do you mean, what do I mean? What do you think I mean? I mean, do you want to go out?'

'Where?'

He shrugged and smiled at her.

She smiled back. 'Yes. OK.'

Later she couldn't believe she'd said it.

·∞·

While Eleanor was washing up she remembered. As she turned to put her plate down on the draining board – she hadn't bothered to use the dishwasher ever since John's accident – she suddenly saw the caption under the photograph in the newspaper as clearly as if she were reading it in front of her. 'Answers Yes or No – But One Question We Daren't Ask Him, Say Parents.' Why did that seem so disturbing? And what question didn't they dare ask?

Eleanor dried her hands and turned away from the sink. For the first time she began to imagine just what it would be like if there really was any awareness inside John. What the hell would she say to him? Would they be able to tell how long he had been aware? For the first few weeks after the accident there had never been any doubt in her mind that as soon as possible she would tell him everything: the thought of his never knowing had been unthinkable. But now, everything was getting hazy. Would she still tell him — and when would she, and what might his reaction be? It was perfectly possible, of course, that he already knew. There had been plenty of times when she and Barbara had been in the room together for a short time as they changed shifts, and more than once they had talked over his head — or talked to Sophie about each other. Eleanor tried to think back over some of the more recent visits and to what had been said within John's earshot.

She wasn't sure if she felt elated or frightened by the thought that there was a possibility of establishing some kind of communication with him. There had been something rather comforting about the period since his accident; a time of enforced limbo, when she had had to take no major decisions about the future, or worry in quite the same way as before about the present. Now his potential reawakening seemed threatening, and she felt the old unease and jealousy begin to stir uncomfortably inside. Supposing he did know that she knew — what then? The thought of it didn't bring her the satisfying vengeful exorcism of her jealousy that she had always imagined. Instead it made her frightened. Maybe he was lying there at this moment planning what he would do once he could make his wishes known. Would he abandon her totally in favour of Barbara? Would he be relieved that the confession had been pre-empted by circumstances? Perhaps Barbara was to be the one wheeling him peacefully along in his wheelchair, Sophie strolling beside them; John looking up gratefully into her eyes; lifting a weak hand onto her arm in loving gratitude. Eleanor despaired as she began to see that either option – John knowing or not knowing – was unbearable.

'No!' she shouted out loud, 'I won't have it. I won't have it.'

·∞·

Sophie carried the two half-pints of beer over to the table in the corner of the pub and pushed Robbie's wheelchair out of the way with one hip as she put them down.

'There,' she said with a smile, 'I told you it wouldn't take me so long this time. They're getting to know me now. I'm not being quite so ignored.'

'Cheers,' Robbie said as he took a sip of beer, then smacked his lips and leant forward to put the glass down again. 'So what's tonight's discussion? Do we continue the story of Sophie's extraordinary family setup, or do we explore the complications of being in a wheelchair?'

'Yes, let's do that,' Sophie smiled. 'Tell me your complications. I'd like to know.'

'Getting trousers on and off. Very tricky.'

'Uh huh. Yes, yes I can see that.'

'Changing the bulbs in ceiling lights. *Extremely* tricky.'

Sophie spluttered into her beer, and slopped some of it over the edge of the glass. 'Oh God – don't make me laugh again. You always do that when I'm just taking a drink.'

'I'm hoping to get your shirt so wet that I can see your nipples.'

'I see. Well, there are easier ways.'

'Sophie!' Robbie opened his eyes in mock surprise. 'Miss Sophie, I'm surprised at you!'

'Why are you so horrible about my name? There's nothing so particularly wonderful about Robbie, but I don't keep on sending you up about it. It's really child-ish.'

'Sorry. Don't take it so seriously. I don't know — it just doesn't seem really you, somehow. Doesn't really seem to suit you.'

Sophie looked at him in as much genuine astonishment as he had been pretending earlier.

'That's absolutely extraordinary. Really amazing.'

'Why?'

'That's just extraordinary.'

'What are you on about?'

'Sophie's not my real name.'

'So?'

'No, I mean I've only been called Sophie for a few months. My real name is Susan.'

'Wait a minute, I don't get this. I don't understand. Do you mean you've changed your name? Why? What for?'

'It'll sound really silly, but — you know the aunt I told you about who isn't my aunt at all?'

'Yeah.'

'She asked me to. She was really kind to me, and helped me to — well, all sorts of things. She bought me clothes and stuff; took me places. Taught me which words not to use, things like that. Showed me things, explained things to me. And she didn't like me being called Susan. So she asked if I minded changing it to Sophie.'

'No! You're kidding.'

'No, I'm not.'

'That's truly weird. She sounds like a snobbish old bitch to me. Taught you what words not to use — what the hell's that all about? And what was wrong with Susan? It's not the prettiest of names, I have to say, but it's a lot more you than Sophie. And what did your mother say? How did she feel about you changing the name she'd given you? Didn't she mind?'

'She didn't really have a say. We don't always — get on very well.'

'Bloody hell, I'd have something to say if my kid started calling herself by some poncy new name!'

'Oh it's not poncy; you've got a real thing about it. You're the snobbish one. What does it matter what name I use, anyway?'

'Well, it's just sort of strange. It must be weird enough for your mum having this other woman hanging about the place, let alone you changing your name to suit the old bird.'

'Yes. Yes, I suppose it must. I didn't really think about that much.'

'Anyway, I'm going to call you Susie. Just to screw you up even more. OK?'

'OK,' Susie laughed.

'Now, Susie, tell me what your plans are for me seeing your nipples without wasting all the beer?'

Susie looked down at her glass for a moment, then

raised her eyebrows and smiled up at him without raising her head. 'Robbie, I've told you so much about myself. About my father and everything. Can I ask you something?'

'What?'

'You won't get angry with me?'

'How do I know if I don't know what you're going to ask me? But I doubt it. I'm not an angry sort of person.'

Susie glanced around the pub for a moment, then leant forward and rested a hand on Robbie's knee as she spoke quietly. 'Can you do it?'

He smiled and looked at her for a second before speaking. 'I thought that's what it was. Well, now, how shall I answer that?'

'Just tell me. Or if you'd rather not, then—'

'Yes.'

'What, yes, you'd rather not tell?'

'No – yes. Yes, I can. And just for that I shall prove it to you.'

Susie gave a little shiver and reached for another sip of beer.

'But there's lots of poor devils in that hospital that can't, I can tell you,' Robbie went on. 'There's a dear old thing there – very disabled, very twisted. Always has been. Hard to understand what she says, but I've got used to her. She's always been in homes and things. She's lived there – in the hospital – for years. And she's never had it. The most exciting thing that happened to her was when one of the porters felt her up. Mucked about with her breasts a bit.'

'That's awful!' said Susie.

'No it's not. Not when that's all you've got. And then he went and now she's got nothing. And she'll never know what it's like. Doing it.'

'That's so sad. Can't they do something?'

'What can they do? She told me she tried to persuade another guy in a chair – not so bad as she is – to try and tip them both over onto the floor so they could try, but of course it didn't work. They both just had to lie there until someone found them. There's lots of people in there like her – that can't get it, I mean. I've got a couple of mates about my age. They're really bad. Won't get out of there, you see. They live in there, and they're desperate. One of them asked one of the nurses to help him bring himself off and—'

'Oh, that's horrible! He shouldn't have done that, surely?'

'Why not? It's easy for you – you can do it whenever you like. Make yourself come, I mean. Imagine how you'd feel if you couldn't—'

'Yes, all right, all right. I get the point. That's so sad.'

'One of them talked to one of the doctors once. He was good – understanding. They talked about how other countries do it. Love houses, or something. But there's nothing he can do. If he brought in a tart he'd be pimping. Not legal. So my mates will probably die without ever having it.'

Sophie put down her beer and reached out a hand to touch Robbie's knee.

'Aren't we lucky?' she said, looking at him seriously, straight in the eye.

'Yeah,' he answered, putting his hand over hers. 'Aren't we just?'

Chapter Nineteen

'What is yes?'

Rae and Eleanor watched John's drooling face closely. It showed nothing — no strain, no confusion, no pleasure, no recognition. But after a couple of seconds the side of his right thumb could be seen to make the tiniest of pushes on the metal flange which Rae held firmly against it. A single bleep slivered into the quietness of the room.

'And what is no?'

Again the pause. Rae leant forward and wiped John's mouth with a crumpled tissue held in her free hand. Eleanor looked again into his face, which remained as blank and immobile as before.

Two bleeps sounded clearly and distinctly.

'Again, John, what is no?'

Pause. Two bleeps.

'And what is yes?'

Pause. One bleep.

'Are you Edward?' Two bleeps.

'Are you John?' One bleep.

Eleanor could feel her heartbeat step up a little with every bleep. She felt a confusing mixture of fear and elation; unsure what this proof of the breakthrough might mean to her, but mesmerised by the drama and tension of what was taking place.

Rae dropped the wet tissue into a metal basin on the table beside the wheelchair, put her hand over John's and rubbed it gently.

'Is this your leg, John?' Two bleeps. 'Is it your head?' Two bleeps. Rae glanced across at Eleanor with a small smile of — what? Triumph? Excitement? Then she turned back to John.

'John, is it your hand?'

One bleep.

'Good, John. Very good. All right, let's take a rest now. You've done quite enough for today. We'll have another go tomorrow, and I might try the alphabet board again, too. Well done, John. That's marvellous.'

As Rae took the bleeper gently from John's lap and stood up to put it away in the small black briefcase, she smiled again at Eleanor.

'You see, Eleanor? You see why I'm so pleased? There is no question now that John is understanding me. I've had these sort of consistent reactions for several sessions now, and he has shown quite clearly that he understands everything I ask him.' She bent down to look into John's face as she spoke to him. 'You do, John, don't you? We're doing very well. Very well indeed. John, I want you to rest now. One of the nurses will be here in a minute to tidy you up and get you into bed. We've done very well this afternoon. I'll see you tomorrow.'

Eleanor gave John a gentle pat on his shoulder and then followed Rae as she walked out of the room.

'Should I – can I talk to him now? Ask him things? Make sure he's all right? What should I say to him?'

'Come into the OT room for a moment.'

She ushered Eleanor into the small room and gestured to her to sit down in front of the desk, while she put the briefcase away on a shelf next to the window. 'Let me have two or three more sessions with him before I leave you on your own, Eleanor. This must be an enormous strain for him and I want to get him as much at ease with the buzzer as possible before I involve you. It's going to be very emotional for him to be able to "talk" directly to you.'

She moved to behind the desk and sat down, gathering some papers that were scattered on its surface and piling them neatly to one side.

'How long do you think he's been aware of what's going on?' Eleanor asked. 'Do you think he's been able to understand everything we say? All the time?'

'I'm really not certain. We did have one client – one of the ones wrongly diagnosed as PVS that I told you about – he'd been in that condition for eight years when he came here. Eight years – extraordinary, isn't it? And he told us things that made it quite clear he'd known exactly what had been going on for at least three or four years. He knew things that he could only have known by being able to hear and understand for all that time.'

'How do you know? I mean, how did you find all that out?'

'By using the alphabet board. The one I'm just starting to try with John. I simply point to the letters one by one and the client gives a single beep when I reach the one he wants. And if the client has no vision, which I fear at the moment may be the case with John, then I say the letters out loud and he beeps when I reach the one he wants. But we're a long way off that with John, Eleanor. I don't want you to get your hopes up too high.'

'No, of course not. I understand.'

Eleanor glanced up at the notice board behind the desk.

'Rae, can I ask you something? About that young man – the one with his parents in the picture?'

Rae twisted round and looked at the cutting behind her. After a moment she smiled back towards Eleanor.

'David. Yes, of course. Anything.'

'What was the question? The one they didn't dare ask?'

Rae stood up and turned to take down the cutting from the board.

'Here,' she said, passing it across the desk. 'Read it. Not an uncommon problem, I'm afraid.'

Eleanor quickly scanned the small piece of newspaper until she found the paragraph she wanted.

'He's very cheerful,' David's mother and father said from his bedside. 'We make jokes about the pretty nurses and his bleeper goes like mad. He's still got his sense of humour. But there's

one question we just daren't ask him. We don't really want to
know you see. Whether he wants to live or not. We just daren't
ask him that.'

'Oh God,' said Eleanor. 'How ghastly. What an awful thought.'

'Yes. These things aren't easy. It will be tough for you, Eleanor. But I'm sure you're able to cope. I don't think I need to tread carefully with you, do I? You're very strong, and I don't want to keep anything from you. I think if you are aware of all the possibilities then you'll be more prepared for some of the — the difficult times that may be ahead. We had one poor therapist here who worked with a young man for many months — he was only nineteen. She got him using the bleeper very successfully, and then moved on to the alphabet board. I'm afraid the first thing he spelt out was "Please kill me." And the second. And the third. It was very distressing for her.'

'Yes. Poor thing. How awful. And for him. Trapped. Inside. But you couldn't do anything, could you? I mean, even if it became absolutely clear that the person really couldn't stand it, really didn't want to live any more, you couldn't stop the food or whatever it is, could you?'

'No, no, of course not. Absolutely not. It's only in cases like the poor Hillsborough boy, when it's completely clear that there is no awareness whatsoever, that the client truly is in a vegetative state, and only when that has been continuing for a number of years, only then can any sort of decision be considered. And I must say, I feel more doubtful all the time about when and if that can truly be said to be definitive. Think of our eight-year vegetative patient. He told us that he had actually heard the doctors and family discussing stopping his nutrition several times during the years before we got through to him. Just imagine that. And he most certainly wanted to live — he was quite definite about that from the first moment he "talked" to us.'

·∞·

Susie was sitting on Robbie's lap in the large armchair. She stroked his hair with one hand and then bent to kiss him gently on the lips. He pulled back a little and looked at her. 'What is it, babe? You're not right, are you? Why are you so quiet? Come on, tell me what the matter is.'

She looked around his small bedsitting room and marvelled, not for the first time, at its neatness. 'God, Robbie, you're so tidy. How do you manage to keep it looking like this, especially in a wheelchair? You're amazing.' She sighed and rested her head on his shoulder. 'It's my dad. He's not a vegetable after all, Robbie. He can understand things. He can feel things. It's so strange.'

'That's great! It's brilliant, isn't it? Why aren't you happy?'

'I just can't bear to think that he knows what he's like. I mean, he can't move — just imagine that? Imagine what it must be like. He can't do anything — *anything*. He just has to lie there until someone does something to him. Or asks him a question. It's unbearable. All the time — right now, while I'm making love to you, or watching television with you, or going shopping, or eating, anything — he's just lying there. They don't think he can even see. Robbie – God, it's awful – just imagine lying there in the dark, and you can't do anything.'

'But you can't know what it's like for him, Susie. It's like me in a way. Before you really knew me you felt sorry for me, didn't you? In the wrong sort of way. You couldn't imagine that my life could ever be as good as yours, or as complete as yours, could you?'

'No, I know, but that's different.'

'No it isn't. Not really. It's all about you judging everything from your point of view.'

'Well, of course I do. How else could I? I'm bound to judge it from my point of view.'

'But you've got to see that you can't know what someone else's point of view might be. Yes, if you – you the way you think and feel now, I mean – were suddenly trapped inside a body that couldn't move or see and all that, then of course you'd find it unbearable. But he's not the old dad trapped inside that body, is he? He's someone different. If you were suddenly put in a wheelchair for the rest of your life with only one arm that worked properly, you'd find that pretty unbearable, too, wouldn't you? Or at least you think you would – you think you'd be fucking miserable, don't you? But you know I'm not, now. You believe I'm as complete a person because this is me, every bit of it. You believe I'm completely Robbie, just like this. So maybe your dad's complete the way he is now. Who's to say?'

'But that's different. You've always been like you are. He remembers what it's like to be—'

289

'How do you know that? You don't. Remember, I've had years of hospitals, doctors and all that. I've seen people in the most terrible state – in ways you wouldn't think anyone would want to go on for a minute. But they do.'

'I just can't believe he's not suffering. He has no quality of life like that. It just can't be worth living, being shut in like that. It's horrible.'

'But who are we to judge his quality of life, as you put it? Why should our lives be any more important? When we run around doing our little important things, my music or your job interviews or shopping, or stuffing food in our mouths or washing or reading newspapers or getting dressed or driving the car or paying bills or reading books or whatever, how can we say they bring us a better quality of life than he has? What exactly is it in any of those things that's so important that his life isn't worth living without it? Or is it sex? Is that what you think he needs to have a reason to live? What about all those nuns and things who've given all that up? To be more spiritual and things? Maybe your dad feels more than any of us; maybe he experiences life in a really kind of intense way. Who are we to say he doesn't? If he can hear a bit of music, or something read to him from a book that really means something to him, or feel you touching him, then who's to say that doesn't mean more to him than all our rushing around doing all the stupid things we do all the time? His world has got really tiny. It's shrunk; but it doesn't mean it's not as important as the world we live in. What about all that stuff about atoms?'

'What stuff?'

'You know, that each one has a whole universe inside it or whatever. Maybe he's really cool. Down to a few atoms to think about. Nearer to the mystery of it all and all that.'

Susie smiled at him. 'You're very clever, Robbie, and I know what you're trying to say. But I still think it's unbearable. He used to be a complete, moving, functioning human being. Now he's a shell. He may be in pain, or frightened. He's a mind without a body – that's no sort of life.'

'I'll tell you one thing, Susie. It's a real lesson to enjoy every minute, isn't it? Grab things while you can.'

Susie took a breath as if about to speak, but then hesitated and after a moment let the breath out again in a small sigh. Suddenly she bent her head down and kissed him, longer and not so gently this time, then held his head in her hands as she looked at him and spoke quietly and seriously. 'Yes. Yes it is. You're right.'

It was a long time since the three of them had been together. Eleanor felt rather uneasy, guessing that Sophie had asked them both to meet her in Barbara's flat for a purpose. She had been so hard to talk to lately, so much colder with her than in the days before the accident. She thought back fondly to their museum visits and shopping trips: Sophie had seemed so completely hers then, so ready to absorb everything she taught her – so grateful. But since the accident something had happened that Eleanor couldn't put her finger on, and although she still clung to the all-important image of the three of them – she, Sophie and whatever was left of John living together in the country – she sensed that it might not be as easy to achieve as she had thought. She patted the chair next to her and spoke as cheerfully and confidently as she could.

'Here, Sophie, come and sit down. You look tired.'

'No, I'll sit over here, thanks Eleanor. Oh – and I've been meaning to say for some time – I'd like to be known by my real name again, if you don't mind. I'm back to Susie from now on.'

'What?' exclaimed Eleanor, filled with more fear than she could account for by the announcement. 'Why on earth do you want to do that? Sophie's a much better name for you – it suits you. It's elegant and – and classy, just as you are.'

'Eleanor, I'm sorry. You were very kind to me and I really appreciate all you've done for me, but, well, I think the shock of Dad's accident, as well as a couple of other things that have been happening, has made me realise that I got a bit lost for a bit. Mum, I'm really, really sorry. There's nothing wrong with Susie – it's a lovely name. And there's nothing wrong with saying "pardon" or talking about your dinner when it's at lunchtime.'

'Oh, Sophie really!' said Eleanor. 'This is childish.'

'No, wait a minute. You were teaching me to be a snob, Eleanor, and I –'

'I was not!'

'Yes you were. Face it. And I don't like it. I don't like

myself for having gone along with it. And the clothes you got me were too smart for me. I like to be more casual, more – more easy. Don't think I'm not grateful, but I just feel you were trying to turn me into something that I'm not.'

'You're talking a lot of nonsense, Sophie.'

'Susie, Eleanor, I'm Susie. Please.'

'You're talking a lot of nonsense and I won't have it. You're the one who's being a snob, my girl. What the hell is wrong with learning how to speak correctly? Clarity, beauty and precision are some of the qualities of the wonderful English language that we are privileged to speak, and if I've begun to teach you how to use it beautifully and correctly then that's nothing to be ashamed of. And you're talking rubbish about the clothes; they're perfect for you and you've begun to look wonderful. Don't spoil it Soph— Susan. Don't throw away all that we've learnt just because this terrible tragedy has confused you. I'll look after you – I'll give you everything you deserve. And when your father gets better we'll all be together and—'

'No!' Susie answered firmly, 'I don't want you to look after me. Can't you see? I've got a wonderful mother and father and you're in the way. He left you because you're old-fashioned and snobbish and cold, and because you didn't—'

'Susie!' interrupted Barbara. 'Don't! Don't talk like that to Eleanor. You mustn't say things like that. You have no right to. What happened between your father and Eleanor and me is very private and personal. I'm sorry it's all been so difficult for you but you've got to understand that these

293

things are much more complicated than you can imagine. You're very upset, and it's been terrible for all of us. But you mustn't take it out on Eleanor.'

'I don't need your help in defending myself, thank you, Barbara,' said Eleanor. 'As it happens, Susan, you are utterly wrong. John never did leave me, as you put it. He's still my husband, morally and legally. He and your mother have been — what do you call it nowadays? — co-habiting for many years, but they were not, are not and never will be married. He is married to me.'

There was a pause. Eleanor expected Susan to break down, to be horrified and shaken by the discovery that her parents had been carrying on an adulterous relationship and that she herself was a ba— was illegitimate. But the girl simply looked calmly back at her in silence for a moment or two, then sighed a little before she spoke.

'I don't think anything you three have done or will do could surprise me any more. I simply don't care. It doesn't matter to me. I am taking charge of my own life now. There's something else I need to tell you. I'm moving in with somebody. I'm going to live with somebody.'

There was a moment's silence, then Barbara smiled over at Susie.

'Is it Robbie, dear? Are you going to live together?'

'Yes, Mum. It's Robbie. And I'm really happy about it. His room's not far from here, Mum, you know that, don't you? And he likes you a lot. So we'll be coming to see you lots of the time. You won't be lonely, I promise you. And then when Dad gets a bit better—'

'NO!' shouted Eleanor. 'Just a minute. Don't I have any

say in this? Who is this boy and why haven't either of you told me about this?'

'You've met him, Eleanor. He's the guy I introduced you to at the hospital. A couple of weeks ago. When we went to have a drink together. Do you remember?'

'No, Susan, I can't say I do. You didn't introduce me to—'

But she stopped, her eyes flicked anxiously at the two of them, and she blinked a few times before going on. 'You only introduced me to one of the patients. The man in the wheelchair.'

Susie said nothing, but gave a small smile and tipped her head on one side as she kept looking at Eleanor.

There was an uncomfortable silence. At last Eleanor took a deep breath and brushed some imaginary crumbs off her lap.

'I can't believe, Susan,' she said, as she kept looking down at her hand as it went on sweeping across the fabric of her skirt, 'that you're seriously suggesting to us that you intend to move in with the young man in the wheelchair that I met briefly downstairs. I'm sure he's a perfectly charming young man, but I can't believe you are stupid enough to take on the problems and responsibilities of such a thing. And I've got nothing against disabled people, you know me well enough to believe that, I'm sure. But you have no idea what you are taking on, Susan. No idea at all. And he's entirely the wrong type for you in any case, I'm sure you can see that.'

'Why, because he's "common"?'

'Oh really, Susan, don't be ridiculous. It's nothing to

do with that. He's just not the right person for you to be with, that's all. I have quite different plans for you. You can't throw away your life like this, Susan. You can't.'

'Eleanor, I've said I'm sorry, and I mean it. I know you imagined everything differently. We all did, I suppose. But everything's changed now – surely you can see that? And you know nothing at all about Robbie. Nothing at all.'

'You're coming to live with me, Susan, you know that. We discussed that. I can give you a far better life than – I can give you the sort of life you deserve. We'll have fun together – we always do, don't we? I want you to meet the sort of young men that I know can make you really happy. And your father is going to need you around; going to need your strength and your love. You wouldn't want to do anything to upset him further, would you? I'll need you there to help me look after him, once we get him home. And I know Barbara would want the best for you. I'm sure she can understand that if I offer to—'

'Eleanor, stop this, please. I don't want the sort of life you were going to give me. I don't think I ever did – even when I was going along with it all. It was just a bit of fun, really.'

Eleanor looked back down at her lap. Something in the girl's tone had suddenly convinced her of the uselessness of her protests and she sat quietly for a moment. When at last she spoke again her words came out muffled and indistinct.

'Sorry?' said Susie.

But Eleanor didn't reply, and after a second or two Susie bent over in her chair and peered up into the woman's face. What she saw made her sit up quickly in painful embarrassment and pity.

'Oh God, Eleanor. Don't cry. Oh don't cry – that's awful.'

'Sorry,' said Eleanor quietly, her voice sounding strangely strangled by the effort to stop crying. 'I just said – you're all I've got now. I can't cope with your father all on my own. Nobody knows what he'll be like when he gets better. I need your help, Susan. I need you with me to— Oh don't leave me, Susan. Please don't leave me.'

'I'm not leaving you, Eleanor. But I won't be black-mailed like this. It's my life and you've taught me to be firm, haven't you? Not to be frightened of what other people want from me? And, anyway, Eleanor, who's to say that Dad will be going back to live with you? If he gets better enough – which nobody knows anyway – who's to say he wouldn't rather go to live with Mum? All the time. Which may be what he's wanted for a long time.'

Eleanor slowly lifted her mottled face and gave Susie a look of absolute terror. The girl had voiced the horror that secretly haunted her, and hearing it spoken out loud gave it a reality that was almost unbearable in its dreadful implications.

Chapter Twenty

'Will I be able to take him home? I mean, if things progress as well as they have been doing; if he continues to be physically stable and so on? Is there any reason why I shouldn't nurse him at home?'

Eleanor looked earnestly into Sister Egan's face and waited anxiously for her reply.

'It's a huge responsibility to take on,' the sister answered. 'Just the physical side of things is enormously hard work.'

'But you don't understand. I'll be able to get him full-time nursing. We are – well, we're what you'd call comfortably off. And the insurance cover John took out was excellent. I'll have plenty to be able to afford proper care for him. Everything it takes to look after him for – for as long as it takes.'

'I see. Well, obviously, it's a possibility. We have several families who have taken their loved ones home in just such circumstances. Some people find it very satisfying to look after their relatives at home. And, of course, in many cases it's far more comfortable – and comforting –

for the patients themselves. There's no particular reason why that shouldn't be possible, Eleanor. But do think carefully about just what you might be taking on.'

'Yes, I will.'

·∽·

Although Eleanor was again uneasy at meeting Susan and Barbara at the same time, at least she was on home ground this time. She sat in the upright chair beside the desk in the small sitting room and looked at the two of them where they sat opposite her in the armchairs. It was the first time Susan had been inside the flat, and Eleanor was enjoying the looks of puzzled incredulity that the girl was still finding it hard to cover.

'So this is your flat,' said Susie, looking around her. 'It's so weird — exactly the same layout, but backwards. And it looks so completely different. And all these years you were just— Oh it's so strange. So very strange.'

'Yes,' answered Eleanor briskly, 'but I don't think it's just the looking-glass layout that makes it look so different, Susan, is it? Good taste. That's what it's called. Something you were well on the way to understanding before you got pulled back into the— Sorry. I'm sorry. I didn't mean to start on that. I don't want to argue with you. With either of you. It's important we all work together for John's sake. To do the right thing for him. Help him. I have no bitterness, now, to either of you.

'Barbara — I shall, of course, see that you continue to receive the allowance John has been giving you all these years. Extraordinary, isn't it, that he could have arranged that so easily and I never suspected anything? It's quite clear, now it's been explained to me, how stupid I was. A little more attention, a little more questioning and I needn't have been kept in the dark all this time, need I? Fancy, even the accountant knowing all about it. How cleverly you all arranged everything, didn't you? But never mind. Don't leave money matters up to the men, Susan, as we did in my day. Make sure you watch every penny — you never know what peculiar doings may be happening right under your nose, do you?'

The other two glanced at each other uneasily. 'Dad would want Mum to have everything she needs, you know that,' said Susie. 'You needn't feel you're doing us any favours. We can go to law to fight for what—'

'Now, now, Susan. Don't be so defensive. They tell me John's will makes adequate provision for all of us. But let's hope it never comes to that. I've just told you I have no intention of stopping your little allowance. Or the payments on your flat. Everything can go on just as before. I want us all to be friends. To work together for John, as I said.'

'Yes, Susie, don't make things difficult. Eleanor's trying to make the best of things. I think we should, too.'

'Thank you, Barbara. Now, there's something very important — and delicate — that I want to discuss with you both. As you know, John is able to answer yes and no to us now. I've watched Rae with him and I think I'm ready to have a go myself. Rae says he has great trouble spelling out words with his buzzer even when she speaks the alphabet out loud to him, so it may well be that the only way he can communicate with us for some time is going to be through answering yes and no to whatever questions we put to him. That obviously puts a huge responsibility onto us. Onto those of us that – she looked directly at Barbara with a strange little smile on her face as she went on – 'that love him. There's something – something very difficult that I want to ask you both.'

'I can't bear it. I can't bear seeing him like that. Poor Dad – I can't help worrying that he's uncomfortable or lonely or frightened. Do you think he's hurting? Do you think he knows what's happened to him?'

'Well, Susan, that's part of what I want to talk about. It started when I saw a newspaper article about a poor young man who was like your father. His parents were able to communicate with him by using just the same buzzer as Rae is using now. And they talked to him about all sorts of things. But they said there was one question – one question that they just didn't dare to ask him.'

There was silence as the other two stared at her.

Then Barbara spoke. 'What, Eleanor? What was it?'

'They didn't dare ask him whether he wanted to live or not.'

There was another silence, even longer this time, and Susie dropped her head onto her chest and closed her eyes. They sat there for a minute, not looking at each other, then Barbara brushed a hand across her forehead and shook her head.

'What, Barbara?' asked Eleanor. 'Did you say something?'

'I was just thinking. I'm not sure we should ever ask

that, either. If that's what you're going to say, Eleanor. I don't think I want to know that. There's nothing we can do, even if he really doesn't want to go on, is there? I mean, there's no way we can—'

'Of course there is,' Eleanor answered firmly. 'There's plenty that can be done. You wouldn't let an animal go on in pain and suffering, would you? There are plenty of ways. And it happens all the time.'

'So what are you saying, Eleanor?' asked Susie.

'I'm saying I think we should be braver than that family. I'm saying I think we should ask him. Just once. And then think about what should be done. If he wants to live, if he can stand it now, then that means he's going to make it; we should be positive and help him to cope with it all. But if not – well, I know what I would do. And I have a feeling Susie feels the same.'

The girl looked at her. 'Oh, wait a minute – I never said that. I mean, it's true, I can't bear to think of him suffering and frightened. I don't want him to suffer, but – Oh God, I don't know. It's horrible. I just can't bear to think about it.'

'I have a suggestion,' said Eleanor. 'I am, after all, his wife. Whatever else may be the complications,' she added quickly, sensing that Barbara was about to interrupt, 'and, as John's wife, I think I should be the one to ask him. I think I should ask him, clearly and straightforwardly, whether he wants to go on—'

'Oh God!' said Barbara, and gave a little smothered sob into her hand.

'—and I think we should abide by whatever he decides.

No, just a minute,' she said firmly, as Susie began to speak. 'Listen to me a minute. If he is happy to go on living, to make the best of whatever may be in the future for him, then I don't feel we should ever ask him that question again. We'll know then that he is capable of coping, and although there'll obviously be bad times ahead, when he'll feel he can't bear it, we'll know that he can. Do you understand? I think we owe it to him. Otherwise he has no way of telling us what it's like for him. If he tells me that he doesn't want to live, then of course we'll have to give him time before we – I mean, in that case we'll have to ask him again, several times, over weeks or months, before we can be sure. And then I'll manage – something. But otherwise, I think I just ask it the once and then we never mention it again. And we don't discuss this with anyone else. If he can't bear it, if he really can't bear it, then I shall find a way. Of – arranging things.'

Barbara looked across at Susie. 'Susie,' she said miserably, 'what do you think? What do we do? I just can't make any decisions. I – oh God, I just miss him so much. I'm sorry, Eleanor, I know I shouldn't say it in front of you, but we've all been through so much together there's no point in pretending, is there? I just miss him so very, very much. He's my world, you see. He's everything – except you, Susie, of course – he's everything I live for.'

'Yes, well,' said Eleanor, not quite succeeding in hiding the look of disgust that was creeping across her face at Barbara's words, 'at least you've got each other, haven't you? At least you've got his child, Barbara. That's more than I have, remember.'

'I think Eleanor is right,' said Susie. 'I hate the whole idea of it, but I think she's being very brave.'

'Thank you, Susan.'

'And I think, if she can bear it, that we should let her do as she says. She should ask him whether – whether – I mean she should ask him. The question.'

·∽·

'Thank you, Rae. I'm fine. You can leave me to it.'

Rae stood up, gave Eleanor a little squeeze on her arm and then walked towards the door of the small side room. 'I'll shut the door,' she said. 'Just for privacy. I'm not far away, Eleanor – just give me a shout if you need me, or ring the bell there. Don't hesitate to call me.'

'I won't,' smiled Eleanor. 'Thank you.'

She watched the woman go out and shut the door, then she turned back to look at John. He was seated in the wheelchair, his head supported in an upright position by the two side pieces of the head rest. The muscles of his face were slack and loose, letting the flesh hang down and to the side. His eyes looked lifeless: the pupils reminded Eleanor of a dead fish in their cloudy dullness. His mouth was slightly open and the ever present string of saliva hung from his lip, lengthening every second as she studied him. She reached for a tissue and made to wipe it away, but then hesitated. She looked down at his lap, where the shiny metal of the buzzer nestled against his thumb, pinioned efficiently into exactly the right position by a piece of crepe bandage. She looked back up into his face again.

'No, John. I think I'll leave it there. Why should I wipe away your slimy mess?'

She kept looking at his face, but could see no flicker of response.

'OK, John, just a little test, I think, before we go any further. I don't want to waste my precious time if you're not functioning, do I? Let's have a little demonstration of your cleverness, shall we?'

She leant forward a little, and spoke slowly and clearly. 'You have your buzzer there, John. On your lap. As usual. Now, tell me, can you understand what I'm saying?'

After a fraction of a pause, a single bleep sounded into the quietness of the room.

'Good. That's excellent. And is your name Henry?'

Two bleeps.

'Richard?'

Two bleeps.

'John?'

One bleep.

'Wonderful. And are you a lying unfaithful bastard, John dear?'

Silence. Eleanor laughed. 'No, well, I didn't really expect an answer to that one, my love. But don't worry, I'll answer it for you. Yes. Yes, John, is the answer to that one. Now, just be patient with me. I have a few things to say to you before I ask you the question you may be longing to hear.' She laughed again, briefly, and rubbed under her nose with one finger. 'Oh dear me, forgive me laughing, John, but it's a funny situation, isn't it? Here we are, me totally in control of you. What a change —

isn't it? Or do you think perhaps I've been in control for longer than you realise? Hm?'

She sat back a minute and looked at him, then her smile dropped as she shifted her chair closer to his and spoke again. 'I know, John. I know all about your grubby little life. About your mistress. Your bastard daughter. Your sordid little lies and excuses. Did you really think you could keep it from me?'

She moved her mouth even closer to his ear. 'And now look at you. You're dribbling again, John. Your nose is messy. How d'you feel about that? You look disgusting. You look like – like your life. Disgusting. Revolting.

'You knew I wanted a child, John, didn't you? Why didn't you give me a child, John? Why did you always tell me you didn't want one? That we were happy as we were? How dare you take that from me? How dare you deny me my right?

'Why did you give that pathetic, common little woman what you'd always denied me? She's nothing, John, she's nothing. How could you do it? How could you touch her – her nasty little body, with its cheap clothes and ugly hair? HOW COULD YOU FUCK HER, YOU BASTARD?

'You've messed up everything. Everything.'

She was hissing, now, spitting into his ear with all the stored-up hatred of the past months; all the frustrations and unhappiness of the past years.

'And then she was coming to me, John. Your child was coming to me – she was going to be mine. I was going to make it all work. I would have let you come back, you see; I would have forgiven you. We could have lived together, made it work. Forgotten your cheap whore and started again. As a family. Watched her marry and have our grandchildren.

'But you couldn't even let that happen, could you? You had to smash into that wretched young man in your hurry to get to your bitch; driving too fast, were you, John, as usual? Only thinking of yourself?

'Well, now look where it's got you. Lovely, isn't it? And you've taken her away from me, John. Your selfishness has taken her away. You have to mess everything up, don't you? Spoil it all with your cheap lust and your thoughtlessness. I would have made it all right, you see. I would have forgiven you. I'm big enough to do that, John. We could have made something out of the mess you'd created. But even that you had to spoil.

'Now she's gone back to that woman. And moved in with a cripple. That's what you've done to her, John.

'But I won't desert you. I'm going to take you home with me. I'm going to look after you, John. And I'll make sure you never see that woman again. Or your ungrateful daughter. You're all I've got now.'

She sat back, exhausted, and looked at him. The string of saliva had reached the collar of his shirt now, and she watched it for a moment as it began to move sideways across the blue fabric. 'Poor old boy,' she said quietly. 'Has wifey been nasty to you?' She sat up again and lifted the crumpled piece of tissue and gently wiped away the mess from his mouth and neck. 'There, there. I'll look after you, Johnny. Eleanor will look after you, don't worry.

'Now then, there may be something you'd like me to

ask you, dear. I shall ask you very slowly and clearly, John, and then — do you know what? — I may never ask you again. So you'd better be very careful what you answer. Think carefully, dear, because this is very important. Are you listening to me, John? Give me a buzz if you are listening to me.'

A single bleep came quickly in response.

'Good. Now then, John, what I shall ask you is very simple. Very simple. Just listen carefully and give me your answer.'

She took a deep breath, then spoke gently but very clearly, enunciating each word crisply and separately so that the short sentence emerged slowly into the still room.

'John: listen to me — *do — you — want — to — live?*'

After the merest hint of a pause the answer came back, echoing in its electronic clarity and definition the way the question had itself been asked.

Bleep. Bleep.

Eleanor looked at John's face for a moment, the face that still betrayed no evidence of emotion or understanding. She smiled at him: the merest hint of an upturn at the corners of her mouth that failed to be reflected in the coldness of her eyes. She stood up and pushed back her chair, then bent to speak closely into his ear, as her smile became a little broader:

'Tough.'

And she turned away and walked out of the room.

Epilogue

Eleanor pushed the wheelchair slowly along the gravel path round the edge of the lawn. The wheels dug into the stones and made it heavy going, and she grunted impatiently with the effort of it.

'Here — do let me have a turn,' said Andrew, leaning forward and reaching for the handles.

'No!' Eleanor pushed his hand away and kept on walking, startling him with the sharpness of her response. 'Sorry, Andrew,' she went on. 'I didn't mean to snap at you. It's just that I like to do everything myself. Only me or the nurse. It makes me feel more secure, somehow. One catch of the wheel in something, or a bump, could just dislodge him and throw him off balance.'

She leant forward and spoke in a cooing little voice directly into the ear of the drooping man in the wheelchair. 'Couldn't it, John?'

'Well, I think you're wonderful, Eleanor,' said Catherine, who was walking a little behind them. 'I'm sure I couldn't do it. If Andrew was like this I'm sure I'd shut him in a home and have done with him!' She laughed, and looked across at Andrew, who smiled back at her a little wanly.

'I like to do it,' said Eleanor.

'And you've been so kind. To – to the woman. You know,' added Catherine, lowering her voice slightly as if mentioning something not suitable for other ears.

'Very forgiving,' muttered Andrew, looking down at the gravel and linking his hands behind his back.

'Well, these things are sent to try us,' smiled Eleanor. 'No doubt it was partly my fault. We can't all have perfectly happy marriages like yours, Catherine.'

'No, well, we're very lucky,' answered Catherine, coming up beside Andrew and slipping her hand through one arm, which forced him to part his hands and let them hang awkwardly at his sides.

'And it all worked out very well, really,' Eleanor said. 'The house on the Devon estate being empty, I mean. Just the right size for the woman on her own. And just the right – sort of place.'

'Yes, yes. Absolutely. Start a new life and all that,' said Andrew. 'And how's he doing? Any improvement? Any more noises or anything?'

'Not really. He does wail a bit, still. Sometimes when I'm trying to get through to him he just cries. They're not sure if it's some sort of reflex, or if it's because he's becoming more aware. More aware of his situation and remembering what's happened and what he used to be like.'

'Poor thing,' said Andrew. 'Poor old John.'

'Yes,' answered Eleanor, bending to tuck the blanket more firmly around John's chest. 'But he's got me. I'm not going to give up on him. He knows I'm here, I'm sure of that.'

And she smiled at the two of them as she went on pushing the chair down the long gravel path back towards the house.

312